VINEET BAJPAI

HARAPPA

CURSE OF THE BLOOD RIVER

TreeShade Books

Published by
TreeShade Books (VB Performance LLP)
Ansal Corporate Park, Sector142, Noida
Uttar Pradesh - 201305, India
Email - publish@TreeShadeBooks.com
www.TreeShadeBooks.com

Printed and Bound in India by
Gopsons Papers Ltd.
A-2 Sector 64, Noida - 201301, India

Cover Design by
Munisha Nanda

HARAPPA
CURSE OF THE BLOOD RIVER

To the one and only,

Munisha

PRAISE FOR HARAPPA

Lending a true Dan Brown-esque vibe, author Vineet Bajpai weaves a gripping narrative...introduces a myriad elements and yet manages to keep them together...brilliant...unputdownable experience for the reader.

- Hindustan Times

Very nicely written...

- Gurudev Sri Sri Ravi Shankar
(Art of Living)

An absolutely delightful story...Harappa is definitely the next Bahubali.

- Mala Ramakrishnan
Chief Commissioner (retd), Income Tax, Mumbai

Vineet's style of narrative and backdrop does remind (the reader) of Dan Brown, but Vineet has surpassed him in terms of vision and imagination.

- ikreatepassions.com

Vineet has raised the bar for fiction writing in India. He is beyond doubt India's new literary superstar.

- Bharat Joshi
Author, Navigating India

Vineet…weaves a whole alter reality with Harappa…a magnum opus!

- 94.3 FM, Radio One

Bajpai sets you up perfectly for the dark revelations…of the great storyline he has created in Harappa.

- thebigfatboho.com

Harappa…a blend of history, mythology, religion and crime.

- afaqs.com

A most promising debut novel from author Vineet Bajpai. Eagerly awaiting the full trilogy.

- Sandhya Iyer
Editor-in-Chief, Jaico Publishing House

Post Harappa, Vineet Bajpai has become a rock-star for every Indian reader who missed out on well-researched, high-quality alternate histories in the Indian literature genre.

- Sumeet Khanna
Chief Executive Officer, Surgivisor

Harappa…fiction fills the gap left by reality…in a Dan Brown fashion.

- Mid Day

Having read Vineet's earlier books on management I could never imagine that something like Harappa could also come from the same author. The narratives and descriptions in Harappa are so well written that they take the reader back to the era of that civilization. The book is exceptionally engaging and deserves to be produced as a movie. It is a great attempt to explore our own civilization, history and culture.

- Pratul Gaur
Chief Financial Officer, TBWA

The writing is lucid, crisp and the story is enriched with complex emotions of love, brotherhood, hatred, lust and trust. The writer ends every chapter on a note that leaves the reader waiting for more. The icing on the cake is the description of Varanasi, which to a traveler soul like me who hasn't visited the city was a perfect delight.

- thereaderscosmos.in

Being among the first few to read the manuscript, I knew instantly that Harappa was going to be a major blockbuster. And the book proved me right within 60 days of release. What a spectacular work of contemporary literature.

- Vivek Merani
Managing Director, Magnon eg+

Harappa…is a mix of history, mythology and fantasy…The story has the visual effect of a screenplay.

- Asian Age

Harappa is a must read title for fiction lovers. The intriguing story line is sure to keep you spellbound as it unfolds across civilizations. Vineet is certainly the finest addition to the world of Indian fiction writing.

- Krishna Mohan
Founder, Nine Triangles

Every few years a book comes along and changes the entire landscape. Indian thriller writing will now be spoken about as before-Harappa and after-Harappa.

- Varun Bajpai
Managing Director, JM Financial

Harappa knits 3,700 years, powerful ancient and modern-day characters, and a nail-biting conspiracy – all in one literary thriller.

- Times of India

Harappa is a masterpiece. It's a great combination of historical and mythological fiction...

- Dipti Patel
Founder, WordFamous Literary Agents

Harappa has been the fastest selling book by a debut Author that we have distributed...has set new benchmarks for the industry.

- Gaurav Sabharwal
Founder, uRead.com

ACKNOWLEDGEMENTS

At the outset, I would like to thank my closest companions that have made Harappa possible – *books*. Yes, you read that right. Books.

It has been possible to envision a tale as expansive as *Harappa* only because of the continuous and incremental learning I have received from the hundreds of books that I have had by my side over the years. I would like to thank all those magnificent authors who have made this world a better place with their passionate imagination and intense hard work.

While the number is too high to name each one of those luminaries, I have to specifically thank a few here. Diana L. Eck for her profound book *Banaras City of Light*. William Dalrymple for all his splendid work. Robert E Svoboda for his brilliant book *Aghora: At the Left Hand of God*. And to many, many other brilliant writers whose writing style has, no doubt, had a rub-off effect on mine - Gregory David Roberts, Dan Brown, Ashwin Sanghi, Arun Shourie, Holger Kersten...thank you all. Learnings from all of the above illustrious writers will find a reflection in *Harappa*. Or so I hope.

There are several fine institutions that I have been associated with over the last three decades, and I feel compelled to thank each one of them. Air Force Bal Bharati School, Hansraj College, Delhi University, Lal Bahadur Shastri Institute of Management, GE Capital, Magnon Group, TBWA, eg+ Worldwide, Omnicom Group, Jaico Publishing House and talentrack. The people I met, studied with and worked alongside at these excellent institutions have shaped my ideas and beliefs, which in turn gave me the intellectual fuel to write *Harappa*.

Some of the people who have helped me at various stages of *Harappa* deserve a special mention here. My beloved wife Munisha for the spectacular cover design. My brother Varun for helping me with the editing process. Tanuj Nanda, Denny Joseph, Apoorve Arya and Rukmini Chawla Kumar for their inputs on the book's blurb. Rahul Kanonia for the excellent type setting. Vivek Merani for being a partner at every single step, and for being the one person who showed most faith in the book becoming a roaring success. Amit Kukreja for his support on the production process. Ashutosh Negi, Nitin Naresh, Ayush Gupta and Denny Joseph (once again!) for the promotional campaigns of the book.

My dear friends Manishi Singh, Gaurav Bhatia, Prashant

Misra, Joydeep Kalra, Naved Aqueel, Sunil Ahuja, Vikas Misra - you are all my strength and my driving force.

There are a few mentors without whom *Harappa,* or most other big and small achievements of my life, would not have been possible. They include Manoj Ghai, Nishish Jha, Navin Chawla and Praveen Puri.

My parents and my family are my universe, the kindle in my soul. I am indebted to them for all the love that surrounds me. My daughter Vandita is the light of my life, and my nieces Vedika and Aditi its sparkling stars.

Utthishtha!

Rise.

Vineet Bajpai

DISCLAIMER

This is a novel, a work of pure imagination and fiction, written with the sole intention of entertaining the reader. While the content has several references to religions, history, institutions, beliefs and myths, it is all presented with the only purpose of making the story richer and more breathtaking. The author is a believer of all religions, and respects them equally and deeply. He makes no claim to the correctness of the historical or mythological references and facts used in the story.

INTRODUCTION

2017, New Delhi:

Vidyut Shastri, a young entrepreneur from Delhi, gets an unexpected summon from his 108 year-old great grandfather who is now on his deathbed. The old *matthadheesh* or clan-leader Brahmin from the ancient Indian city of Kashi (Banaras) wants to reveal the secret of a prehistoric curse to Vidyut. A curse that not just destroyed an entire civilization thousands of years ago, but also obliterated its very truth.

Until now.

The dying Brahmin, Dwarka Shastri, is the last among a lineage of guardians of a hidden cellar in the complex maze of a Shiva temple in Banaras. There lies buried a 3,500 year-old encrypted and preserved hand-written scroll. It has a lone

Sanskrit couplet written on it, along with a prophecy that during a specific sacred hour in the *Rohini Nakshatra* (constellation) on the *purnima* or full-moon as per the *shaka-samvat* or Hindu calendar, a person of their own bloodline, yet unblemished by the sins of his ancestors, will unfurl the dark secret. He will put an end to the most horrifying curse in the history of mankind.

There is a reason why Vidyut hears from his great grandfather.

The sacred hour has arrived.

Vidyut has been kept away from Kashi by his previous three generations because they are bearers of a spell – the curse. It was none other than their own ancestor, Vivasvan Pujari, who betrayed his own people and his own civilization 3,700 years ago. He paved way for the destruction of planet Earth's first metropolis – Harappa.

But most unforgivable of all – he betrayed the great *River of the Wise*. He turned it into the *Blood River*.

1700 BCE, Harappa:

Harappa is the mightiest city on planet Earth and is run by the wise and righteous Vedic way-of-life. Vivasvan Pujari is about to be announced as the chief priest of Harappa – the most powerful position in all of *Aryavarta* or the land of the mighty Aryans. He has worked for half a century to reach this pious and coveted position.

But something goes horribly wrong.

His friend turned archrival, the wise Pundit Chandrad-har and his bewitchingly beautiful wife use the dark forces of the three long-faced magicians with empty eye-sockets from Mesopotamia. They get Vivasvan Pujari entangled in a dreadful controversy of being the cold blooded murderer of Nayantara, the enchanting dancing-girl known for her up-per-arm bangles that covered her elbow and then were worn right up to her shoulder. That's all she wore while perform-ing for her most powerful and intimate guests.

Vivasvan Pujari is condemned in a public court and is thrown into the dark cellars of Harappa's *Mrit Kaaraavaas* (dungeons of the dead), where he swears vengeance. Not against Chan-dradhar. Not against his venomous conspirator. Not against the judge who declared him guilty or the black-magicians from Mesopotamia. He swears vengeance against the whole of Harappa! His public trial is held at the *Great Bath*. He is spat upon and pelted with stones by the very people of the great city for whom he had dedicated his whole life. His property is seized and his beloved family exiled to barren and deathly lands. He screams with hate and paints the word *pratishodh* (retribution!) on the wall of his dark cell - with his own blood.

1578 AD, Portugal:

King Immannoel the Vth of Portugal receives an urgent let-ter from the Vatican. In the letter the Big Man himself refers to an ominous truth that when discovered will change the world forever. That secret buried in the sands of a western-Indian port-village must be found & wiped-out from the face of the Earth. It is once again about the lost city that once prospered on the banks of the fabled river. Once again! This chapter of human history must be destroyed forever. The very existence of the Church leadership depends on it.

The emperor is advised to use the fiercest force of the sword to achieve this end. King Immannoel sends a lethal fleet of two hundred warships to the quiet and peaceful Indian region of Goa. The natives were unaware of the prized remnant of mankind's greatest secret that lay buried in the deep chambers of popular yet fiercely guarded Goan temples. And little did they know that they awaited the bloodiest pages in the story of the sub-continent.

·||卐||·

1856 AD, Barrackpore:

The British sociologist and employee of the East India Company, Wayne Ashbrook, seeks a midnight meeting with his superior, Colonel Mark Sanders. He has made a discovery that cannot wait. It is a reality diametrically opposite to what he has been asked to record in his India diaries and documents. It is the biggest lie on the face of the Earth. It is about the Aryan invasion he has been indoctrinated with. It is about the racial superiority of this creed that arrived into India and colonized the natives. He has now unveiled scriptures and sources that point to an unbelievable truth about the mighty Aryans. Wayne knew this startling revelation would alter the very fundamental dynamics of religious and political discourses of the world.

To his utter shock, Wayne is warned of dire consequences by Colonel Sanders who wants Wayne to quietly document the false data and forget that he ever unearthed anything about the Aryans. He tells Wayne that he has no idea of the scale and implications of this reality, and the forces behind it. Wayne nods and takes leave of Sanders, but his conscience does not allow him to do as told. He tries to get the truth published in the *Calcutta Tribune*.

Wayne's mutilated body is found hanging on a tree outside the Writers' Building secretariat the next morning. The newspapers declare it an act of violence by two Indian sepoys. But the truth is something else. Something terrible.

The prophesied blood-thirst is about to raise its head again.

PROLOGUE

1700 BCE

He was the only human for miles. He could hardly see in the dark of that unusually fearsome, stormy night. Especially with the heavy trickle of his blood, tears and sweat mixed with the muddy waters of the unseasonal, torrential rain blurring his vision. In the pitch-black night the bald, bare-chested Brahmin struck with his axe back and forth at a feverish yet futile pace. He was attempting to cut at least one of the thick jute ropes that bound one pillar of the freshly built, man-made mountain of brick and bronze. Although made with the objective of diverting the course of a river, the enormous mound of stone, brick, metal and wooden blocks appeared threatening enough to alter the assault of even the bold tsunamis of a rogue sea. But then the river under question was no less than the mighty oceans themselves.

Muttering to himself under the roar of the downpour, like a man possessed, he used every ounce of strength from his body hardened by years of penance and Vedic discipline. He pounded the cable-like rope furiously even as his fingers splayed and started to bleed. When he couldn't breathe anymore he threw his head back and looked up once to let the heavy raindrops slap his face angrily. With the unsympathetic water washing the red mud off his eyelids, he let out a ghastly, sky-piercing scream. It was perhaps an attempt by his recently blackened soul to make the Gods hear his indescribable angst. But he knew it was too late. The Gods were horrified at his deeds and would not forgive him. Or anyone.

He started cutting the rope with his short axe again, more menacingly than before. He knew he had been trying to cut one coupling knot for over an hour now. The ropes were specially made, upon his own instructions. He knew there were 998 more brick, bronze and stone pillars held together by thousands of similar rope-knots that forged the unbreakable mount. And that it would take weeks to disassemble it if a thousand men worked day and night. The 999 strategically engineered and reinforced pillars were built as per his own careful architectural and astrologic guidelines. *What was he doing? Had he gone mad?* He knew he could not undo the giant mound even one bit. And yet he fired away his axe incessantly, hopelessly.

A solitary figure in the lonely miles of empty land ravaged by a mid-night cloudburst, Vivasvan Pujari, a man worshipped for decades as a *devta* (half-human, half-God), revered as the

Sun of Harappa, looked liked a ghost. He felt extreme pain and a sinking regret at the sinister consequence he knew could not be averted. He kept weeping, kept mumbling and kept chopping away. And then he heard it.

It had begun.

The ominous rumble of the mighty river gushing into an unnatural course, somewhere distant but not too far, made his blood curdle. The once generous, loving and nurturing Mother River had incarnated into a thirsty *Rakt-Dhaara* (Blood River) lunging towards devouring her very own children. The *River of the Wise* was betrayed by one of her favorite sons. She was betrayed by her devta son, Vivasvan Pujari.

The once righteous and indomitable Vivasvan Pujari let the axe slip from his hand and it fell on the slushy mud with a wet thud. He stood frozen gazing towards the direction he knew his now-manic Mother would appear in her demonic form. He knew it then. He knew he was going to be the first blood at her altar. Suddenly, he wanted it that way.

He slowly felt a sense of ease and relief spreading within him. He felt hope. Maybe his Mother would claw out his life but spare the millions of others. He dropped to his knees, stretched out arms in submission by his sides and opened his palms. The rain washed his taut and wounded body as if finally helping him cleanse his badly knotted conscience. As if pitying Vivasvan Pujari and offering him his last bath.

"Take my life, O mighty Mother! I have earned your wrath. And I submit myself to thee!", he yelled out as the night sky lit-up with an angry clap of thunder. It was as if the Gods were reject-

ing this fallen devta's plea.

He screamed again, this time his voice splitting with desperation and heavy sobbing, *"Do you not listen to your crestfallen son, O mighty Mother?! Take my life but forgive the others! They have not sinned as your son has. Take me!!!"*

The sky lit up again. It was nearly daylight for a few moments. The silent lightning flashed on Vivasvan Pujari's bleeding, sweating and deranged face. And then it followed. The delayed noise of the thunder was as loud as an exploding sun.

The Gods were saying NO!

Vivasvan Pujari felt a powerful gust of wind on his face as he saw the giant water-mountain appear from the corner of the far mound, turning directly towards the path where he sat crumbled on his knees. It looked like an enormous hydra dragon turning its head towards its prey. The din of the river was louder than the thunder that roared a few moments ago. Vivasvan Pujari sat there dazed, as he looked up at the mountain-high torrent casting a looming shadow even in the darkness. He appeared as small as an ant would in front of Mount Sumeru, as the sky-high tsunami of his Mother River was all but a few moments away from engulfing him.

Vivasvan Pujari had faltered in the last few days. He lost the glory of a lifetime in a few days of the blinding revenge he sought. But he was Vivasvan Pujari. A devta! Like all men of advanced *yogic* learning, he instantly summoned and centered his soul within his *kundalini*, he froze his heartbeat and prepared his mortal body for death. Even as he did that and was getting swept off the ground with the force of the invading water, he whispered a calm, last prayer.

"Mother, forgive them. Don't let them perish for my sins. Forgive them, Mother!"

The devastating river swallowed the devta Vivasvan Pujari like a mammoth tornado erases the existence of a dry twig. The Gods, the murderous blood-river, the dark night, the thunder of *Indra* (the God of lightning and storm), the vast expanse of land and the merciless rain stood witness to the end of the greatest man of his time. But the death of Vivasvan Pujari was not going to be the end of his impact on this planet. It was the beginning. He was going to live on in hatred, deceit, conspiracy and violent conflicts for thousands of years. He would haunt not just Aryavarta but the whole world with never-ending bloodshed and killing in the name of the very Gods that abandoned him. Even his death would not liberate him or human kind from the curse.

She maintained her unrelenting course. Despite Vivasvan Pujari's dying plea, the blood-river was not going to forgive them.

The *Saraswati* was going to devour the mighty city of Harappa, along with every last one of its inhabitants.

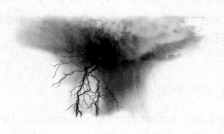

Delhi, 2017

VIDYUT

The mobile phone wouldn't stop ringing. Both Vidyut and Damini were in deep sleep and neither of them had the energy to get up and take the call. It was 4.30 am. The phone continued to ring incessantly. Damini shook Vidyut slowly.

'Vidyut…get up *na*. Its your phone.'

'Hmm…' mumbled Vidyut.

'*Arey* get up *please*,' Damini insisted with her eyes still closed.

Vidyut reached out for his phone, his hand groping for it on the bedside table.

'Who calls at such a God forsaken hour man?! Hello…!'

Vidyut nearly barked into the phone as he took the call.

There was silence in the room. Vidyut sat up on the bed and was listening to whoever was on the other side of the call very intently. His muscular body appeared as tense as his brow.

'All okay, baby?' enquired Damini.

Vidyut squeezed her wrist gently, indicating that he wanted complete silence. Damini knew Vidyut well. She opened her eyes and looked at Vidyut holding the phone tightly against his ear, teeth clenched, eyes shut in concentration.

'But Purohit ji, why didn't you tell me sooner?' said Vidyut to the person on the phone. Damini had no idea who Purohit ji was and why Vidyut looked so anxious suddenly. She got up on her elbow as she listened carefully.

'How much time does he have, Purohit ji?' asked Vidyut pensively. After a few seconds pause he said, 'I'll be there by this evening.'

·‖卐‖·

Vidyut hung-up the phone and rested his head on the bed's backrest, his eyes fixed on the ceiling. His well built chest, arms and shoulders combined with the rare glow of his fair skin gave him the appearance of royalty, of an august lineage. His long, light-brown hair complimented his chiseled features and penetrating eyes well. Vidyut looked every bit his name — *vidyut* or electricity! But there was infinitely more to his persona than just his Greek-God looks.

Damini knew she loved a strange and strong man, and while she never spoke about it to him, somewhere deep down she hoped to get married to him one day. She knew Vidyut was different from all the other boys and men she had met at the premier Hansraj College of the north campus of Delhi University, and the world in general. Apart from her deep and secret delight of *owning* this man who was pleasantly complexioned, well built, with deep-brown eyes like those of a Biblical conqueror and the intense facial expression of a man born to lead the world, she was convinced that Vidyut was uncommonly gifted. And he was. Vidyut was an inferno of talent, skill, spirituality and ambition. He was an entrepreneur par excellence at his young age of 34. He was a musician, a poet, a writer, a painter, a martial artist, a party-maker and a natural leader of men. His friends lovingly called him Video. What worried Damini sometimes was the kind of friends he had.

'Baby you okay?' she enquired gently after a minute. 'Who is this Purohit ji and where do you have to be by this evening?'

'Varanasi. Or Kashi or Banaras…as most people call it,' replied Vidyut, still gazing at the ceiling.

'Why Banaras, love? Out of the blue…?'

'Not really out of the blue, Damini…but I wasn't expecting to be called like this. I was supposed to *never* return to Kashi.'

There was silence in the room. Damini listened with disbelief at the mysterious and disconnected statements Vidyut was speaking in. It wasn't like him. And it wasn't like her assertive journalist self to keep waiting till eternity for the answers she wanted quickly. She sat up fully attentive, tied her hair swiftly in a bun while holding a hairpin between her teeth like only beautiful and confident women do, and fired her questions, politely yet firmly.

'Kashi? You mean Banaras…or Varanasi…or whatever! Why do you have to go there, baby? What were you not expecting? And for God's sake…why were you to *never* return to that place? And what do you mean return? When were you there in the first place? And how on earth have we never spoken about all this? Can you please tell me everything?' Damini was now as curious as she was edgy.

Vidyut turned to look at her, as if noticing her presence for the first time since his phone rang.

'We have not spoken about it because it was not important. Kashi was a closed chapter for me. For years when I tried to claw my way back there, I was prohibited from doing so. And now when I have learnt to live without the phantoms of the past, they give me a call?!' said Vidyut with a laugh of disbelief.

Before Damini could organize her thoughts, Vidyut sprung up from the bed and walked to his wardrobe. He took out a cigarette box and lit a cigarette. Now Damini was really nervous. It was after nine months that Vidyut had put a cigarette to his lips. And it was now she knew something was really not right. Her eyes silently followed Vidyut as he walked out to the balcony of his sprawling penthouse in tony Gurgaon where she lived with him. She quietly followed and stood next to him leaning against the railing of the balcony. She wore a very light and short negligee that accentuated her slim and attractive figure. Damini was as beautiful physically as she was intelligent. She did not utter a word. Vidyut was in a trance. And for the first time since she knew him, Vidyut looked afraid. Of what, she knew not.

·|| ॐ ||·

Kashi is the holiest city in Hinduism, perhaps the most ancient religion and way-of-life on Earth. Originally called both Kashi and Varanasi, as hundreds and thousands of years passed the name changed first to *Baraansi* and then to Banaras under the influence of Pali literature. Hindu mythological scriptures have it that when the great floods destroy the whole world in the final judgment-day deluge called *pralay*, Lord Shiva Himself will protect the city of Kashi by raising it on the tip of his mighty trident or *trishul*. A city that has seen over 10,000 winters, Varanasi is said to be home to some of the greatest occult practitioners and powers of this world, *and all others*. It is also the keeper of the planet's most sinister secrets.

It was a 90-minute flight from New Delhi to Varanasi. Vidyut was going to take the 3 pm flight so as to be with Purohit ji by 6 pm. He had a devoted set of friends and colleagues who took care of everything for him. And vice versa. Vidyut and his core team operated like one single organism that needed very little conversation among them. Most things got done with the exchange of a glance or two words on a phone text. Vidyut's dear friend Bala, short for Balakrishnan, was his closest confidante and perhaps the only man Vidyut fully trusted. Bala was not only Vidyut's next in command at the company, he was also Vidyut's best friend. He was ex-military, a highly decorated army officer during his short service commission. Bala could crack complex financial models with the same ease with which he could bust the ribs of an opponent in unarmed combat. And he worshipped Vidyut. He loved Vidyut.

Vidyut ran a corporate security company that protected its large multinational clients against technology-based competitive espionage. Vidyut launched his company as a small start-up, which was now among the leading industrial security companies in India. The success of his company made Vidyut a very sought-after man, and gave him access to the movers and shakers of corporate India. Powerful politicians, who perhaps needed more technology-based security than even business houses, swiftly noticed the use of his company's products and services. Vidyut was soon a speed-dial for many of them. They took pride in having Vidyut at their social lunches and garden dinners. At a very young age Vidyut was a very influential man. But for people who knew his lineage, for people like Purohit ji, this came as no surprise. Vidyut was no ordinary man. He wasn't supposed to be one.

·||卐||·

Wearing a casual grey t-shirt and blue jeans, Vidyut looked much younger than he actually was. He was packing light, just for a day or two. Damini was worried about all that was happening, but maintained a brave and smiling face. Vidyut looked at her every now and then, and flashed his disarming smile or winked at her playfully. He wanted to comfort her and show her that everything was normal. They both knew it wasn't.

After he was done with the quick packing, Vidyut paused for a while and stood staring out of the window. By this time Bala had entered the house and made himself comfortable with a carton of coconut water from the fridge. He sat on one of the dining chairs and sipped at his sweet coconut water silently. Both Vidyut and Damini were used to Bala's presence in their home, and they loved it. He was family.

Vidyut noticed Bala.

'Hi Bala.'

'Hey Video'.

'Whassup man? *Khaana khaaya?* Had lunch?' enquired Vidyut.

'Yea yea…' Bala responded without looking at his friend. This was enough show of affection for the day. But it meant the world to Vidyut.

What happened next was something Damini dreaded and couldn't imagine happening. Vidyut walked to the safe in his study and pulled out the *maha-panchaanng* – the Hindu or *Sanatana* calendar and planner. Damini froze with fear and her mouth went dry. The last time Vidyut had taken out this advanced *panchaanng* was his life's worst day. It was the day he had lost his beloved mother! Despite his modern clothing and appearance, despite his flashy cars and his technology company - Vidyut was an expert practitioner of Vedic astrology. He could read the *kundalis* (horoscopes) of people with the same prowess with which he often scanned through software codes.

·||ॐ||·

Damini protested by covering her open mouth with both her hands and by allowing an expression of horror to envelope her face. Vidyut noticed it but made no effort to comfort her. He seemed to be in a trance again. He spread the panchaanng out on the dining table next to where Bala sat, chanted a silent Sanskrit mantra in his mouth and leaned over the large chart. His *panchaanng* was more detailed than the regular thing available in the market. Every year his dear friend Gopal from a Hindu monastery in the Himalayas sent him this authentic *panchaanng*. It was the real deal. It could be interpreted, studied and put to use only by the grandmasters of Vedic astrology. Vidyut was one of them. And Gopal was among the many friends of Vidyut that mystified Damini.

Bala could see the panic on Damini's face and the tears welling up in her eyes. He put his hand on Vidyut's and asked softly yet firmly, 'What are you doing man? Why do you need *this* now?'

Vidyut did not respond. Damini could not take it any more. She ran to Vidyut's side, held him tightly by his arm and pulled him to face her.

'What are you doing, baby?' she yelled at him, her voice ready to burst into a sob.

There was momentary irritation in Vidyut at being disturbed like this, but he quickly regained his composure. He realized that an explanation was now overdue. He had been behaving strangely ever since he took Purohit ji's call, and his love for Damini demanded that he shares everything with her. Or *almost* everything.

'Come here baby,' said Vidyut as he affectionately pulled Damini by her arm and made her sit on a couch close to the dining table. 'I can tell you what is important in two minutes, or try and tell you everything in the greatest detail. But for that even two days will fall short,' he continued.

Damini just stared lovingly at Vidyut, her eyes wet and her beautiful face slightly contorted as she tried very hard to hold back a barrage of tears.

'Even if I tell you everything Damini, you will not be able to believe it. You will probably think Vidyut has lost it. You will probably want me to meet a psychiatric consultant, if you don't want me to contact one already!' Vidyut laughed meekly as he tried to add some humor to the tense situation – in vain. Damini kept staring at him with the same disbelief and fear.

'Baby just tell me what is going on. Your woman is a strong woman. She can handle it,' said Damini as matter-of-factly as possible. 'I didn't want to push you till now, but I know you so well. You would never pull out the *panchaanng* if something was not seriously out of place.'

Vidyut was silent for a moment. He then took Damini's soft and artistic fingers in his hands and sat down on his knees on the floor in front of the sofa she sat on. He looked at her with a charming tilt of his head and a genuine smile, this time for real. He kissed her hands and said simply, 'Damini, *I am half-human, half-God.*'

Paris, 2017

'KILL THAT BLOODY ARYAN-BOY.'

Reg Mariani's Lufthansa flight landed at the Charles De Gaulle Airport. He peered out of his first-class window at the rainy Paris evening. He did not really relish the inviting sight. He had work to do.

A tall and handsome man in his mid-forties, Reg strode briskly through the airport exit, stepped out of gate number 6 and slipped into a waiting black Mercedes Benz S 500. He instructed the chauffeur to drive him to the lovely Hotel Regina at the Rue De Rivoli. After a fifty-minute drive and a courteous check-in, Reg was in the most luxurious suite of the posh Parisian hotel overlooking the *Musee du Louvre*. Money was the last thing Reg had to worry about. He was funded by the world's richest institution. *Ever.*

After a quick shower, the finest Italian suit and an anxious cigarette, Reg was on his way to his dinner rendezvous with a man known not by his name but by his title - the *Maschera Bianca* – someone Reg considered to be the most dangerous man in the world. Or second most dangerous maybe. The *most* dangerous man was the one who had sent Reg from Rome to Paris. With a hand-written note.

·‖卐‖·

The *Maschera Bianca* was a 40-year-old dashing man, with beautiful, almost feminine features, and penetrating eyes that could burn a hole into metal. He sat alone and relaxed in the expensive *brasserie*, sipping on his vodka and smoking an Indian brand of cigarettes. An acquaintance from India regularly sent him a supply of his favorite Indian tobacco. The brasserie was filled with fine people, though more men than women. The *Maschera* welcomed Reg with a warm smile and a wave as soon as the latter entered the restaurant. This was not the first time the two were meeting.

Reg was greeted by a warm handshake and an order for double vodka, the finest on the menu. The Maschera offered Reg a cigarette from his Indian pack. Reg obliged with a smile and asked a bit hesitantly, 'So you are still in touch with your Indian employee?' The Maschera lit Reg's cigarette and replied smiling, 'Not an employee. A friend! I only work with friends, Reg. You should know that.'

Reg nodded with a grin. He knew the Maschera had no

friends.

·||ॐ||·

'So how can I help you?' asked the Maschera.

'You know who I work for. And you know what has been bothering my mentor and employer for so many years.'

The Maschera nodded profusely as a sign of his complete understanding of the situation. While the Maschera looked very calm, Reg was uneasy about how a man of his stature and profession was sitting alone in a public brasserie. Reg expected the Maschera to be more guarded than the President of the United States. He continued nevertheless.

'Clearly the situation has now become serious. They have called *him* to the clan HQ'.

The Maschera stopped nodding and his eyes became still. A man of his extreme intellect could sense that the prophesied hour had finally arrived.

'So what does the big man want?' asked the Maschera after a pause, referring to Reg's employer as the 'big man'.

Reg quietly took out the hand-written note he had carried from Rome in a sealed envelope and handed it over to the Maschera. The latter opened the note, read its contents in less than a second and handed it back to Reg. Stopping for a moment to think, the Maschera picked-up his glass of vodka and emptied it in one gulp. He puffed the last drag from his Indian cigarette and extinguished it in the ashtray.

After a few seconds of pause the Maschera spoke referring

again to Reg's employer, 'the big fellow knows this is not going to be easy right? This…this…*man* cannot be harmed without the greatest of effort.'

'Yes he knows,' replied Reg. 'He knows because he tried to use his own craft first. It didn't work. He would not ask me to meet you, of all people, to take care of someone ordinary.'

The Maschera looked deep into Reg's eyes with his cold and fearsome gaze. After a few seconds he smiled and said, 'Consider this done, Reg. Tell the big man.'

Saying this the Maschera got up from his chair and shook Reg's hand like a regular old friend. As soon as he turned to walk away, Reg and four other guests were stunned to see the entire restaurant get up from their seats. It was only then Reg realized that 45 out of the 50 guests of the brasserie were the Maschera's security detail. They all got up in unison and walked out of the brasserie, the Maschera lost somewhere amidst them. Reg knew now that there were more than one hundred concealed automatic guns in that brasserie all this while they were speaking. From past dealings he knew that each of the Maschera's fighters carried a minimum of two deadly weapons on their person at any time.

Reg was always afraid of the Maschera. Despite knowing that the Maschera was Europe's most dreaded and mystical Mafia boss, Reg still found something amiss about the man. Something eerie.

Reg's attention went to the crumpled note the Maschera had returned to him. He picked it up and saw the familiar hand-writing of his powerful mentor.

He did not flinch as he read the five words written on that note – *Kill that bloody Aryan-boy.*

Banaras, 2017

KASHI: THE ANCIENT CITY

Varanasi's Lal Bahadur Shastri International Airport at Babatpur is about 26 kilometers to the northwest of the main city. Vidyut got off the plane and walked straight to a waiting cab that had been arranged by his office. His team knew Vidyut treated his time as precious currency and was not one to waste even a minute searching for a taxi. He counted every minute and valued every moment. He expected a fast and classy cab to be parked for him. It was there. And he expected the driver to know where exactly he wanted to go. The driver did.

Vidyut's Executive Assistant Rhea was well trained. More than that, she truly adored and respected Vidyut. And his time. And she was madly in love with him. Vidyut had that effect on any woman he spent time with. Just like one of his illustrious ancestors did about 3,700 years ago, in a different and distant land.

The white-colored BMW SUV moved swiftly out of the airport and covered the first few kilometers in no time. Vidyut sat in front next to the driver. He wore a black tee, blue jeans, reflecting sunglasses and a sparkling Rolex. The driver of the car was as excited as he was uneasy. He had never ferried a passenger like Vidyut. He could not fully understand it, but he could sense a powerful energy-wave emanating from his customer for the day. Paras could not hold himself back.

'Sir, you are from Delhi?'

'Hmm,' mumbled Vidyut as he speedily responded to business emails on his smartphone.

'Sir you come to Banaras for holiday?'

'No.'

The driver of the cab could sense his customer was in no mood for a conversation. He persisted nevertheless. For some unknown reason he wanted this intense and handsome man to acknowledge his presence.

'Sir myself Paras Pandey.'

Vidyut now turned and smiled generously at Paras Pandey. Much as he was busy and engulfed by the powers and demons of his own world and life, Vidyut was exceptionally kind to people. He could sense Paras' effort to start a chat and the man Vidyut was, he would never let anyone down as far as he could help it. Paras was delighted by the show of civility by his clearly rich and mysteriously powerful customer.

'Hello Paras. I am Vidyut,' said Vidyut extending his hand out to Paras, who grabbed it with great enthusiasm and eagerness. He grinned widely at Vidyut as they shook hands, but something made him revere this hand he held. It was not the first time he had felt that nearly divine touch.

'Sir, how long you stay in Banaras?' enquired Paras in the typically broken but supremely effective English that expert tourism business-folk use in India.

'*Ek din*. One day,' replied Vidyut.

'*Arey* no Sir…you will not be allowed to leave Banaras, the city of Lord *Bholenath* (another loving name for Lord Shiva), till the time He himself permits you to,' said Paras jovially.

Little did Paras know that his casual words would turn out to be dangerously prophetic, for Vidyut was not supposed to leave Varanasi alive.

·‖ॐ‖·

Banaras' colonies and localities have the most tongue-twisting names – *Naati-imli, Lahura-beer, Kabeer-chaura, Vishwanath-gali, Baans-phaatak, Dhoop-chandi, Assi, Gadauliya, Lanka* and more. But very few people know that each name has a profound history and a story that is as old as humankind itself. For example, Kabeer-chaura is located where the followers of the legendary philosopher and ascetic-poet Kabeer built a hermitage in his memory (although quite contrary to the teachings of the great Kabeer himself, who spurned institutions that attempted to act as conduits between the Almighty and His subjects). Similarly Assi was named after the ancient Assi river and the associated sacrificial *ghaat* or pier. The name Varanasi itself was derived from the primordial river *Varana*. Nothing in Varanasi was frivolous or trivial. Nothing. The only frivolity was in the skeptical eyes of the uninformed observer.

Paras knew Vidyut's destination in the city was the most powerful and secretive Hindu monastery in all of Varanasi – the *Dev-Raakshasa Matth* – or the God-Demon Monastery. He was petrified because the host involved was none other than the mystical, the worshipped and the dreaded Brahmin priest – Dwarka Shastri, who led this powerful matth. While most of Varanasi's monasteries or *matths*, training-grounds or *akhadas* and educational hostels or *gurukuls* had a strange mystique or secrecy about them, the matth that was led by Dwarka Shastri was exceptionally feared. And this modern, boyish, city-bred man Vidyut wanted to get dropped in the very heart of the hell-fire. Paras felt the urge to warn this seemingly naïve gentleman.

'Vidyut Sir, why you go to this place please? It is very… you know…*daraavna* (scary),' advised Paras, though it sounded more like a frightened warning. He continued, 'Dwarka Shastri ji is a saint…but very short-tempered. He curses frequently now, you see? And his curse never go wrong.'

Paras was perplexed because his customer seemed unmoved by this subtle yet dark caution. Vidyut's gaze on the road ahead did not flicker for even a split-second. Paras wondered if the man next to him was fearless or foolish. Or something *else*.

॥ ☩ ॥

Varanasi is not everyone's cup of tea. A lot of it is stinky, ugly, dusty, crowded, jammed, poor and repulsive. It represents everything that is not right with humankind. And yet it is undoubtedly the most beautiful city in the whole world. Just an inch below its horrendous outer skin, lie the most profound and the most spiritually powerful mysteries and philosophies man has ever known. In that sense, it is quite like the universe in which we live - dark and cruel on its outside material crust, yet calm and immortal in its inner realm. The ancient city of Kashi was meant to represent this duality since the beginning of time. But only the gifted seeker could spot this fine Godly construct.

॥ ☩ ॥

Paras stopped his car when it could go no further into the typical narrow lanes of the city. He dropped Vidyut very close to Dwarka Shastri's matth, which itself was in close vicinity of the city's greatest Shiva temple – the majestic *Kashi-Vishwanath Mandir*. Despite the unstoppable rush of people and the screaming of bicycle-rickshaw horns, the place had universally accepted holiness. Even as Paras pulled out his car from the drop-point, he touched his forehead with his fingers and submitted a small prayer to the very air of the place, a common Hindu gesture in reverence of the Almighty. Even as he drove out of the narrow alley, Paras leaned his head out of the window and called out to Vidyut, 'Vidyut *babu*, my number is 98456738917…please call me if you need anything.' Vidyut smiled and nodded in response. He had a near photographic memory…or phonographic at that.

With the small rucksack on his back, Vidyut walked steadily into the really narrow and wet alleys leading towards the secretive and feared monastery. Vidyut was here after two and a half decades, but he remembered every path like the back of his hand. Nothing had changed. The same constricted lanes between residential buildings built hundreds of years ago. Almost every wall painted with sceneries and portraits of Hindu Gods and Goddesses, each painting expressing boundless love and devotion in the form of bright colors. The same fragrance of marigold flowers mixed with temple incense. Almost every home in Varanasi had a small temple, and it was cleaned and anointed every day. The same kind of people walked past him, visibly poor but strangely content. Every third person who passed by was a priest or a holy-man. Vidyut knew where his destination was, and *vice versa*! Aware of every step he took and after a few minutes of walking, Vidyut knew he was very close. He felt his pulse racing faster as he advanced closer and closer to his goal. It was not the pulse of a man nervous or afraid. It was the happy heart-thumping one feels when coming to family after a long time. And Vidyut knew he was coming home – his *real* home.

Vidyut reached the massive stone-carved *dwaar* or archway that marked the entrance to the *Dev-Raakshasa Matth*. The archway was beautifully and intricately chiseled into fine designs, patterns and figures. It looked awe-inspiring at once, but the real narrative lay in the small stone figures and figurines carved into it. A close inspection would uncover the powerful, haunting and immortal legends those figures told. However, for Vidyut there was no fear or power associated to this archway. There was only love, only a warm embrace. He stepped close to one of the ends of the archway and caressed it gently with his fingers, like an infant touches the cheek of a beloved grandparent. Even as Vidyut immersed himself in the memories and affection this gate held for him, a rough and loud voice barked, 'How dare you lay your hands on the *dwaar*?'

Vidyut turned to see a young man in his late twenties, well built and clad in the flowing traditional saffron attire of Hindu monks, charging towards him. He sported a big *tilak* or vermillion paste on his large forehead. Most ominously, he carried in his hands a short but battle-ready trishul or trident that had three spearheads made of shining steel at its attacking end, held by a thick, polished bamboo stick. Vidyut was unfazed.

'Who the hell are you and how on Earth did you dare to touch this pious pillar?' demanded the young fellow. Vidyut observed that he was a good-looking man with honest features and expression.

'How much do you know about this pillar and this archway, brother?' enquired Vidyut with a soft smile.

The young man was taken aback by the fearlessness and insolence of this stranger. But he also sensed something familiar about Vidyut. He couldn't tell what it was.

'This gate is over 800 years old,' replied the young man with no letting-up in the anger in his voice.

'And…?' asked Vidyut.

'What do you mean *and*?! It is made of a very rare kind of stone.'

'And…?'

'And I am going to break your big-city face if you don't walk away right now!' growled the young man.

Vidyut looked straight into the eyes of this fine young fellow, paused for a few moments and then spoke with supreme confidence.

'This gateway was built in the year 1253 under the steward-ship of the then matthadheesh Shri Bhairava Shastri. The stone-block used to carve this magnificent archway was a gift from the King of Kannauj, and weighed an incredible 1008 tonnes. The primary architect of the gateway was Pundit Ramakant Deekshit who employed 27 fine craftsmen from Mathura, and they worked continuously for 3 years to complete this masterpiece. It was erected and commissioned in the winter of year 1256 and was inaugurated by none other than the *Kashi-naresh* (King of Kashi) himself. '

The young man stood dumbstruck. 'Who are you?' were the only words that escaped his mouth.

'My name is Vidyut Shastri.'

The young man froze with disbelief. In a few quick moments Vidyut could see his eyes welling-up with tears. Before Vidyut could say anything, the young man crumbled and fell at his feet. Vidyut was bewildered as he could feel the man's hands wrapped around his ankles in a show of complete submission and devotion. Even before Vidyut could bend down to lift the man up, he had sprung to his feet and run towards the inner sanctum of the monastery like a man possessed.

'He has arrived! He has arrived! He has arrived!' the young man kept yelling at the top of his voice as he vanished into one of the lanes leading to the matth.

They were waiting for Vidyut's arrival. For centuries.

Harappa, 1700 BCE

THE LAST DEVTA

Vivasvan Pujari bathed himself in the pious and sparkling waters of the *Sindhu*, a small tributary of the mighty Saraswati River, that ran next to Harappa. Harappa worshipped the powerful river as the very giver of life and knowledge. Inhabitants of the massive metropolis loved the river as much as they revered it, and the most affectionate among them called her *Sara Maa* or Sara the Mother.

The very existence of Harappa and both its close and distant provinces like Mohenjo Daro and Lothal depended on the Saraswati. She provided them with drinking water, irrigation, transport, fish, medicine, protection against invading armies and sacred banks for advanced Vedic rituals. She was the very soul of the Harappan society.

The day after tomorrow was going to be the biggest day of Vivasvan Pujari's life. A man of fifty-five years, he looked not a day older than thirty-five. His ivory skin radiated an unusual glow and he had the broad forehead of a powerful monarch. Hailed as the *Surya* (Sun) of Harappa for the brilliance of his triumphs, he had the eyes of a very kind man, who also enjoyed unquestioned authority. His built was as stone-cast as that of an expert athlete and his muscles glistened under his fine *angavastram* (upper body robe). Vivasvan Pujari was not only a grandmaster of ancient scriptures, mantras and hymns, he was also one of the authors of the profound and intense *Vedas* – the most contemporary work of literature, nature sciences and spirituality. He was said to be the recipient of divine blessings from the primordial *Rishis* who were the causal forces of *creation* itself, along with *Shiva* and *Shakti*. Vivasvan Pujari was not a man. He was a divine phenomenon. He was the last devta ever to be born on planet Earth.

Or so they believed then.

Chandradhar was pacing up and down his grand study. While he wasn't too happy about the turn of events himself, his real worry was something else. Chandradhar was exceptionally wise and a master of all the spiritual and scientific learning of his time. He was the second most influential man across the vast plains of the mammoth Harappan settlements. He was the chief treasurer of the state. He was also the acting head of the priestly council. Most importantly, he was chief of the *Gopaalaks* or the raisers of Harappa's greatest wealth, the divine milk-bearing livestock. Anyone who controlled *this* fortune, controlled all of Harappa. And yet the second most influential man in all of the state was envious. He was envious of the first most influential man in all of Harappa. He was envious of his best friend, his very own brother-in-law.

Chandradhar was envious of none other than the mighty Vivasvan Pujari.

But Chandradhar's real worry was something else. His real worry was his wife - Priyamvada or the soft-spoken. Unfortunately his wife was anything but that. She was his life's greatest choler. Unlike his own large-hearted self, Priyamvada hated everything and everyone. Chandradhar feared that the rub-off of her emotional venom was slowly transforming him into a monstrous soul, something Harappa had never known. He hated her. And yet, deep down he loved her madly. He couldn't live without her.

Priyamvada entered the study where he was pacing frantically. He could see her profound hatred veiled well under her beautiful and smiling face.

'Congratulations Pundit Chandradhar,' she said cheerily, and then hissed like a witch - 'You've lost again, you fool!'

·‖卐‖·

Vivasvan climbed the steps of the sacred *Sindhu-Saraswati ghaat* (pier) towards the posse of state-guards waiting for him in utmost attention, holding his signature banner of the shining Sun high. It was their duty to protect Vivasvan Pujari under all circumstances. But more than considering this their duty, they felt blessed to be in this position of closeness to Vivasvan Pujari, the greatest treasure of the Harappan civilization.

Apart from being the man who brought the ten warring tribes of Aryavarta together into the historic peace accord, Vivasvan Pujari was credited with the most profound contribution to Harappa. He was the one who rode the first five thousand battle-beasts or *ashvas* (horses) into Harappa, making it the most powerful military in the world. This was immediately after he had defeated the mighty Sura, the powerful warlord from the far west, where they spoke the strange *a-bhasha* (un-language). Vivasvan Pujari was the most revered man across all of the vast plains and people knew he was not just another ordinary mortal. No mortal could achieve and deliver what Vivasvan Pujari had. He was indeed a devta – half-human, half-God.

Vivasvan was elated today. He was going to be declared the Chief Priest of Harappa the morning after next by the blessings of the highest council of the divine-seven, or the *Saptarishi*, which would make him virtually the emperor of the nation-state. 'Emperor' was not really a welcome term in the powerful democracy that Vivasvan Pujari and Pundit Chandradhar had painstakingly carved Harappa into, but the Chief Priest practically controlled everything.

However, not everyone was taking this coronation of sorts lightly.

Definitely not Priyamvada.

||ॐ||

Vivasvan Pujari entered his massive yet simple home. It was a gigantic structure in the heart of Harappa that stated in no unclear terms what stature Vivasvan Pujari commanded in the metropolis. And yet it appeared to be nothing more than a gentle hermitage – the abode of a family that lived its life in intense austerity, in the service of God and His people.

As soon as he entered his house, Vivasvan was greeted by Sanjna, his graceful and devoted wife. She was widely loved and revered both as Vivasvan Pujari's better half, as well as for her own charisma, social service and profound Vedic learning.

Sanjna served Vivasvan's morning repast in which his son Manu joined him. Manu was named after the first man in Vedic scriptures, and was a handsome, strapping young lad of twenty-two. He was immensely proud of his father, and vice versa.

'So how is your learning of *Atharva Veda* progressing, Manu?' asked Vivasvan gently while scooping up his *kheer* (rice-porridge) from the fresh banana-leaf plate using his fingers. 'You know it is among the most important sciences you need to learn, as it deals with occult practices and knowledge of the ethereal world?'

'Yes father, I am concentrating a lot on it, as it interests me deeply,' replied Manu. 'Although there are some scary elements of the spirit-world that I will need to learn directly from you,' continued Manu with an element of jest in his tone. He very well knew that the dark-sciences were out of bounds for all young practitioners. He enjoyed teasing his father, the great Vivasvan Pujari, nevertheless.

'You'll get one tight slap from me one of these days. How many years has it been since I gave you one?' enquired Vivasvan jovially. He knew his son was having fun. Both of them shared a hearty laugh, followed by a doting caress from Vivasvan on Manu's shaven head. He loved Manu and Sanjna more than his life.

Sanjna sat next to Manu, transferring some more *kheer,* potato curry and *pooris* onto her son's banana leaf every couple of minutes. Her life's greatest joy was to see Vivasvan and Manu bond like the sun and light. The family of Vivasvan Pujari was a model of love, trust, simplicity and togetherness. It was as if Sara Maa and the Gods themselves had fashioned this beautiful family. Sanjna spent several hours every day expressing her gratitude to the Gods and seeking their continued blessings.

But the Gods were about to fail Sanjna. Terribly.

·||ॐ||·

A dark force had begun its ominous work against this powerful yet gentle, pious family. A distant forest-cave was witness to the commencement of a cruel black-magic ritual. The three Mesopotamian *andh-maayaavi* (blind magicians) cackled maniacally and bathed in human blood and wine, as they began the ghastly rites. Their growling chants resonated in the forest, killing every animal, bird, plant and insect in the vicinity. The three of them had to summon and combine their entire army of dark forces and violent, dissatisfied spirits in this one last do-or-die quest.

It was not going to be easy to vanquish the devta himself.

Banaras, 2017

ROMI PEREIRA

It was sweltering hot and humid in that sardine-can of a railway coach. The skinny, bespectacled young man was being pushed around in the unreserved second-class compartment of the train. He looked so vulnerable that almost everyone in that angry coach kicked him around. He had changed many trains in order to reach Banaras from his current living quarters in Pondicherry. Romi looked like a software geek straight from the hostels of India's famous engineering colleges. He was scrawny, had thick black-rimmed glasses, unkempt hair, fair skin and an innocent, handsome face.

Romi had a very insecure, very subdued personality. He could not stand up to anyone, especially since he could never confront his brutally punishing ex-Mumbai-police father. With a troubled childhood bruised regularly by a drunk and violent Dad, Romi grew up to be a very gentle yet complex character. He was afraid of everything and everyone. He stammered before every word that he spoke in his soft and endearing voice.

His father had died in a bizarre domestic accident when Romi was just thirteen. Romi's mother had anyway abandoned him and her half-mad husband just two years after Romi's birth. Being from a landed family, Romi inherited a lot of estate after his father's demise. He did not shed a single tear as he led the last rites of the drunk, fallen man. His distant relatives figured it was understandably deep shock.

Romi topped his engineering batch. He had no friends in school or at his engineering college. He was the laughing stock of his entire class. Even Priya laughed at him along with them. *Even Priya.* Romi was a master at the English language and when Rahul, the most handsome and popular student of their class inexplicably committed suicide, they asked Romi to write his obituary. Romi left the beautifully written note under Priya's girls' hostel room. They loved his gesture, since Priya was Rahul's girlfriend. They continued to laugh at him nevertheless.

What they failed to notice was that Romi's father and Priya's boyfriend had both died mysteriously. Brutally.

As the train made its brief halt at the massive Varanasi railway station, Romi struggled to make his way out of the train compartment. His slim and scared figure tried to squeeze out of the compartment door, apologizing to everyone on the way. As he was moving out he stepped on a large dark man's toe. In the heat of the moment that burly figure turned, mouthed expletives and slapped Romi across his face. Romi's thick black specs almost flew out of his childishly handsome face.

'Sorry sir,' said Romi to the dark man, almost crying and trying to get his glasses back to his face. The thick dark man in the purple shirt frowned, inebriated by the confidence he felt as a victorious warrior. Everyone around looked away as if nothing just happened.

Romi was almost thrown out from the coach on to the Varanasi railway platform number 3. He could barely maintain his balance as his poor, weak figure managed to get hold of his backpack. Romi was in tears as he regained his composure, wiped his wet eyes and unsurely trudged along the railway platform. He was a pathetic sight. As everyone knew, Romi was a complete loser who had no strength or talent whatsoever.

As the train moved along, the dark man in the purple shirt gurgled in his own blood. In the chaos of the crowd, an expert killer had slit his throat in just a centimeter long gash. But a gash that was sure to kill the man, slowly and painfully.

Everyone knew Romi was a complete loser who had no strength or talent whatsoever.

Except that he was among the world's most sophisticated and ruthless assassins.

And the *Maschera Bianca,* or the Italian *White Mask,* had taken notice.

Banaras, 2017

'NOBODY MISSED YOU...?'

The piping hot *kachoris* and sweet orange colored *jalebis* piled-up in front of Vidyut were irresistible. They had been supplied by the famous Basant Mahal *halwaai* (caterer). Vidyut's last two hours had been a merry reminder of his childhood days at the matth.

The young man's screaming had resulted in Purohit ji's hasty emergence at the gate of the matth. He had broken down as he had caught the first glimpse of Vidyut. He looked at Vidyut and burst into childlike sobs, like those of a long lost love. And why not? Vidyut was like a son to him. Purohit ji had been the first and only father-like figure Vidyut had ever felt the protection of, ever since he lost his father Kartikeya.

After the intense exchange of affection and tight hugs; after the complains and counter-accusations of two people trying to prove who loves the other more were over, Purohit ji had welcomed Vidyut into the very sanctum sanctorum of the Dev-Raakshasa matth. While entry to this area was carefully restricted, Purohit ji had no doubt in his mind whatsoever. Vidyut was the ultimate master and commander of this clan anyway, and had been summoned by the spiritual force of the matth to come and take his rightful place.

·||卐||·

And so it began with the feeding. Just like a mother treats her beloved child returning from a distant land, Purohit ji and his henchmen spared no effort in pampering Vidyut with a mountain of goodies on his table. Varanasi is a food-lover's paradise and Vidyut was served an assortment of the city's most delectable vegetarian delicacies.

It started with the *kachoris* – round, deep-fried puffs stuffed with minced and spiced lentils. These taste much better than it sounds. Followed by the ubiquitous *samosa* – a pyramidal shaped patty of refined flour stuffed with a spicy potato paste. Again deep-fried. Again simply delicious. Then came the signature *tamaatar-chaap* or the tomato-mince of Banaras – a thick batter of fried tomatoes, potatoes, peppercorn, onions and finest Indian spices. Shallow fried for a change. Delicious nevertheless. Vidyut was forced to consume *two* portions of each of the above delights. And then arrived the famous Banaras sweetmeats or *mithai*.

A whole epic can be written about the dairy based sweets of Banaras. Perhaps Calcutta (now Kolkata) is the only other

Asian city that can match Banaras' variety and finesse when it comes to sweets. The experienced and discerning culinary expert can identify a Banaras *mithai* by only its appearance or even fragrance. For Vidyut there was the unique *launglataa*...the clove-flavored delight with a spiced stuffing of extra-condensed milk. Then the *jalebis* and the *kheel-kadam* - cottage cheese in fragrant sugar syrup wrapped inside a dumpling of powdered *khoya*.

Vidyut was a supremely fit man who swam miles every day during summers and ran near-marathons on his treadmill in winters. He also practiced advanced *pranayama* (yogic controlled-breathing exercises) every morning. His fitness level was so high that no amount of Banaras oil or *mithai* could beat him. And yet Vidyut was unable to move after this calorie tempest! He enjoyed every moment of it, especially the love that came along with the food.

He was living Banaras like he did nearly three decades ago.

Vidyut was reintroduced to a lot of his childhood friends. The young man with the ominous trident was none other than Sonu, Purohit ji's son. By now he was totally in awe of Vidyut and threw himself repeatedly into the latter's hugs many times. All Vidyut could do was to laugh out loud every time Sonu innocently did that. Then there was Balvanta, the 'humanoid' as Vidyut used to call him playfully as a child. He was the beastly looking, forever-frowning *Kshatriya* fighter. He would never smile. He didn't know what a laugh was. He was alien to the concept of human happiness. But he was a protector. And a master artist of *Kalaripayattu*, the ancient Indian martial art said to have been founded by none other than the mighty ascetic-warrior *Parashuram* himself.

Thereafter Vidyut met Govardhan dada - the semi-blind ayurvedic master-pharmacologist. He had not changed a bit, except for his hair turning snow white. Then Vidyut met his nursery school friend Biji, who had now become a school-master. They all met him with great affection and awe.

And then he saw the stunning Naina.

Vidyut was momentarily smitten as he saw Naina's almond brown eyes and her arrogant yet soulful submission. She walked right into him boldly and bowed deeply in a *namaste* without taking her eyes away from his even for a second. Under normal circumstances Vidyut would have embraced her in a warm hug. But this was the matth. And Vidyut was here after decades. He wanted to be sure of what was the accepted norm here nowadays, even if Naina was his child-hood friend.

Naina looked nothing like what Vidyut would have expected. For a girl from a comparatively upcoming city like Banaras, especially when she grew up in the most conservative Brah-minical upbringing, Naina was enchantingly attractive. She had glowing tanned skin and the features of a celestial god-dess. Her eyes were large and piercing. She had a full mouth, a small but sharp nose and dark brown hair that curled nat-urally at the ends. Her clothing was simple, full...and yet conveyed something deeply sensual. But most of all, it was Naina's unusual confidence that struck Vidyut. She carried herself as if she was the empress of everything and everyone around.

'*Namaste* Vidyut', said Naina with her palms folded and her eyes sparkling.

'*Namaste* Naina', replied Vidyut with a broad grin.

'So how come the star of Delhi's corporate world finally found time for us lesser mortals?'

Vidyut laughed out loud and said, 'Well, looks like nobody missed me here.'

Naina tilted her head to one side and said with a naughty yet enquiring smirk, 'so sure *haan* Vidyut? *Nobody* missed you?'

Suddenly Purohit ji called out for Vidyut.

Naina turned away slowly, stopping her gaze at Vidyut a moment longer than needed.

·||卐||·

Purohit ji had a hearty laugh as Vidyut described the culinary onslaught he had just been subjected to.

'I will need a really potent digestive, Purohit ji,' said Vidyut while merrily rubbing his bloated yet strong abdomen.

'Don't worry. Govardhan will have something for you,' replied Purohit ji still laughing.

Then slowly Purohit ji turned serious. Wiping his face with his *angavastram,* as if to erase his own grin, he said, 'Vidyut, you need to prepare yourself.'

'For what, Purohit ji?'

Purohit ji stared at Vidyut, with a mildly admonishing expression.

'For your meeting, Vidyut.'

'Which meeting, Purohit ji?' enquired Vidyut plainly.

Purohit ji paused for a moment to compose himself. He was evidently concerned. After a short breather he said, 'Your meeting with the mighty Dwarka Shastri ji, Vidyut. Your meeting with your great grandfather.'

Vidyut always knew there was more to meeting the dreaded Dwarka Shastri than a great grandson meeting an elder. But he asked nevertheless, 'What preparation do I need to do, Purohit ji?'

'You need to perform a *yajna* (a holy ritual around a sacrificial fire) and chant the divine mantra 1008 times through the night.'

Vidyut winced. 'But Purohit ji, I am a regular meditator, an advanced *taantric*, a practitioner of *pranayama* and I have mastered all the eight *siddhis* (divine proficiencies) you began teaching me as a child. What *yajna* do *I* need to perform?' exclaimed Vidyut with a bit of exasperation and a bit of conceit, something he almost never came near to.

Purohit ji anchored his fiery gaze at Vidyut's eyes, unable to control his temper. In a sudden and uncharacteristic outburst he flared up, 'Do you know *who* you are going to meet, you arrogant fool?! Dwarka Shastri is the most powerful spirit on planet Earth today. Even if he is on his deathbed now, you will not be able to handle the intensity of our master's persona, Vidyut!' By now Purohit ji was screaming at the top of his voice.

There was silence for a few moments. Vidyut knew he had overstepped. The calm and supremely wise Purohit ji would never lose his cool like this, unless the situation truly demanded it.

Regaining his composure Purohit ji continued in a soft tone, 'I know who you are, Vidyut. I know you are destined to be a devta like your great ancestor Vivasvan Pujari. But don't forget for a moment, my son – Dwarka Shastri is an ethereal combination of a man, a yogi, a devta and a *raakshasa*. No one can match his power.'

Purohit ji kept a loving hand on Vidyut's shoulder and continued, 'No one can withstand his wrath, Vidyut. Not even you.'

There was silence for a few moments. Vidyut looked at Purohit ji and nodded respectfully, finally showing full understanding and agreement. Choosing to retire for the day and to prepare for the big meeting, he folded his hands and bid farewell to Purohit ji. He decided to abide by every instruction given to him by the great hermit. Irrespective of his confidence and conviction about his own abilities, Vidyut knew he would need to be in prime spiritual strength when he faces the dying matthadheesh.

There was something causing butterflies in Vidyut's stomach even as he walked towards his living quarters in the matth. All this while, even during the intense and heated exchange with Purohit ji, even with the looming pressure of meeting the mighty Dwarka Shastri...there was something that was distracting him continuously.

Not something in fact. *Someone*.

Naina.

Harappa, 1700 BCE

SAPTARISHI

Vivasvan Pujari dismounted from his massive white steed. His trusted bodyguard and he had galloped for six straight hours to reach the beautiful abode of the mighty Saptarishi or the Seven Sages. Despite being the devta himself, Vivasvan Pujari was nervous at the prospect of being face to face with the Saptarishi themselves. It was the last day before they went into their divine retreat for the lunar year.

The mighty Saptarishi were no ordinary sages. No one knew from where or when they arrived on the planet. No one knew what the purpose of their existence was. No one had an idea from where they drew their boundless power. Everyone knew they controlled everything – the forests, the beasts, the skies, the rivers and even the Gods. The only thing that at times seemed inexplicably out-of-bounds for the Saptarishi…was free human will.

Yet despite the boundless power the Sages wielded, they were the gentlest and the most loving benefactors of Harappa and its people. It was said that even the sight of one of them was enough to cleanse the karmic-debt of a thousand rebirths. A divine glance from them could heal the most dreadful of ailments. Their incessant penance protected the crop of Harappa, the livestock of the metropolis and the well being of its inhabitants. But most of all, they were the loving sons of the mighty Saraswati river. She adored them. She listened to them. They were everything to her.

·‖ॐ‖·

The stunning snow-capped mountains towards the far east of Harappa were where the Saptarishi resided. Vivasvan Pujari could sense their dominating presence in everything around him. They were present in the trees, in the gushing rivulet, in the pebbles under his feet, in the breeze and in the mighty peaks. The Saptarishi were believed to be the guardians left behind on planet Earth by the primordial *Rishis*, after they completed the initiation of creation itself. The Saptarishi were not everyday humans. They were not even devtas. They were extraordinary mortals reinforced with the fiery strength of ultimate penance. With a streak of the Gods in them, they were the last real presence of the Creator on planet Earth.

Vivasvan Pujari folded his hands and fell on his knees. He loved the Saptarishi and vice versa. With smiling tenderness and deep reverence, he summoned the divine Seven, 'O great Sages; O protectors of Harappa; O defenders of the Vedas; O older brothers of this servant; O Saptarishi…show yourself to this humble being.'

The chilly breeze of the beautiful riverbed surrounded by enormous peaks blew itself cheerily on Vivasvan Pujari's face. Someone was responding to his call and the elements of nature were carrying the message. And then Vivasvan heard what he did every single time he paid a visit to the Sages. He heard the forest, the mountains, the stream, the birds and the breeze come in unison, resonating the most powerful sound of the Universe – *Oum*.

The Sages were about to present themselves.

·||卐||·

Vivasvan Pujari sat on one knee, head bowed and hands folded in profound respect as one after the other the Saptarishi emerged from their Earthly dwelling. They did not walk up to him. They did not suddenly appear out of nowhere. They seemed to be one with the mountains and the forest. They seemed to rise up seamlessly from the pebbles under the flowing stream. They branched out in human shape from the barks of mighty conifers. They took shape from the mouths of hidden caves in the greyish-blue mountains. Whether the Saptarishi were truly Gods or master-illusionists, no one could say.

'Rise, O Surya of Harappa, rise, O great devta', said one of the Sages in a voice as soothing as the healing touch of a loving Mother. Vivasvan looked up with misty eyes. One glance at the Saptarishi was more peace giving than a hundred years of deep meditation. This was not the first time Vivasvan Pujari was meeting the Sages, and he could not thank his stars enough. His love for the great Sages was second to none.

'O great Sages, O benefactors of your people, O Saptarishi…your humble servant bows to you with deepest affection and veneration', said Vivasvan Pujari as all of his bodyguard stood stunned in awe and disbelief. The new ones among them had seen the Saptarishi for the first time. They knew that in Harappa this opportunity was considered no less than the most hallowed of pilgrimages. *Darshana* (or the sighting of the Lord) of the Saptarishi was a matter of finest fortune. And it brought the devotee a step closer to gaining the love and blessings of the deific Mother Saraswati – the one believed to have given divine birth to the Seven Sages.

'What brings you here, revered devta?' asked one of the Sages.

'The insatiable thirst for your *darshana* and your blessings, O great Sages', replied Vivasvan, now smiling at the Saptarishi like a child. He was experiencing a deep sense of peace and satisfaction in the vicinity of the Sages. Their inner spiritual power radiated for miles around them, offering rejuvenation and life-energy to every living organism. Being face-to-face with them meant absorbing their indescribable vitality from the very epicenter. Vivasvan Pujari was soaking in every wave of that invisible but potent nectar. He knew how to.

'The day after tomorrow this devotee of yours will be granted the duty of leading Harappa as the Chief Priest. Bless him with your gracious presence at the sacred ceremony on the banks of Sara Maa herself,' continued Vivasvan.

The Seven Sages smiled all at once, and then spoke in unison as if they were seven voices emanating from the same one being, 'Our affection for you is boundless, O devta. But never use the name of the one and only Saraswati, our divine Mother, until absolutely necessary.'

Vivasvan Pujari was stunned as he heard these words. He never meant to use Sara Maa's name unduly. But somehow the Saptarishi appeared to be overly sensitive about the Mother. Everything about the great Sages was an extremity – their love, their benevolence, their patience, their power… and their wrath.

Vivasvan wasted no time and without debating whether or not he was understood correctly, he fell prostrate on the pebbly banks of the gushing stream, with his hands still folded towards the feet of the Saptarishi.

'Forgive me, O great Sage. My intention was not to invoke Sara Maa's name needlessly.' Pausing for a moment Vivasvan continued, 'While she may not have given birth to me, I consider myself to be her child.'

The Sages grinned, and the entire universe broke into a smile with them. The birds broke into a chirpy flight. The river stream seemed to have raised the decibels of its bubbling. The flowers appeared to be blossoming all at once, and the horses of Vivasvan Pujari's bodyguard danced and neighed in strange symphony.

'You really are the noblest of them all, Vivasvan Pujari,' said one among the beautifully laughing Sages.

Vivasvan Pujari raised his head, thankful at being forgiven so quickly, though still wondering what he had said so wrong.

'You don't need us or Mother Saraswati's waters to be physically present at your grand appointment, Vivasvan,' continued one of the Sages. 'It may give you some happiness to know that the brotherhood of the Saptarishi has decided to embrace you as one of our own.'

Vivasvan Pujari could not believe what he had just heard. He stood up in a slow, dazed motion, dusting the sand off his face.

'Do not be amazed, O mighty devta. You have earned this position and you honor us with your esteemed presence amidst us as a brother...now and forever. Soon the Saptarishi will be known as the *Ashtarishi* (the Eight Sages).'

The seven smiling Saptarishi bent down together with their right hands scooping up some water from the gushing stream. They took the water in their arms outstretched from their right shoulders, shut their eyes once again in synchronized action and announced in a practiced chant -

'We pronounce you our brother, O great Vivasvan Pujari,' said the glowing sages with soft smiles beaming from their gentle, bearded faces. 'You will hereon be counted one amongst us. Our wise and loving Mother, Saraswati Maa, will now be your mother as well.'

Vivasvan Pujari could not believe his ears. He broke into tears of devotion and fell at the feet of the divine Sages with reverence that cannot be measured. He was overwhelmed at the assurance that once he was done delivering his material duties of this life, he would find enlightenment as one of the Ashtarishi. No human or devta could ask for more.

Banaras, 2017

THE DYING BRAHMIN
CHIEFTAIN

The outer periphery of the Dev-Raakshasa Matth looked like a haunted ancient castle to the unacquainted. It had vast courtyards surrounded by dark corridors and monstrous-looking sculptures. The stone cut figure of a man with the head of a bloodthirsty lion was a rendition of the fierce *Narsimha* avatar of Lord Vishnu. The terrifying and massive statue of an eagle with a muscular human body represented *Garuda*, the mighty celestial bird. There were several pits blackened with years of soot from the fires of dark taantric rituals. Menacing sentries dressed in saffron and black, and armed with scimitars, tridents and old Enfield rifles stood guard at every corner. Smoke, dark walls, barren yards, fearsome chanting, negative forces and angry faces - this entire area was called the *Raakshasa Khand* or the Demon Sanctum.

For those who considered the matth their home and their place of spiritual learning, it presented itself in a tender and beautiful form. These select few men and women had access to the inner sanctum or *Dev Khand* of the matth. This section of the matth looked diametrically opposite to the outer periphery. It had beautiful gardens, flowerbeds, lotus ponds and *havan kundas* or ritual pits for divine Vedic *yajnas*. The air was fragrant with rose and marigold scents and one could see learned priests performing various advanced sacraments around holy fires. There were various corners where handsome young boys with shaven heads recited divine hymns in unison. The entire sanctum resounded with sacred chants of Vedic and *Puranical* couplets. The Dev Khand was truly among the most divine and spiritual places in the whole world.

The inner and outer sectors of the matth were not in their present forms by accident. They were an outcome of meticulous planning by the great Dwarka Shastri and his powerful ancestors, in line with the very core objectives of the matth's establishment. While the world was made to believe that the matth was a center of spiritual learning and dark-arts, the reason behind the founding of this powerful monastery was something very different. It was built as a spiritual cantonment, an impregnable fortress armed with the ability to withstand and counter every otherworldly assault that could be imagined. It was established to protect a bloodline. Vivasvan Pujari's bloodline.

Very few people know that Varanasi or Kashi itself is placed at the center of seven concentric holy circles. Each circle represents a group of potent deities, primarily *Ganesha*, and is dotted by shrines and temples. For the common visitor or pilgrim these 56 temples represent simple centers of divinity and are places of worship. Millions of pilgrims throng to Kashi every year and circumambulate these circles and shrines barefoot, over days of tireless treks. Only a handful of mystical priests and *yogis* of Kashi know that these seven circles exist for thousands of years, and are strong celestial force fields against black occult originating half the globe away.

At the heart of the circles lies the ancient city of Kashi. At the core of Kashi, in the vicinity of the Vishwanath temple, stood the Dev-Raakshasa Matth. At the very nucleus of the matth, surrounded by vast gardens and massive statues of Lord Shiva on all four sides, stood Dwarka Shastri's majestic cottage. Constructed with perfect *vaastu* (ancient Indian architectural science) and astrological precision, this cottage was built at the world's most ethereally secure spot. And it was home to the world's most powerful taantric and most profound yogi.

·||卐||·

As Vidyut entered the dim, vast and lamp-lit chambers of the great Dwarka Shastri, he sensed the presence of power he had never felt before. He could sense the presence of over a hundred, maybe thousand unearthly beings in this large room where Dwarka Shastri lay propped-up with half a dozen pillows on a massive bed.

The grandmaster looked as old as his age, yet his heavily wrinkled face radiated with the vitality of someone much younger. His thick, snow-white hair was thrown back and gave his towering personality the appearance of a battle-scarred Mohican chieftain. He had a large red *teeka* or vermillion smearing at the center of his forehead, and he was adorned with several garlands of pure *rudraksha* (beads believed to be the teardrops of *Rudra* or Shiva himself, its biological term being Elaeocarpus Ganitrus). He wore white robes and his fingers constantly flipped the beads of a rosary. In all, he looked like a galactic warlord.

While there was complete silence in this vast hall of a room, Vidyut could almost hear the faint hissing of an invisible *Brahma-Raakshasa*. There was nothing ordinary or Earthly about this place. Vidyut stood frozen, wondering whether his great grandfather was a hermit, a devta, a *raakshasa* or a dangerous combination of all.

'Do you know the Atharva Veda by heart, Vidyut?,' enquired the great Dwarka Shastri in a voice that reverberated across the room like the grumble of a raging fire-dragon.

'Yes Baba...*Atharva Veda*, *Yajur Veda*, *Sama Veda* and *Rig Veda*...I know all four Vedas by rote,' replied Vidyut without any show of pride. Although he had never expected any show of love from his great grandfather, Vidyut was somewhat hurt at the complete absence of affection from the only blood relative he had left.

'Hmmm...' came the acknowledgement from Dwarka Shastri. It sounded like the hum of a massive diesel engine. 'Why are you here?'

'Baba, Purohit ji informed me that you were not keeping well.'

'Now will that Purohit decide when Dwarka Shastri *himself* is well or unwell?' growled the grand old man angrily as he sputtered into a painful coughing bout. Vidyut stepped forward to show his concern. 'Stand back!' yelled the breathless master. Vidyut froze where he stood.

'Listen to me, boy,' continued Dwarka Shastri. 'Now that you have come, I see it is quite at an opportune time. Now with me gone, *they* will come for you.' Dwarka Shastri's voice was uncharacteristically shaken. It had traces of an emotion that was never even remotely associated with the grand old man over the hundred plus years that he lived and ruled. It had traces of *fear*.

Vidyut felt a cold sweat breaking on his forehead and temples. He had a faint inkling of who his grandfather was referring to. And if the grandmaster's words came true, nothing was going to remain the same for Vidyut, for the matth, for his beloved Damini or even for the entire human race. That would mean that a prehistoric prophecy long forgotten was about to raise its brutal head. A war infected by the ancient curse was going to rage again. War in the name of God. War between the proverbial devtas and demons.

And like everyone at the matth believed, and the Order in Rome was sure of - *Vidyut was the last devta left.*

Harappa, 1700 BCE

SHAV-SAADHANA

It was a horrifying sight.

The three hollow-eyed Mesopotamian magicians sat inside a dark cave that was lit by a lone torch flickering in one corner. Their posture was crooked and their empty eye-sockets looked like black holes leading into an evil infinity. Their jaws drooped and they looked like hideous creatures from another world.

The stink from the stale human blood that they had poured over themselves during their black-ritual against Vivasvan Pujari made it impossible to stand and breathe in the cave. But their feisty employer stood her ground firmly. Despite being a woman of exceptional beauty and evident royalty, she looked more dreadful than the three fiends. She was burning with violent rage.

'What happened, O mighty magicians from the West?' she asked in a scathing whisper.

Her devoted guards in red hoods stood around the three magicians, their swords unsheathed, gleaming alarmingly in the dim light. Just a flick of a finger from their powerful mistress would have meant a swift beheading of the three conjurers of black magic. The single source of light threw monstrous shadows of this vile gathering on the stone walls of the dank cave. The three blind sorcerers sat frozen and battered with defeat.

'What….happened…?' the woman enquired again, slowly.

'Zzzzzaaaaaaaarrggghhhhh…..uuuuurrggghh……bbbbrrrrr-rrggghhh…….' the three scoundrels began growling in unison, in voices that didn't belong to them. Their long and dirty fingernails were clawing their own faces and necks, peeling skin and flesh. They were clearly still under the control of the angry spirits that possessed them.

Then one of them spoke, in a horrifying voice that sounded like someone extremely old, in an accent of a very distant land. It was the most sinister voice that the royal lady and her guards had ever heard.

'*Shav….sssshhhhaaavv……*' spoke the horrible voice through the magicians open mouth, as his face twisted and distorted into a lunatic expression.

Shav meant a dead body. The ethereal being inside the malevolent magician was asking for a human corpse.

·‖ 卐 ‖·

The devta was unbeatable. The three black-magicians – *Gun*, *Sha* & *Ap* as they were ridiculously called, had tried a powerful exorcism on Vivasvan Pujari. The practice of exorcism was known and feared across the known world, and most believed that it could prove to be deadly effective. It basically stole the soul of the target and replaced it with a violent and dissatisfied spirit from the netherworld. For most ordinary people, this meant the end of life and physical existence, as they knew it. But Vivasvan Pujari was not an ordinary mortal.

The exorcism had backfired. The devta's soul was so spectacularly evolved and blessed, that no evil spirit could overpower it. Decades of intense meditation, penance and an unparalleled mastery of the Atharva Veda (Veda of occult) had made Vivasvan Pujari indomitable. Even without his conscious knowledge, Vivasvan's powerful soul had repelled the assault. The evil spirits had come back even angrier, and housed themselves in the bodies of the three magicians. And they sought revenge.

Shav-saadhana or corpse-practice was the darkest and most horrendous of all occult rituals. It meant the ceremonial use of a fresh human cadaver that concluded with inviting the most insatiable spirits into it. Half the taantrics that attempted this malicious ritual died while trying. Shav-saadhana was prohibited in the virtuous scriptures of Harappa, because it went against the very central rule of creation.

Shav-saadhana brought back the dead to life.

Illegitimate life.

·||✳||·

'Who is that dancing girl that wears the famous bangles during her performances?' enquired the beautiful yet witch-like woman. None of her guards responded, although they all knew well whom she was referring to.

'Did you hear what I asked?' she said again, 'Ranga!' this time raising her eyebrows at the captain of her personal bodyguard.

'Pardon your servant, my lady…but I don't know who you are referring to.'

She laughed. And she looked so pretty that even the Gods wished her soul shared at least a bit of the beauty of her face.

'Really? Is she not the bitch that every man in Harappa wants to feed on?' she barked with an arrogant and authoritative tilt of her head. 'Answer me!' she thundered.

'Nayantara, my lady…her name is Nayantara,' replied Ranga hastily. Much as his reputation was one of dread across Harappa, in the presence of his mistress the giant Ranga was no better than a wet puppy.

She laughed again. Then her face slowly turned to a stony expression. She appeared demented with hate and envy.

'Use her. Bring these three dogs the corpse of a young girl. Then use it to capture this Nayantara's soul. She is the only one who can corrupt the incorruptible Vivasvan Pujari.'

Upon hearing this Gun cackled like a wicked witch. Sha growled in hideous delight. Ap was already chanting something incomprehensible yet menacing. They looked worse than the worst nightmare any human could have.

Ranga and his men gasped in horror, but the lady walked out of the cold cave unfazed. Pundit Chandradhar's wife was not as righteous as he was. Priyamvada's blood was no better than the yellow venom of the cobra.

Banaras, 2017

MANKIND'S GREATEST UNTRUTH – PART 1

'Harappa?!' exclaimed Vidyut as he now sat next to his great grandfather's bed.

They had been alone together in Dwarka Shastri's cottage for nearly six hours now, barring one interruption by Govardhan, the monastery's physician. These were the most terrifying yet transcendent six hours in Vidyut's entire life. He now knew why Pujari ji had asked him to perform certain nerve-control rituals before this meeting. Vidyut was a whisker away from his head exploding like a fireball.

Over the six hours Dwarka Shastri had narrated one part of the gripping and cruel tale of the mighty Vivasvan Pujari, Chandradhar, Nayantara, Priyamvada, Manu, Sanjna, Somdutt, the Saraswati river, the Saptarishi and Harappa in great detail. He described the city of Harappa, its culture and how the great *Sanatana Dharma* (the world's most ancient religion followed by people of the Hindu way of life) originated on the banks of the venerated Saraswati. Vidyut found it hard to believe that he was hearing a true story that unfolded itself in Harappa thousands of years ago, a civilization he had only read about in the schoolbooks of history.

Vidyut was unsure how to react. Had it been anyone other than his powerful great grandfather, Vidyut would have laughed off the episode as a wild figment of some storyteller's imagination. But it was Dwarka Shastri who was narrating this fantastic and horrifying tale. And Dwarka Shastri was no storyteller.

'But Baba, since childhood we have been taught that Harappa and Mohenjo Daro were pre-historic cities, preceding even the Vedas and *Puranas*.'

Dwarka Shastri held his gaze on Vidyut's face as he allowed his great grandson to continue.

'I mean I'm sorry Baba, but all this is sounding ridiculously contradictory to everything that has been established, propagated and taught all over the world about the Indus Valley civilization. I mean, look at how you described Vivasvan Pujari riding at the spearhead of five thousand mounts, bringing the horses into Harappa's army. However, it is now widely believed that horses never even existed in Harappa. And that they came in with the great Aryan invasion.'

Vidyut gave a flabbergasted look to the grandmaster in front of him. Dwarka Shastri smiled with sarcasm.

'Notice the terms you use Vidyut, when you speak about Harappa and what you call the Indus Valley civilization. Note what words you used - *established*, *propagated*, *taught* and err…what else…oh yes, *believed*.' Dwarka Shastri paused for a moment before continuing, 'Now tell me young man, *who* has established this belief? *Who* has propagated it? *Why* is it being taught? *How* have you and billions of people over the last one and a half millennia been fooled into believing the greatest untruth in the story of mankind?!'

'But Baba, how can you say that the Indus Valley civili…'

'Enough!' yelled the old grandmaster midway between Vidyut's sentences. 'Stop using that conspiratorial term, Indus Valley civilization!'

Dwarka Shastri broke into a bout of violent coughing once again. But that did not stop him from angrily screaming out his next words.

'Don't you understand even now, you dimwit boy? Harappa was not about the Sindhu (Indus) or its valley!'

He paused for a moment to see if Vidyut was getting his drift, and then nearly whispered with exhaustion.

'Harappa was the Saraswati civilization, Vidyut!'

It was time for Dwarka Shastri's daily incantations in the worship of his protecting deity, Lord Shiva. Vidyut had been glued to his chair ever since his conversation with his Baba began. He was baffled, dumbstruck and agitated. His great grandfather had told him the beginning of the Harappa tale, and something about the Indus Valley civilization actually being a massive settlement on the banks of the vanished river Saraswati. But Vidyut had no clue how all that was related to him or even to his great grandfather. He wanted to know more…he wanted to know everything! But he had to leave the room as Dwarka Shastri's trusted staff entered the grand chambers to prepare their master for his daily ritual.

Vidyut walked out of the cottage into the sprawling lawns surrounding it. He desperately needed a cigarette. His head was spinning and it was only the comfort of nicotine that could keep him steady. He had to find a cigarette somewhere. He had about one hour and he decided to step out of the matth. He walked straight out of the Dev-Khand into the outer sector of the matth. He met and nodded at Purohit ji and Naina on the way. 'A walk to the *ghaats* (piers), Purohit ji,' was all he could mutter to them.

Purohit ji was astute enough to know Vidyut needed time and space. Time to digest what he had heard, because this was just the beginning of the dark intrigue and violent conflict that awaited him.

It was afternoon by now and Vidyut decided to take a cycle-rickshaw to the closest ghaat of the holy Ganges (or *Ganga* as it is lovingly called by a billion Indians). The ghaats of the revered river were nothing less than a wonder of the world. If there was any place on Earth that congregated so much colour in the form of millions of people of different shades, sizes, classes and creeds, it was the ghaats of the Ganga in Kashi.

This stretch of the riverbank, converted into numerous blocks and sections of unimaginable heritage and richness, had names that were equally loaded with history. Sometimes tough to pronounce for someone unfamiliar with Hindi and Sanskrit, the ghaats carried names that were eternal witnesses to the sands of time. The *Dashashwamedh Ghaat* translates into the 'Pier of the Ten Sacrificed Horses'. The *Tulsi Ghaat* is where the immortal poet and author of the profound epic *Ramcharitamaanas* once lived. The Ramcharitamaanas is credited with bringing the epic-tale of Lord Rama to the common man, because it broke free from hard Sanskrit and was written in the language of the masses.

The *Manikarnika Ghaat* is perhaps the most mystical and morose place in the whole universe. This ghaat is by far the busiest cremation ground for the Hindus. It is believed that there have been funeral pyres burning continuously at this ghaat for more than ten thousand years. Never a moment had lapsed in all this time when the flesh of a deceased human being was not being incandesced into amber and ashes at the Manikarnika Ghaat. It is said that a jewel from the earring of Lord Vishnu had fallen at this precise location, making it the most sanctified *crossover* bridge.

Vidyut got off the rickshaw at a crowded spot closest to the famous steps of the Dashashwamedh Ghaat. He left a hundred rupees bill in the hands of the rickshaw puller, over four times the regular fare for this short journey. He quickly bought a pack of the best available cigarettes at one of the many modest shops around, and walked down the steps to the first broad platform on the ghaat. As is common practice for the millions of visitors and pilgrims that visit these hallowed piers, Vidyut too offered a short prayer to Ganga *maiyya*, as the Ganges is referred to by the locals, *maiyya* being a loving term for Mother. There is something that connects Indians with their rivers. Some deep, indescribable bond.

·||ॐ||·

Vidyut sat on the stairs, looking at the mighty Ganges flowing in its full glory. The sight was surreal. Almost nothing had changed since Vidyut was here last, except for the ghaat being much cleaner and better maintained. He once again witnessed what had been etched in his memory for decades, ever since he was a small child. He saw human faith and unquestioned devotion at its pinnacle. There were old women, older than you would believe could exist, hobbling down the steps of the pious ghaat just to touch the water with their shriveled finger-tips. There were young mothers carrying bawling babies tirelessly, right up to the mother river, just to anoint their infants' foreheads with the holiest of drops. Then there were the bereaved, who had come to take a dip in the divine water, as a final duty to their departed loved ones. Every soul on the ghaat had the look of absolute submission on their faces. The Ganga was truly nectar, the giver of boundless blessings and the cleanser of sins of a million births.

As Vidyut took out a cigarette and held it between his lips, he realized he had nothing to light it with. Even before he could figure out what to do, a hand with a silver zippo lighter lit his cigarette for him. Vidyut looked up to see a lean, handsome young man smiling at him while slipping his expensive lighter back into his jeans pocket.

'You…mind if I join you?' asked the gentle looking fellow in stammering yet chiseled English, and with a disarming grin.

'Of course,' Vidyut replied welcomingly.

The young man sat down next to Vidyut, smoking a cigarette himself. They sat there for a couple of minutes without speaking, staring at the mesmerizing and muscular flow of the mighty Ganges. Vidyut could manage to notice that while the man next to him was almost his own age, he was very pleasant and nearly boyish looking. It was like someone had picked up Harry Potter, made him all grown up, but had done so without losing the innocence of childhood.

Vidyut finished one cigarette and took out another one. He needed the release. His neighbor instantly took out the zippo again and lit Vidyut's second cigarette. He was about to keep the lighter back into his blue jeans, but then slipped it into Vidyut's hand.

'The way…you are going with puffing these babies, you're going to need this more than me,' said the gentle stranger with a nice laugh.

Vidyut laughed out loud. He was quite charmed by the seemingly shy but bright young man sitting next to him. As the early evening breeze of the Dashashwamedh ghaat caressed their faces and hair, Vidyut warmly stretched out his hand to introduce himself, 'Hi, I'm Vidyut. Nice to meet you.'

The handsome fellow clasped Vidyut's outstretched hand, smiled and responded, 'Hi I'm Romi. Romi Pereira'.

Harappa, 1700 BCE

PRALAY

'Intoxicate him with your most potent mix of *datura* (Devil's Apple), crushed pearls and rice wine,' said Priyamvada to the now half-manic but indescribably pretty Nayantara. 'But most of all, use the temptation of your flesh.'

Nayantara nodded like a gorgeous but deranged doll. She was not herself. Literally. Thousands of years later such a condition would be described by terms like Schizophrenia or substance-induced psychosis.

But in 1700 BC, amidst the vast stretches of the Harappan civilization, the condition of Nayantara was nothing but the outcome of the shav-saadhana conducted by Gun, Sha & Ap. Nayantara was possessed by an angry *daakini* (spirit of an untimely dead woman) that had never been beaten.

·‖卐‖·

The grisly ritual had begun at the abandoned *smashaan* or cremation-ground at the outskirts of Harappa. Sha, Ap & Gun, the three dark conjurers of spells and spirits, began the preparations of the shav-saadhana. The captain of Priyamvada's bodyguard had sourced a fresh cadaver from the city mortuary. It was of a young, fair and beautiful woman of perhaps thirty years of age.

The three evil Mesopotamian magicians had travelled for seven months to reach the sprawling city of Harappa. They were here on the invitation of Priyamvada, one of the city's most powerful women. She had summoned them because their notoriety as matchless artists of the dark forces had spread far and wide. Priyamvada was aware that no one from Harappa or even the far provinces would dare attack the great Vivasvan Pujari. She had to seek and hire specialists from distant and unknown lands.

Sha stretched the beautiful corpse naked next to the ritual fire. Ap poured human blood on the ground from an earthen container, circling the ritual area. Gun placed the most powerful human skull he had on a jar that held an offering of wine in it. They then placed the raw meat of five different animals in mud-plates and placed them on the ground in a pre-decided configuration. The scene was set.

The chanting began. The gruesome ritual was aimed at pleasing *Smashaan-Tara*, the divine Goddess of the cremation realm. But the fearsome yet benevolent Tara was never going to respond to these beastly creatures. She saved her blessings for the true taantric. But as the horrifying chanting continued into the wee hours of the dark morning, it began attracting several daakinis or dissatisfied female spirit forms. One particularly powerful daakini decided to take the body of the beautiful fair corpse.

·||ॐ||·

Gun, Ap & Sha looked at each other with their hollow eyes in manic delight, as they saw the corpse first shiver and then begin growling in a horrifying unearthly voice. The daakini was entering the flesh and struggling to take control against the laws of nature. It was only if she entered a corpse first, that she would be able to transmit herself into a living human, Nayantara in this case.

The lifeless body of the young woman was now trying to get up from the prostrate position, scowling and growling unstoppably. Sha pinned her back to the ground with a tight strangle on her neck and hard strikes from a ritual femur (human bone). The demonic chanting continued. The daakini was slowly but surely entering the now undead body.

The magicians knew they were now very close to stealing and replacing the soul of the beautiful Nayantara. The prohibited shav-saadhana was about to be concluded successfully.

The three evil fiends were now certain that they would be appointed as the chief priests of Harappa, making them the most powerful men in the world. They had been promised.

Even these wretches underestimated the darkness that resided in Priyamvada's heart.

·||ॐ||·

The famous exotic dancer of Harappa, the ravishing Nayantara was dead. Her physical form was still alive.

The first casualty of an exorcism via the shav-saadhana route was the soul of the victim. While Nayantara's was not an evil spirit, years of worldly suffering, material hunger and subduing of her conscience had weakened it substantially. Which in turn enabled the daakini to easily vanquish it and take over her mortal body. Some of Harappan and Kashi folklore for centuries attributed this dramatic change in Nayantara to simply an overdose of an unknown datura concoction. No one knows what really happened.

Nayantara was now dressing and behaving even more sensually than before. The daakini that possessed her was well versed with these earthly tricks, as she had exposure to much higher crafts of the spirit world. She knew what little and ephemeral things humans fall for. Even her servants were startled to see the new enchanting avatar of Nayantara. Her female accomplices joked with her that if her new form attracted *them* so much, what devastating effect would it have on the rich and powerful men of Harappa!

Nayantara knew she had to entice only one man - the richest and the most powerful in the entire state. She laid out an elaborate quagmire for Vivasvan Pujari. She sought justice for an act of molestation that never happened. She registered a complaint with the city magistrate that a young man named Manu Pujari attempted to take her by force. Her loyal staff was readied as witnesses to the false accusation and a malicious rumour was unleashed. Given the stringent Harappan laws safeguarding its women, such an allegation could not be ignored. She, the daakini, knew where to attack Vivasvan Pujari. She knew what his weak spot was.

·‖ॐ‖·

Sanjna could not believe her eyes as she read the summons from the city court. Vivasvan Pujari sat next to her, his eyes shut and his fingers flipping the beads of a rosary. Manu stood in a corner of the same room. He looked perplexed, bewildered, and yet unquestionably righteous. He knew it was a mistake.

'What do we do now, Vivasvan?' enquired Sanjna anxiously. The calmness she saw on her husband's face was worsening her nervousness and angst. Her son's composed posture was also bothering her. *Didn't they remember that in Harappa court summons meant a public hearing?!*

Vivasvan Pujari opened his eyes and turned to his son.

'Manu, pardon me for asking this my son. I know by even questioning you on something so despicable I do you great injustice. But I have to ask for the sake of propriety,' he continued. 'Did you visit the quarters of this lady Nayantara?'

Manu stood steadfast, listening to his beloved father and letting him finish. At that time neither young Manu nor his celebrated father knew that one day Manu was going to change the fate of not just Aryavarta, but of all of mankind.

'No, father.'

'Thank you my son. And once again, forgive me for ever subjecting you to this enquiry.'

'You only do your duty, father. I would expect nothing less from you,' replied Manu with grace and confidence.

Vivasvan Pujari smiled. He stood up from his seat and walked a few steps to hug his son. As they locked into a soulful embrace that only a loving father and a devoted son can share, Sanjna felt mildly relieved. But she could still not share the relaxed demeanor her husband and son were displaying. She could only remember the brutal public court hearings of Harappa.

If there was anything even remotely uncivilized about the great metropolis, it was the public spectacle that its criminal proceedings made. For all its grace and luminous Vedic way of life, both the justice as well as the prison systems in Harappa seemed untouched by the civility. These were the only things that Sanjna ever dreaded. And these were now knocking at her family's hallowed doors.

'Okay, so what now, you two?' exclaimed Sanjna. She looked visibly worried.

Both Vivasvan and Manu burst out laughing at the way Sanjna looked. They were unafraid. Their confidence emanated from the glowing torch of their impeccable character and their faith in the harsh yet honest judicial machinery of Harappa. In fact Vivasvan Pujari and Pundit Chandradhar were among the guardians of the metropolis who had purposefully engineered the justice framework into a huge deterrent. However, sometimes when someone is too deeply immersed within the picture, he misses seeing the dark imperfections. Sanjna could sense the threat that Vivasvan and Manu were carelessly unheeding of.

'I will go and meet this Nayantara tomorrow morning,' said Vivasvan Pujari, casually flicking the summons document to a nearby table.

Even before Vivasvan could complete these words, the Earth moved. The city of Harappa shook along with every house, every temple and every living being within it. The clouds burst into violent thunder and Manu had to jump and grab his mother's arm to prevent her from ramming her head into a nearby pillar. The vast Saraswati settlement was witnessing the greatest tectonic shift of all times. And the Harappans had never witnessed this phenomenon before.

Was it the Gods trying to warn their last devta against what he had just decided to do? Were they foretelling the disastrous consequences of Vivasvan's meeting with the possessed Nayantara? This quake of the Earth and this deafening clap of the skies was nothing compared to the destruction in store for all generations of mankind, should the black daakini within Nayantara succeed in her blind and evil quest.

And no one knew at that time, not even Vivasvan Pujari and Chandradhar, that the massive shift in the inner Earth was the first sign of the mighty Saraswati inching towards the most powerful river-Tsunami humankind was to ever witness.

These were all horrifying omens of a dark age approaching fast. It seemed like the Gods were preparing planet Earth for its worst and never-ending nightmare. It was as if the prophesied *pralay* or the *Great Deluge* was finally coming.

Banaras & Somewhere in the
Swiss alps, 2017

'HE CANNOT BE KILLED.'

Dwarka Shastri looked somewhat refreshed. But it was evident that an illness was slowly and surely eating into him. He was a strange combination of a tired body and an enflamed spirit. But most of all, his eyes burned through everything they inspected. His eyes were unusually penetrating.

Vidyut was back from his short sojourn at the ghaats. He was about to enter the chambers of his great grandfather again, that his phone rang.

'Yes, Rhea,' said Vidyut. It was his executive assistant calling.

'Vidyut where have you been *yaa*? Damini has been trying to get in touch with you. I believe she has tried your phone more than a dozen times.'

'Shit,' exclaimed Vidyut. 'She's gonna kill me.'

Rhea waited patiently for Vidyut's next set of instructions. She could wait for Vidyut till eternity. Even as she heard nothing, she could smell his strong cologne. She could count the hair-tips on his rugged stubble. She knew he liked his americano more than a cappuccino, and that Jiu Jitsu was his favourite martial-art form right after *kalaripayattu*. She knew what he liked to eat, what he liked to wear, how he liked his breakfast eggs and what made him laugh. Rhea knew everything about Vidyut. And she hated that Vidyut knew almost nothing about her. But she was mistaken. Vidyut knew a lot about her. But not everything.

'Tell her I am with someone important right now and that I will call her back as soon as I can'. He added, 'Tell her I am well and everything is okay.'

'Who are you with, Vidyut?' asked Rhea.

Vidyut was a bit taken aback. It was not Rhea's mandate to ask him for information he did not care to offer himself. And she knew that well.

'No one you know Rhea, thanks,' said Vidyut and disconnected the call. *Why did she want to know who I am with?*

But Vidyut quickly lost the thought as he had a lot to deal with at this point.

The Maschera Bianca was not used to listening to such words. He maintained his composure nevertheless.

'How can you say that? He is after all just human,' said the Maschera through the advanced satellite phone he was using, from one of his operational bases somewhere deep in the Swiss Alps.

'That's the...point...Maschera. He is *not* just...human,' said the polite, stammering voice on the other side. It was Romi, calling his employer to give an update.

'I sat next to him today. He is something...*different*. He cannot be killed. He radiates this unknown energy that will unnerve even the most capable adversary.'

'Are you saying he has unnerved you, Romi?'

'No, Maschera.'

There was a brief pause from both ends.

'Remember who you are, Romi,' the Maschera broke the silence. 'Remember your profound work in that speeding tunnel of Paris. It was 1997. You were what...only 16 then?'

'Yes Maschera,' replied Romi. His did not have fond memories of that project. That graceful lady had the most beautiful face in the world and she did not deserve to die. But there was no choice. The Order needed her dead.

'Remember Istanbul, Paris, Delhi, Damascus...you are unstoppable Romi. You are the Order's most valuable asset.'

Romi grimaced. He did not like what the Maschera just said.

'I have told you before I am not your Order's asset, Maschera,' said Romi with uncharacteristic coldness. 'I am an independent specialist and I only undertake work that I truly believe in.'

He continued, 'it is only a matter of chance that the Order and I have many areas of overlap in our beliefs.'

'Yes of course, Romi,' replied the Maschera instantly. 'All I meant was that the Order has found you very useful whenever the need arose.'

'Yes, Maschera.' Romi was back to his gentle tone. 'And all I meant to say was that Vidyut is nothing like the other projects I have delivered. He is strong, fearless…and…'

'And…?'

'There is a profound force that I sense around him,' said Romi. 'You would agree that my years of successful work have been possible because I have this unique gift of foreknowing the impending death of my projects. I can see it.'

'You do have a rare gift, Romi.'

'Precisely. But I am unable to foresee Vidyut's end Maschera. Something inexplicable is protecting him.'

The silence was longer this time. The Maschera had never seen his prized hit man so unsure of himself. He also realized he had never spoken to Romi this long. For the first time the Maschera sensed something he had never witnessed before. *Romi was losing his nerve.*

'Nothing can protect him from you, Romi,' said the Maschera matter-of-factly into his sat-phone. 'You are an artist. Vidyut is just another ordinary guy.'

'Thank you for the confidence you have in me, Maschera. It

is very kind of you.'

'Now do what you have to, Romi. I'm sending some of my elite unit, just to be sure. I know you don't need them, but only as a back up. Vidyut must not leave that wicked city alive.'

'He won't, Maschera.'

Both Romi and the Maschera Bianca knew Vidyut was not just another ordinary guy.

·||ॐ||·

Vidyut entered his Baba's chamber and stood waiting for the grand old man's signal. Dwarka Shastri was back on his bed, surrounded by the massive pillows. His eyes were shut, as if in deep trance. Vidyut waited patiently even as he stared lovingly at his great grandfather. It was after decades that he had got the chance to be with his Baba. The initial phase of fear and tension was now giving way to an affectionate comfort that Vidyut felt in Dwarka Shastri's towering presence.

A few minutes later the matthadheesh opened his eyes and signaled Vidyut to come and sit beside him. Vidyut was keenly waiting for Dwarka Shastri to narrate the next part of the gripping and portentous tale of his ancestors, even though he was still a bit shell-shocked at everything he had heard so far.

Vidyut stepped forward to touch his great grandfather's feet, as is customary even today in millions of Hindu families. Touching of the elders' feet is symbolic of deep respect and absolute submission. In return one wins showers of blessings.

Vidyut bent forward and pressed his fingertips on Dwarka Shastri's left foot. As soon as his fingers touched Dwarka Shastri's wrinkled skin, the old man turned to look at Vidyut with a sudden expression of alarm. Even before Vidyut could ask what had happened, the expression on the great Dwarka Shastri's face transformed from alarm to one of horror!

The old man grabbed Vidyut's wrist in a tight grip and shot several questions in one shaken burst.

'Where did you go just now, Vidyut? Tell me exactly! Who did you meet? Did a stranger touch you? Did anyone give you anything? Who did you meet boy? Answer me!' By now Dwarka Shastri was shivering with fear and anger.

'Sorry if I did something wrong, Baba,' replied Vidyut in an uncertain tone. 'I...I just went to the Dashashwamedh Ghaat, Baba. Just...for some fresh air. I did not meet anyone.'

'Yes you did, you fool. There is something you are carrying on your person that is alien to the secure precincts of the matth.'

Dwarka Shastri's laser-like eyes were now looking straight into Vidyut's, but it seemed they were looking beyond them. As if Dwarka Shastri was reading Vidyut's space-time continuum.

Vidyut was baffled with what was happening. And then he suddenly remembered the flip-top lighter that handsome fellow from the ghaat had given him. Hesitating momentarily since revealing the lighter would have meant a confession of his smoking in front of his great grandfather, Vidyut quickly concluded that there were things far more serious at play. He took out the lighter slowly from his pocket.

'A stranger gave me this at the ghaat, Baba.'

Dwarka Shastri froze for a few seconds. And then all hell broke loose.

The grandmaster tugged violently at a thick chord that hung right next to his bed. The pull activated a lever and hammer that struck a massive tower-bell atop the dome of his cottage. It was a SOS call from the matthadheesh to his fellowship. Within moments the door of Dwarka Shastri's cottage flung open, with Balvanta storming in. He held a pair of ominous short-swords one in each hand, and had a double-barreled shotgun slung behind his back. To his belt were strapped several rounds of ammunition. Also came running Pujari ji and his son Sonu, the latter's trident at the ready. Through the windows Vidyut could see the cottage being surrounded by warrior-monks of the Hindu monastery. Each one of them was armed with blades and modern weapons. The Dev-Raakshasa Matth was indeed ready to scramble for war at a moment's notice.

'What happened, *Gurudev*?' enquired Purohit ji, referring to the matthadheesh as his gurudev, or God-master. Balvanta looked like a panther ready to pounce on its prey even as he inspected every corner of the cottage with his darting eyes.

By now Dwarka Shastri was panting with anxiety, but his face had firmed-up into a hard cast. His eyes were blood-shot.

'They are here, Purohit,' said the grandmaster. 'It has begun'.

Harappa, 1700 BCE

HOW CAN A MOTHER LET THIS HAPPEN?

'Five villages have been inundated overnight, my Lords,' said the chief civil engineer of Harappa.

The shaking of the Earth had deeply unnerved the entire populace of the mighty city, including its leaders. Such bloodcurdling rumble and rippling of the ground had never been experienced or heard of before. No ancient scriptures or texts of science had any reference to something so terrifying. And even the Saptarishi were in their most intense month of penance and were unreachable. Their presence was being particularly missed, because along with the quake of the Earth there had been an unexpected occurrence. Eyewitnesses claimed that they saw the ever tender and reliable

Saraswati throw mountainous waves towards the shore, which had instantly flooded several villages in the nearest vicinity. Such a violent tumult of the Saraswati waters was again unheard of. The mother river was a giver of life for the Harappan people. She would never harm her flock.

A late night meeting had been summoned. Every important person of the metropolis was present at it. The meeting was being presided over by Vivasvan Pujari, with Pundit Chandradhar seated on his immediate right. This duo of Vivasvan and Chandradhar was the most capable, potent and trusted leadership Harappa had ever found. They were also brothers-in-law. Vivasvan's wife Sanjna was Chandradhar's younger sister. But most importantly, the two were dearest of friends. Together they had pulled Harappa out of innumerable grave dangers, and had propelled the city to its present glory. And in less than thirty-six hours, Vivasvan Pujari was going to be appointed as the Chief Priest, officially making him the most powerful man of the metropolis.

'How many people witnessed this upsurge of the waves?' enquired Vivasvan Pujari.

'My lord, since it happened in almost a flash and that too several hours after sunset, there were only a few trade travellers returning from their long journey from the land of the pyramid tombs. Their caravan was a few miles away from the riverside when they saw the monstrous waves in the light of the half-moon.'

'A few *miles* away did you say...?' asked Chandradhar in a tone of disbelief.

'Yes my lord. Traders from the caravan say the waves were higher than a mountain and darkened the skies in their vast shadow. Over two hundred men, women and children have perished. They didn't know what struck them.'

There was deathly silence in the room as the engineer paused for a few moments.

'My lords, the villages were swept away like they were made not of baked brick, but of dry straw,' he continued. 'The locals of the area have now started calling the mother river with a different name. They are calling her the *Rakt-Dhaara* (River of Blood).'

The last statement from the chief engineer sent a chill down everyone's spine. Blank looks were exchanged. Every priest-leader sitting in the gathering knew that the Saraswati carried enormous volumes of water in its flow, more than any other river in the known world. While the mother river had taken care of them for centuries, none of the wise men in the room underestimated the raw strength of her holy flow. If that river had thrown up waves as high as mountains, like the traders had described, it was very bad news.

·||卐||·

Four hours had passed since the engineer had broken the news of the tsunami. While a couple of the priests opined that the whole episode be treated as a rogue and one-time occurrence, the majority voted otherwise. There were strange signs presenting themselves. Across the vast plains and valleys, the wind was blowing with unnatural strength and in unexpected directions. Migratory birds had flown away hours before the quake, months before their annual season of flight. Domestic pets and beasts of burden were visibly uneasy and afraid, tears flowing from their terrified eyes. The skies were covered with thick clouds of red and purple, something the Harappans had never seen before. These ominous signs were enough to convince the wise priests that the worst was not over. That they needed to prepare for an eventuality far more perilous.

The large walls of the meeting room were now pinned with vast charts of both geographic as well as astrological drawings. After giving directions for the last rites of the demised and for relief teams to reach the five flooded villages immediately, Vivasvan Pujari had immersed himself in a rigorous discussion with the engineers and town-planners. He wanted to explore all the possibilities they had at hand to take protective measures. On the other hand Pundit Chandradhar was working on the *panchanng* and other astrological frameworks to understand why such dark clouds of misfortune had engulfed them all of a sudden. In Harappa human endeavor was the paramount philosophy of survival and growth. But divine intervention was never undermined.

'Our towns are reasonably safe against the shifting of the Earth, my lord,' said Somdutt, one of the most accomplished chief engineers of Harappa, and a close friend of the devta. He was responding to a barrage of questions from Vivasvan Pujari.

'Our buildings are made with high-quality baked brick and are seldom more than three stories high. Even if the ground moves, none of the buildings will fall.'

'I am relieved to hear that, Somdutt. Are you sure the large granaries and copper smelting workshops are also equipped to handle this unnatural phenomenon?' asked the devta.

'The granaries will be fine. The copper units should be advised to halt work till we know better what we are dealing with,' replied Somdutt.

'It will be done.' Vivasvan Pujari nodded at one of the priests who were responsible for all copper and bronze works of the settlement. The priest bowed and left the room to execute what had just been advised.

'Okay let's move to Sara Maa now,' said Vivasvan Pujari, looking at a different chart that laid out the trajectory of the river. He was still referring to her lovingly as *Maa* or mother. Deep down he was annoyed with her. The lives of two hundred innocent Harappans were lost as they slept. Why did she unleash such a curse? *How can a mother let his happen??*

He was stunned to see that the engineers had nothing to say. They stood staring at their feet in complete silence as the devta looked up from the chart to inspect their faces one after the other.

'What happened, Somdutt? You and your fine team are here to offer solutions so we can safeguard millions of our countrymen. Your silence is not appreciated!' said the devta sternly.

'Forgive us, my lord, but we really don't know what can be done to counter the assault of a storm from the Saraswati.

We calculated to the best of our abilities. If the traders who witnessed the tsunami are to be believed, there is nothing we can do against the might of the river. A wave as high and powerful as what has been described will deliver a blow so devastating that it cannot be measured in even advanced mathematics.'

Vivasvan Pujari couldn't believe his ears. He was relying on his engineers to offer a solution, no matter how daunting it was. But here they were, giving up at the very outset.

'So what are you saying, Somdutt? Do we just wait and watch our homes and our people get washed away?!' asked Vivasvan angrily, almost shouting.

Even before Somdutt could reply, the room echoed with a loud metallic ring. Everyone turned in the direction of the sound, only to see that Pundit Chandradhar had dropped a large copper inkpot on the floor. He stood gazing at the astrological chart, as if frozen.

'Chandradhar...' called out Vivasvan without moving from his position.

There was no response from his friend.

'What happened, my friend?' called out the devta again. Chandradhar did not turn or speak. He was staring at the *panchanng* as if hypnotized by it.

Vivasvan Pujari walked up to him, held his shoulders and turned his friend around to face him. He was taken aback at what he saw. Pundit Chandradhar was petrified. His face was contorted in horrifying terror and he was not blinking. The devta had never seen his formidable friend in this state, not even in the face of imminent death in battle. Pundit Chandradhar was as righteous and fearless as the devta himself.

Vivasvan shook his friend gently and spoke in a very calm voice.

'What happened, Chandra? What have you seen in the *panchanng* my friend?'

Chandradhar turned slowly to look at the devta. His wide eyes were full of horror and angst. He raised one of his shaking hands to grab hold of Vivasvan's shoulder and clasped it tightly. He looked straight into his friend's eyes.

'Vivasvan…the end is here.'

·‖卐‖·

Vivasvan Pujari tried to comfort his anxious friend with a feeble attempt at a smile. 'Nothing is ending, Chandradhar. We will fight it together like we have many times in the past,' he said reassuringly.

Chandradhar now gave a painful smile. By now everyone in the room was looking at him and there was pin-drop silence. He was slowly gaining back some of his signature composure. After a moment or two he cleared his throat and wiped the tears from his eyes with his fingertips. He then turned to Vivasvan Pujari and spoke in a loud voice for everyone to hear.

'The charts have never been wrong. The *panchanng* has never been so unforgiving. I am unable to believe what I am reading and deciphering.'

Everyone was listening in rapt attention and growing concern. The *panchanng* and the astrological charts were of grave importance. And their study and interpretation by Pundit Chandradhar were legendary. Never once had his prediction gone wrong.

Chandradhar did not want to delay the bad news. He spoke simply and clearly.

'Gentlemen, within one cycle of the moon, Harappa will fall. Never to rise again.'

Banaras, 2017

'I'M HALF-HUMAN, HALF-GOD.'

'What is the matter, Purohit ji?' enquired Vidyut.

Purohit ji looked at Govardhan, the monastery's physician and chemist.

'Mercury fulminate,' said Govardhan.

While Vidyut ran a cyber security company, he was well aware of what that was. But he kept quiet.

'It is used in hand-grenades and other forms of friction-based explosives.'

The three of them exchanged uncertain glances.

Govardhan continued.

'They are trying to kill you, Vidyut.'

·||ॐ||·

Dwarka Shastri's alarm had resulted in the matth unleashing hard defense measures of every kind. After all they had been preparing for this day for hundreds of years. The 'object' that Vidyut accepted from the stranger at the ghaat, was subjected to scrutiny of all kinds. Govardhan and his team carefully disassembled the flip-top lighter and studied its contents scientifically. On the other hand, Pujari ji and his team performed a *dhaatu-pareeksha* (metal-examination) using an ancient occult practice to identify the presence of evil in a substance. Both examinations delivered the same result.

The *raakshasa cult* had arrived. And they wanted to kill Vidyut…at any cost.

·||ॐ||·

'The mercury fulminate would have exploded in your face if you had used it only three or four times more Vidyut,' announced Govardhan in the *sabha* (conference) hall of the Dev-Raakshasa Matth.

The great Dwarka Shastri presided over the meeting. His condition had not improved, but he outright refused to visit a hospital. His heavy and labored breathing could be heard across the hall. His fingers clasped a small bundle of herbs tied into a cloth, that the matthadheesh inhaled into every now and then. The bundle held a mixture of ayurvedic extracts trusted with longevity and palliative properties.

Govardhan had drawn a simple yet clear diagram on the whiteboard at one end of the hall. It depicted the internal mechanism of the flip-top device.

'Mercury fulminate is very sensitive to friction. This cigarette lighter operates on the principle of mechanics - heat being generated by the strong friction that is caused between two metallic, heavily ribbed surfaces.'

By now everyone had fully understood this simple yet lethal modus operandi of the enemy. Govardhan delivered the final message nevertheless.

'This device is packed with so much mercury fulminate, that it would blow-up the head of a man to smithereens even if he was wearing a driving helmet.'

·||﷽||·

There was silence in the hall. Balwanta stood with his eyes still bloodshot. He seemed to be trying to burn a hole in the floor with his intense gaze. In his mind he knew he was on the verge of playing a decisive role in the final God-demon war of planet Earth.

Sonu was breathing heavily, rage overtaking his face and body language. He pounded the base of his trident gently but repeatedly on the ground, as if preparing for a full-out battle.

Purohit ji was in an intense state of calm and calculation. His eyes appeared like those of a yogi in trance. His clenched teeth and pulsating temple gave him the appearance of a war-veteran preparing for a major offensive.

Naina, who was representing and leading the very important and very revered women-folk of the matth, looked worried and ready to burst into tears. It was very unlike her to display this vulnerability. She liked to show she was as strong as Balwanta himself. She probably was. But here it was Vidyut under question.

Dwarka Shastri was tired, very sick, with his mortal body pleading for release. For three quarters of a century he had led all the earthly and otherworldly battles of the matth. But now his awaited successor had arrived, to lead them in the greatest war of all times. He simply turned and called out to his grandson in a loud, rusty voice.

'Vidyuuuuut!' The grandmaster's voice reverberated across the hall.

Vidyut stood up and folded his hands as a gesture of respect to his Baba.

'*Utthishtha!*' thundered the grand matthadheesh throwing both his arms up in the air above his shoulders. What he said in Sanskrit meant one single word.

Rise.

He was beckoning his great grandson to answer his calling.

He was urging the devta in Vidyut to show himself.

·||卐||·

Vidyut stood facing the righteous and powerful gathering of Hindu monks and priestesses. He could see their eyes and faces filled with hope and expectation. He could sense their indescribable and probably undeserved devotion to him. He knew that the hour of meaning that he had always searched for his entire life, was here and now.

'My veins carry the blood of my great ancestor Vivasvan Pujari,' began Vidyut. 'Your Vidyut is the son of the legendary warrior-monk Kartikeya Shastri and my divine mother Pooja. I have the privilege of being the great grandson of the mighty Dwarka Shastri. My soul enjoys the blessings of all of you, and of every ancestor and matth elder for hundreds, perhaps thousands of years. While I am still unaware of the full ancient tale behind this impending dev-raakshasa conflict, I promise you this…'

The men and women sitting in the *sabha* were now glued to Vidyut and every word this divine man was uttering. Their moist eyes made them believe they could see a faint halo around Vidyut's persona. They could see he was the true bloodline of the mythical Vivasvan Pujari. It was crystal clear that Vidyut was the awaited savior. They now knew he was the promised last devta.

Vidyut continued in an emotional, lofty yet humble tone.

'I will punish the man who tried to kill me. And I will stop anyone and everyone who tries to harm me, or anyone from this great institution. For now I know one thing for sure, my dear well-wishers.'

The audience was listening in rapt attention. Dwarka Shastri was hearing every word like it was a balm on his troubled soul. He could see his great grandson coming of age. He could see Vidyut finding himself. He could now allow his soul to liberate itself from his mortal body and duties.

Vidyut made his concluding statement.

'My revered fraternity, know this – *I am half-human, half-God.*'

MOUNTAINS OF BRICK AND BRONZE

The priestly council reassembled after a short break of dry fruit and saffron milk. Each one of them had to come to terms with what Pundit Chandradhar had prophesied. All of them were capable astrologers themselves, and they used these minutes to verify and re-verify the prediction. It was absolutely correct. The planetary configuration was darker than anyone of them had ever imagined. The chances of such juxtaposition were one in a million, but it was happening. As per Vedic astrology, this was the perfect storm. There was no way Harappa, the five thousand year old civilization, was going to survive more than thirty days.

'We must abandon the city and flee while there is time,' said one of the engineers. His words were greeted with nods of agreement across the grand meeting room of the priestly council. Several of the Harappan luminaries in their flowing robes sat around the gigantic wooden table spanning across the length of the room. The others stood around it in groups of twos and threes. The setting appeared not very different from what a prehistoric *Senatus Romanus* would have looked like.

'We could travel eastwards. The horses, bull-carts and elephants can be used for the women, children and the disabled, while everyone else can travel on foot,' suggested one of the council members.

Yes! Yes...came the response from the congregation in the room.

'The escape must begin at sunrise. We could leave the prisoners of the *mrit kaaraavaas* (dungeons of the dead) behind,' said another. 'Let their sins be washed in the deluge.'

'Yes...yes...let's warn our families and pack our valuables,' came several suggestions in favor of the exodus. The room soon became chaotic with the noises and animated chatter of the accomplished people in it. One could hardly hear what was being said in the commotion.

THWAAAACK!

A loud and tearing thud startled everyone into silence. They then saw the mighty devta Vivasvan Pujari leaning over his large gleaming dagger that he had dug on top of the center table, his hand still grabbing hold of the blue lapis lazuli handle of the blade. His muscular frame stretched across from where he stood to where the dagger had found its mark. He eyes were surveying the assembly from face to face in evident disgust.

·||࿕||·

'What is the matter with all of you?!' yelled the devta author-itatively.

'We are the mighty Harappans! We are rulers of entire Aryavarta! We are the writers of the profound Vedas, the riders of the great *ashvas* and the founders of advanced met-allurgy. Are we going to run away like cowards just because we are faced with an adversity??' thundered Vivasvan Pujari, his powerful voice echoing across the tall ceilings of the hall.

No one had the courage to respond, let alone counter the devta. They remained silent. Vivasvan Pujari could make out his fellowmen were more intimidated than convinced. He immediately pulled out his dagger and put it back into its leather scabbard. He stood straight up and spoke in a low yet emphatic tone.

'We have built a civilization more painstakingly than our de-scendants would ever believe. Each one of us has bled and sacrificed for this great nation. Would history believe that we tore out metals like copper and bronze from the very heart of the land? Would they credit us for building the most ad-vanced cities of this planet? Would anyone remember that it was we, the Harappans, who could pump water even against the pull of the Earth? And will we leave all this glory and run like mice just because a river challenges us??'

There was silence in the room. The council members, the priests, the engineers and the military commanders, were all listening intently. Vivasvan Pujari continued.

'We are together the most powerful force on the planet. We have soldiers, engineers, astrologers, metallurgists, physicians, alchemists, architects and more. What can we not achieve together? Maybe this is a test. Maybe the Gods want us to show them that we are worthy of their benevolence!'

'What the Gods want is clear from the *panchaanng* and the *nakshatras* Vivasvan,' said one of the high priests. 'You know this better than I do my friend, my leader...this planetary formation is unprecedented. It is screaming out death and destruction.'

'Be that as it may, my friend, I believe we can prevent this calamity. Or stand in its way and fight! The collective will of our people can endure more onslaughts than the ranges of the Hindukush.'

Vivasvan Pujari looked around the room again. He was disappointed to see drooping shoulders and unsure eyes. He felt as if he was standing amidst strangers. He had never seen such timidity and escapism in the brilliant and fierce leaders of Harappa. *Were these the people he believed to be the finest on Earth? Were these the people he had appointed as the priest-leaders and guardians of his beloved city?*

'Do you have a plan, Vivasvan?'

Vivasvan Pujari turned with delight to see his friend and partner Chandradhar finally participating in the debate. He was relieved.

'Do you have a plan?' repeated Pundit Chandradhar as he made his way to the center of the assembly.

'Yes I do, Chandradhar,' replied the devta. 'As long as I have the support of this esteemed gathering.'

Chandradhar smiled. He looked like he was saying 'You stubborn idiot!' to his devta friend. He didn't say anything.

'Tell us what you have in mind, O great devta. You have been our savior numerous times in the past. You are the *Surya* of Harappa. We have no reason or stature to question your fine judgment,' said Chandradhar with a respectful bow and a great amount of officiousness. He meant every word. He wanted to remind everyone in the gathering who they were speaking to. Vivasvan Pujari had pulled off impossible victories from the claws of defeat on more occasions than he could count. Chandradhar was not going to let them forget their debt to the devta.

'Thank you, Pundit Chandradhar - my friend and my able partner,' replied Vivasvan with equal formality. 'I do have a plan. It will sound ridiculous at first, but I promise you I will make it work.'

·||卐||·

'But this is absurd Vivasvan!' exclaimed Chandradhar. The other people in the room could not believe the audacity of the plan Vivasvan Pujari had suggested, and there were cries and moans of disagreement across the hall.

'It may sound absurd, Chandra, but this is the only option we have. And tell me, why can't our engineers and architects, who have built sprawling cities and modern towns, build these structures?'

Chandradhar didn't know what to say. On one end he was trying to grasp what Vivasvan was proposing. On the other he could see people in the room exchanging mocking glances and silent snickers. He continued the discussion nevertheless.

'So tell me again, what exactly do you want to build?' he asked.

'How and why do rivers change their course gentlemen?' Vivasvan replied with a question directed to everyone in the gathering. 'It is great mountains or giant rocks that force even powerful rivers to divert the direction of flow. Moreover, if water from a stream can be filled into a bucket by placing it at the right place and at the right angle, then water from a river can also be collected in a giant reservoir. The science is the same. The scale is different.'

There were more groans and grumbles of disbelief in the room.

'Today you say you will halt the flow of water. Tomorrow you will say crafts made of metal will fly in the sky!' one of the senior engineers shouted scornfully, hiding his face so as to not offend the devta.

'If the course of a river can be changed, then probably wind will also be harnessed one day to light up villages!' another voice came. It was followed by subdued laughter.

Vivasvan Pujari was unfazed. He knew he could save Harappa, irrespective of the new-found cowardice and skepticism of his colleagues. He, however, couldn't help but notice that some of the engineers and army commanders in the room were new faces. He also observed strange and unexpected insolence in the demeanor of some of the attendees he knew for long, something no one could dare show in front of the devta himself. But he ignored all of it. There was a mountain of a task ahead. Literally. He would deal with them for their misbehavior later. It was this clarity of thought and priority that made the devta who he was.

·||ॐ||·

'We will build mountains of brick and bronze, and change the course of the mighty Saraswati!' concluded Vivasvan Pujari.

There was stunned silence in the room. Chandradhar and Somdutt were amazed at both the ambition as well as the simplicity of the proposed plan. Little did they know then, that the devta had just drawn out the blueprint for the planet's first river dam.

'I need a thousand horses, two hundred elephants, four thousand men and the entire supply of bronze, brick, wood, copper and rope till this undertaking is complete. I will lead this project myself and will camp on the riverbank. If Sara Maa chooses to swallow her children again, I will be the first at her altar.' The devta did not believe in half measures. He also forgot momentarily that the cosmos is always listening.

There were murmurs in the room. The plan that Vivasvan Pujari had proposed was hard to reject. But it was equally outrageous to accept and implement.

After a few minutes of deliberation Pundit Chandradhar stood up from his wooden stump seat. He raised both his hands in a plea for silence. It was only after a couple of minutes of cajoling that he could command the silence and attention he wanted. Harappa's otherwise able and dignified leadership was behaving uncharacteristically uncouth today. Something was not right about any of this.

'My brothers and friends,' said Chandradhar, 'devta Vivasvan Pujari has rescued us from the darkest of hours, not once but many times. Do we forget it was he who defeated the warlord Sura's armies and rode back to Harappa with the first five thousand *ashvas?* Do we not remember that he subjected himself to the forces of the netherworld and co-authored the often-frightening Atharva Veda, when none of us could withstand the dark occult rituals? I clearly remember when he fought twelve of Sura's ace swordsmen alone on the ghaats of Kashi and crushed them singlehandedly. He did that to save me…'

Reminiscing about Vivasvan Pujari's contributions and achievements made Chandradhar emotional for a few moments. He pressed his chin against his chest to hold back the tears. He then raised his head and announced with deep conviction and influence.

'If the devta says we will build mountains, we will! If he says we can change the course of the mother river, we can! Friends and brothers, we will build mountains of brick and bronze!'

'It will be done, my lady. The dancing girl shall be made to rest pinned to her great bed as soon as the devta leaves her private quarters. And yes, all cisterns of saffron milk were spiked with the concoction provided by the sickening swines, Sha, Gun & Ap. Yes, all the council members, engineers and commanders were affected.'

This was the vile progress report Ranga whispered into the meticulously carved grill of the regal Priyamvada's secret chamber. She stood listening even as the purple and red skies threw distorted and ugly shadows on her hidden face. To a common observer Ranga appeared as if worshipping the idol of a goddess at a dilapidated temple. No one knew that the black soul of Priyamvada stood listening on the other side.

As Ranga was about to take leave, his evil mistress murmured out her last commandment.

'Make sure Ranga, what has happened to the priests and engineers today, should happen to all of Harappa starting tomorrow. Every well, every tank and every fountain of the city should be poisoned with the potent Mesopotamian salt of Sha, Gun & Ap!'

'Yes, my lady,' responded Ranga. He was wondering what his mistress really wanted from the general populace of the city. He didn't have to wait long.

'In two days Harappa should be a city of zombies and madmen!' hissed Priyamvada.

Goa (16th Century)

THE DARKEST CRUSADE

The wildly gasping and panting man ran like only a man running from his death can run. Or a man who is willing to give his life for the cause he believes in. On this dark and stormy night Valmiki had both these reasons behind his manic dash through the narrow lanes of Bopdev, the Konkan coastal village he grew up in.

He was running from Cristovao and Agostinho, the two most brutal Portuguese executioners who were trailing him by only a few corners and turns amidst the village huts on this ominous night. These black-hooded executioners with guillotine like axes were more fearsome than the Reaper himself. Known to have unnatural fangs forged from sharpened metal, they never failed to use these savagely on the throats, scalps and faces of their unfortunate prey. They were filled with demonic hatred for the dark-skinned Goan, and in the last few months Cristovao and Agostinho had earned the reputation of being incarnates of the devil himself. But there was more. Valmiki was carrying a 3,300 year old precious treasure that could not fall in the hands of the Portuguese at any cost. Even if it meant that Valmiki died a horrible death tonight. Even if it meant that entire Bopdev and its 800 inhabitants got torched to ashes.

It had all started with the vast fleet of battle ships dropping anchor at the coast of Goa. In the sixteenth century these were the forces of one of the most powerful monarchs of Europe at that time. This mammoth marine army fought for none other than King Immannoel the Vth of Portugal. And Immannoel fought for none other than the Order and the Big Man from Rome.

The initial assault was subdued and camouflaged. The fleet of Portugal sent more priests and 'saints' to the quiet shores than it sent soldiers. The people of Goa were baffled to see prayer meetings and religious gatherings being organized by these priests, when a massive and impatient army waited just a few waves away. There was much talk of the love of a fairer God, when the bloodthirsty swords of Portuguese soldiers glistened even in the distance. There were discourses on the merits of one God over another, which was a completely alien concept for the simple-living masses of this peaceful settlement. They were happy with their Gods.

Amidst all this forced love, what became slowly but vividly evident was the uncanny effort of these priests and their missionaries to scan and search every religious institution and building of Goa. They would not only visit these places, but camp at them for days, sometimes weeks together. No one had the courage to object. No one could ignore the lethal swarm of ships anchored at the shore.

One thing was clear. These priests, these saints, and these men in clean white robes…they were looking for something.

Something they wanted badly. At all cost.

·‖ ꣼ ‖·

Valmiki turned around a corner only to be greeted by a slash of Cristovao's gleaming axe. The blade tore through Valmiki's chest, which spurted blood almost instantly. The brave Goan fell on the slushy mud, the crimson red liquid now flowing out from his bosom freely. The Portuguese executioner stepped forward and raised his axe to deliver the final blow. He was going to cut Valmiki into two halves.

The rain was now violent, pouring down on this black night like a cloudburst. Valmiki could see this mindless animal preparing to strike. The lightning lit-up Cristovao momentarily, with his metallic fangs shining like the devil's claws. He appeared more monstrous than death itself.

Valmiki could not let himself perish. He cared little for his life. But the scroll sewn into his waistcoat was more precious than all the treasure in the world. It was the only hope for mankind. Even this mindless killing by the Portuguese in the name of God was nothing compared to the violent destiny that awaited the human race. The scroll was the only hope. It held the only secret that could save planet Earth.

As he scrambled backwards on the ground facing imminent death, Valmiki drew upon his last reservoir of energy. His hand bumped into a rock, which he immediately picked up and attacked Cristovao with. The rock struck home. Propelled by a dying man's final burst of strength, the rock smashed the Portuguese's face into a pulp. The beast Cristovao crumbled on the ground with his lower jaw dislocated. He was dead.

Valmiki stood panting, fully aware that Agostinho would arrive at any moment. He also knew his end was near. The blood loss from the deep gash on his chest was making him dizzy. He had to deliver the scroll into the safe hands of the only man he could trust in all of Goa. He had to deliver it to the only Hindu monk who could stand in the way of the Portuguese pogrom.

He had to deliver it to the doorstep of the great Markandeya Shastri.

·‖卐‖·

The banging on the door was desperate. The thunderous night was overpowering all other sounds, yet the hammering on the door woke up Markandeya Shastri rudely. He rushed to open the door, only to find his dear friend Valmiki drenched in blood. He was dying.

Markandeya lifted his Goan friend on his shoulders and carried him into the small thatched hut he called home. He lit a lantern to inspect the wounds of his friend. He was distraught at what he saw. Valmiki's torso was slashed across its full length, from the shoulder to the waist. His friend was not going to last more than a few breaths.

'They are going to break it down, Markandeya! They are going to raze our Shiva temple…' said Valmiki, coughing blood almost immediately.

'It's all right. You take it easy. Let's talk about it in the morning.' Markandeya Shastri lied to his friend. He knew Valmiki was not going to see another morning.

'Stop fooling with me, Markandeya. We both know I don't have that much time.'

Markandeya Shastri was the leader of a small clan of Hindu monks settled in Goa. Legend had it that his ancestors had travelled thousands of miles on horseback to reach this land. Whether they were escaping a great flood or a great adversary, none could say. They were believed to be bearers of a great secret. They carried immense wealth with them, and used it with utmost righteousness. Their clan built several grand Shiva and Vishnu temples, and created philanthropic institutions around them. Soon the people of this vast coastal settlement began to revere this clan deeply. The belief regarding their ancient secret was slowly lost in the sands of time. Several generations passed and Goa accepted Markandeya Shastri's lineage as its own.

'They were inches away from finding it Markandeya, when I used the key, broke the seal, and took the scripture out,' explained Valmiki.

'You are very brave, my friend. Your name will be immortal one day,' replied Markandeya calmly, his arms holding his dying friend in a close embrace.

'You will...find it...in my waistcoat, Markandeya...' continued Valmiki, now clearly in unbearable pain. His mutilated body was twisting and writhing with suffering.

Markandeya was weeping quietly. He could not bear to see his friend in such agony, especially when he knew Valmiki was yet another sacrifice at the altar of mankind's larger good.

Valmiki could not speak any more. He could not breathe. The world was turning dark for him. As he prepared to leave his mortal body, his bloodstained hand rose up to touch Markandeya Shastri's face, smearing it in blood from forehead to chin. Valmiki whispered his last words.

'They are going to build a dominating structure...in place of our temple, Markandeya...and call it holy. These wretches kill and destroy in the name of a fair shepherd, who spoke only of love and sacrificed *himself* for them.'

Valmiki was now sobbing...as much in physical pain as at his disbelief at the monstrosity of human beings.

'Save us, Markandeya. Save us. Leave tonight. Leave now. Go far eastwards my friend, towards lands closer to Java and Sumatra. Take the scroll with you.'

Markandeya did not know how to react. The whole situation was overwhelming. On one end there was nothing more important than protecting the scroll. On the other he had no idea where to escape.

'Yes I will Valmiki, my brother. I will try. But don't be so sure. What makes you think I can save us from this mammoth bloodbath?'

'Because…because…Markandeya…' gasped Valmiki and raised his head in a final effort before he whispered something and sank lifeless in Markandeya's arms.

His last words kept ringing in Markandeya's mind for several long moments after his friend had passed away.

'Markandeya…*you are half-human, half-God.*'

This duel was not between equals.

Agostinho wore almost an impregnable armor, strapped from his shoulders to his thighs. He held two gigantic, menacing swords that he swung like feathers in his powerful hands. A helmet made from Greek metal protected his head. He had several razor-sharp daggers hanging from his belt. And last but not the least, his iron fangs still had traces of human flesh clinging to their edges.

Markandeya Shastri on the other hand, stood unarmed and bare bodied till his waist. As he stood staring at his adversary, the unending downpour washed his sculptured body, cleansing his sense of purpose. He was burning with a desire for vengeance. Valmiki's corpse still lay in Markandeya's hut, waiting for its final rites.

Agostinho charged at Markandeya like a raging bull, swinging his brutal swords in massive sweeps. Markandeya Shastri stood unfazed. A split moment before Agostinho's swords could hit their target, Markandeya stepped on one side in an expert move to dodge the mad man's assault. In one seamless flow of trained *kalaripayattu* routine, he landed his fist in a claw-formation into the Portuguese bulldog's gut. Markandeya's fingers were equipped with lethal tiger-claw hooks. Within moments he disemboweled Agostinho, tearing out his heart along with his intestines.

This duel was not between equals.

Harappa, 1700 BCE

NAYANTARA

The famous and respected father and son duo of Vivasvan Pujari and Manu stood tall, proud and authoritative in the palatial lobby of Nayantara's rich and classy mansion. They had ridden their muscular horses into the courtyard of that large villa, followed by a guard of one hundred cavalry.

There was much weighing on Vivasvan Pujari's mind from the last night at the council meeting, especially around the doomsday prophecy of Chandradhar. After much deliberation and cajoling by the devta, the decision had been taken to build massive structures of stone, wood and bronze - manmade mountains so large that they could divert the course of the raging Saraswati, and even its demonic waves. Vivasvan Pujari had then spent the remainder of the night with the architects, military commanders and council members of Harappa. With careful precision and a stunning command over engineering and Vedic mathematics, the devta had drawn out the first blueprint of the ambitious plan he had proposed. The plan scrolls had been left with Somdutt and his engineers to study, till they met again later today to discuss the detailed and arduous execution. Vivasvan's plan was to quickly settle this irritating matter of Nayantara's complaint and return to his duty of fighting for Harappa's safety till his last breath.

The devta was secretly stunned at the opulence of this beautiful reception master-hall. The shining floor was glossy as polished metal mirrors. The pillars were adorned with the most beautiful and intricately carved stone tiles. The corners of the hall housed tall statues of the most erotic sculptures Vivasvan Pujari had seen in all his travels. The air of the mansion was fragrant with fresh flowers and exotic herbs. The sparkling fountains used the fall of water from higher ground to gain propulsion, and were placed at the center of the series of large halls. Beautiful choirs played harps and other musical instruments, rendering the air with enchanting symphonies.

But what dazzled the devta more than the beauty of the residence he was standing in, was the divine and unmatched splendor of its owner. The gorgeous Nayantara made such a ravishing appearance that she momentarily enraptured even the devta himself.

Vivasvan Pujari could not believe his eyes. Nayantara looked nothing less than an *apsara* straight from the heavens. Everything about her was crafted to perfection. Her hair was straight and brown, tied in a casual bun behind her chiseled neck and shoulders. Her fairest skin glowed like it had just been bathed in rose, saffron and milk, and her full lips carried a natural pout that attracted every beholder to them. Her eyes were large yet drunk with divine nectar, with her long-curved eyelashes punctuating her striking beauty with natural kohl.

Manu instantly figured it was not his place to remain in that hall, especially when Nayantara had presented herself in all her infinite beauty. He bowed and folded his hands towards both Vivasvan and Nayantara, and left the building. In all this while, Nayantara had not taken her eyes off Vivasvan Pujari even for a moment.

Vivasvan noticed that Nayantara stood in front of him in unabashed sensuality, with her slender and bangled hand resting on her hips. She wore a white and incredibly thin robe that did little to hide her slim yet perfectly voluptuous body. The robe threw itself casually from her left shoulder right down to her upper thighs, revealing her bejeweled red underclothing quite clearly. Rest of her flesh, from her right shoulder and collarbone to most of her full bosom, her slim waist and her legs…was bare and unclothed. Vivasvan admired her unbelievable attractiveness and charm, but he was not tempted. The devta had absolute control over his senses.

·||ॐ||·

'This palace hall is not worthy of you, the Sun, my lord,' said Nayantara. 'Please allow me to welcome the great devta's lotus feet into my private chambers', she added coyly.

Vivasvan Pujari found the request inappropriate. But he did

not flinch.

'As you please dear lady,' he responded.

'Please call your servant Nayantara. Or Nayan as most of her patrons call her lovingly.'

'All right, Nayantara. Can we now discuss the court summons my fine son Manu has received from the city judge? There seems to be a mistake.'

'Your servant is a bundle of mistakes, by lord,' giggled Nayantara beautifully.

She turned to walk towards her private chambers, glancing into Vivasvan's eyes, indicating that he should follow her. Vivasvan Pujari obliged. He had nothing to fear. Not even himself.

·||卐||·

Nayantara's bedchamber was nothing short of a coital paradise. The air was perfumed with fresh flowers, camphor and incense. The massive white and turquoise curtains made the sunlight turn silken as it entered this pleasure den from its various windows and sunroofs. A massive chandelier of rare and uncut crystal hung over what looked like an ornate fountainhead of scented wine. Large cushioned seats with rich blue bolsters and intricately crafted yellow-metal frames were placed towards one end of the large room. The other end displayed the most opulent round bed draped in black silk.

'Please come in to my humble love nest, O great devta,'

whispered Nayantara huskily as soon as Vivasvan entered her bedroom and she shut the chamber's doors behind her. She now had a naughty twinkle in her intoxicating eyes.

Vivasvan stood still, deciding not to react to any of this tricky woman's antics.

'Why was there a summons, Nayantara?' he demanded, sternly this time.

The chamber rang with the most musical laughter Vivasvan Pujari had ever heard. Even Nayantara's laugh sounded like a thousand heavenly harps twang their strings in symphony.

She now walked towards Vivasvan Pujari and stood daringly close to him, her body nearly brushing against his muscular frame, and her raised lips close to caressing his chin. She stared straight into his eyes. Vivasvan Pujari could now see her gorgeous face closely and could smell the intense perfume of Nayantara's skin. He had to admit to himself that this was a heady concoction, and that he would need to brace himself more than usual. He was after all, half human.

'Would my lord have given his humble servant the chance to come this close without the summons?' Her fragrant breath was now heaving warmly on Vivasvan Pujari's face.

Vivasvan Pujari stepped back in angry objection, startled at the audacity of this young enchantress. Even before he could say anything, Nayantara undid her thin white robe and let it slip to the shining floor. In one practiced move she stepped forward boldly, flung her arms around Vivasvan Pujari and pressed her lips thirstily against his.

Banaras, 2017

NAINA

It was a new and enviable fellowship. Vidyut sat in the center of the Dev-Raakshasa matth's armory. It was a dark hall in the basement of the matth, one among many such hidden chambers in the monastery. Vidyut was smoking continuously. He didn't care anymore. All he could think about was the cute boyish face he saw at the ghaat. And how he was going to make him pay.

They sat in a circle with an assortment of weapons kept in the center. It was a kind of presentation being made by the dreaded warrior Balwanta. In the inventory there were old Enfield bolt-action guns and a few Winchester rifles. There were shotguns, pistols and revolvers of the finest makes, ranging from Colt, to Beretta to Webley Scott. And then there were the blades – the favorite armaments of the *kalar-*

ipayattu champions.

Vidyut was stunned to see the battery of arms and ammunition in front of him. The matth was truly equipped for a small-scale war.

'Why don't we have Kalashnikovs and Chinese grenades, Balwanta dada?' enquired Vidyut in jest.

'Because we are not terrorists, Vidyut', replied Balwanta matter-of-factly. 'We are protectors, not destroyers.'

He continued, 'Every weapon you see here has been legitimately sourced, has a government license and can be traced back to its purchase mostly from either retired British officers or Indian government servants. These friends of the matth trusted us with these weapons to be used strictly as defense infrastructure, not offence.'

Vidyut was impressed to find a deep sense of responsibility and righteousness in even the war General of the matth. He couldn't, however, stop himself from probing further.

'But why does the matth need so much weaponry, dada? Who are we preparing to fight?'

Balwanta nodded, looking enquiringly into Vidyut's eyes. He didn't know where to start.

'This matth has survived for hundreds of years Vidyut. It has witnessed and withstood attacks from sultans and marauders, from invaders to imperialists. When every building, every home and every temple including the great Kashi Vishwanath was razed to the ground by these violent and mindless forces, the matth stood its ground. Over the centuries a couple of hundred Hindu warrior-monks have repeatedly repelled armies of thousands.'

Everyone was now listening intently to Balwanta, with the sudden realization that the Dev-Raakshasa matth was over 1,600 years old.

'We have fought wars that are not even recorded in history. These guns and swords are our last line of defense against a conspiracy encircling us at a scale that is unimaginable. You see Vidyut, *we are all alone.*'

'What conspiracy, dada? What do you mean alone?' asked Vidyut, a bit perturbed at Balwanta's last statement.

'Let your Baba tell you about it, Vidyut. He would know best how to initiate you into this surreptitious reality.'

Vidyut nodded. He desperately needed another audience with the great Dwarka Shastri. Much was to be learned. Much seemed to be at stake.

·||ॐ||·

In the ring Balwanta sat to the immediate left of Vidyut. There was Sonu, devoted unquestionably to this scion of the Shastri and Pujari bloodline. Naina sat to the right of Vidyut, with her shoulders intermittently rubbing against his. There was Govardhan, adding maturity and experience to the group. The only new and external entrant into the bunch was Bala, Vidyut's trusted friend. He had flown-in from Delhi at a four-hour notice earlier that morning.

'So what's the plan, Video?' enquired Bala looking at Vidyut.

The others in the huddle were quite delighted to see the warm irreverence Bala had in his tone as he addressed Vidyut like a buddy. They were convinced very quickly that the two were dearest of friends.

'I'm going to find and kill that bastard', replied Vidyut even as he inspected a neat Walther PPK automatic pistol.

'Whoa…whoa…sure we will find him, Vids. And we will make him pay. But what's with this *kill* him etc, buddy?' said Bala. 'We are not in 1,700 BCE anymore, bro.'

Vidyut grinned in a tired manner. 'Ya ya…I know, Bala. You know what I mean, man.'

'Of course we kill,' interrupted Balwanta in broken English. He looked angry and perplexed at this indecisive discussion around whether or not to kill the enemy. As far as he knew, the only way ahead was to deal in body bags.

Bala now took closer notice of the Neanderthal looking character sitting across him, with short-swords resting on both sides. He burst into a laugh, riddled with disbelief at this strange looking man's complete disregard for the law of the land.

'Balwinder Sir…murder is illegal, sir', said Bala in a jovial and typical Dilli-wala tone so as to not offend the cave man. He failed miserably.

Balwanta was seething with anger at Bala taking his name wrongly, when Sonu intervened with a loud laugh and corrected the ex-military veteran, 'Not Balwinder, Bala brother…our commander-in-chief is called Balwanta'.

'Balwanta…Balwinder…same thing…*kyun,* Sir?' Bala winked at Balwanta, pressing on with the teasing.

Everyone laughed, with Vidyut putting his hand on Balwanta's knee, calming down the warrior chief. Naina rested her head for a moment on Vidyut's shoulder even as she broke into a beautiful laughter that turned her face red. Balwanta had already started disliking Bala. Bala on the other hand had developed great interest in this creature that was ready to kill for Vidyut.

·||卐||·

Vidyut picked up a cup of tea from the matth's canteen and walked up to the second floor terrace. He lit a cigarette and took a sip of the cinnamon flavored, fragrant tea. The dusty, bustling town of old Varanasi spread out in front of him, with thousands of small jointed homes and temples in a continuous crisscross of lanes. Even as he took the first long drag from his Marlboro, someone flicked the cigarette off his lips. He turned to see the gorgeous Naina standing right next to him, taking a deep puff from his cigarette. Even before she completed the deep drag, she turned to him and winked naughtily. Vidyut gave her a scowl of protest. Deep down he was delighted to see her. At the same moment he remembered Damini. He quickly shrug off the magnetic attraction he was feeling towards Naina.

Naina took out the cigarette from her lips, her mild lipstick leaving a clear impression on the stub. Without permission, without hesitation she put the cigarette between Vidyut's lips. She didn't leave it there. She didn't turn to Vidyut. She expected him to take a pull at the cigarette while it was still in her fingers. It was a strange yet extremely effective way for her to show two things. One, that she felt great physical comfort with Vidyut. And two, that she did not need his permission.

'Didn't know you smoked, Naina,' said Vidyut after taking a long drag from the cigarette in her fingers.

'What *do* you know about me, Vidyut?' she quickly responded with her eyebrows raised. She looked stunning. And annoyed.

Vidyut just laughed, embarrassed at her question. She was right. He had not kept in touch despite them being best of friends in their early childhood. He realized she was prettier than anyone he had ever seen. The breeze on the terrace made a lock of hair flutter over her beautiful face. Her eyes seemed moist all the time, even when she laughed. That gave her an inexplicable look of vulnerability. Vidyut knew Naina lost her parents in childhood, and that she was a brilliant scholar and martial artist. But here, at this time, she was just a beautiful girl he could not help but admire more than he wanted to.

'No really, Vidyut, how could you do this to me? I wrote perhaps a hundred letters to you without a single reply. I have been waiting for you for years, yaa. Not *one* phone call? Not *one* short note?' Naina was now staring into Vidyut's eyes with a complaining and demanding expression.

'Well don't blame me, Naina. You see the girls in Delhi were so fashionable. And you…you were a little plump, if I may say?!' said Vidyut, now mischievously pulling Naina's leg. He didn't know what else to say anyway.

'You cheapo, you…!' exclaimed Naina in a display of artificial anger and landed a few soft punches on Vidyut's muscular arm as her sign of protest. Her soft green *dupatta* (stole) slipped off her shoulder in the process, but she didn't care. She didn't seem to notice. But Vidyut did. Naina only looked prettier without the dupatta around her. Her dangling jade earrings were now accentuating the feminine attraction of her unusually lovely face and her long, slender neck made her look like the perfect storybook girl-next-door. While she was in her early-thirties just like Vidyut, this gorgeous, teasing and vivacious girl from Kashi looked nothing more than nineteen.

Vidyut was now laughing fully and hopping around the terrace to escape the volley of the playful fists Naina was landing on him. Naina chased him around amidst peels of laughter, just like she did when they were children. Only that this time around there was clearly more amorous chemistry between them, despite Vidyut's repeated yet ineffective attempts against it.

'Okay stop, enough!' said Vidyut, still laughing and panting as a result of the friendly pursuit.

They both paused the chase, and rested with their hands on their knees, catching their breath and laughing like old friends.

'Okay then say you're sorry!' demanded Naina, panting heavily, which made her look more desirable than ever. Her face was flushed red after the entire running around. She was laughing along with Vidyut, but appeared strangely emotional. All this was not a game for her.

'Yes, yes…I'm sorry *yaa*! I'm sorry, *Nainu*…' said Vidyut, folding his hands in full surrender. He did not realize he had called her Nainu - a name that he lovingly used for her many many years ago.

Naina froze. This name was more special to her than she could ever tell anyone. This was her name when she was alone. This was what she called herself while speaking to herself in the mirror. She tilted her head slightly, and looked at Vidyut's eyes as if imploring him for his love.

'And say that you will never leave me alone again?' she now whispered softly, her laugh slowly transforming into a plea, smiling and crying all at once.

Vidyut was dumbfounded for a moment or two. On one hand all he wanted to do was to take this girl meant for love into his arms. On the other he knew he was spoken for. Damini was the love of his life.

He said after a few seconds of pause, 'Naina…my dear Naina…much as I care for…'

'Shhhh…' Naina suddenly put her soft and slender fingers on Vidyut's lips.

'Not Naina, Vidyut. Call me what you just did', she moved closer to him and whispered into his ears. She was looking into his eyes enquiringly, as her cheek brushed against Vidyut's, and her slightly open mouth touched Vidyut's lips for a split second.

Vidyut could feel her tender and fragrant breath on his face. He could see her yearning eyes ready to break into passionate tears.

Even before he could say anything, Naina stepped forward boldly, flung her arms around Vidyut and pressed her lips thirstily against his.

Harappa, 1700 BCE

SIN LIKE A HUMAN.
REPENT LIKE A GOD.

Vivasvan Pujari was riding his stead faster than ever before. He was angry, both at himself as well as at the circumstances. It was the first time in his life that he had struck a woman, and he was not ready to pardon himself for this deplorable deed. In a fit of rage he had momentarily forgotten his own strength. A slap from the devta was too punishing for the delicate Nayantara. She had fallen on the floor with a painful cry, her lower lip bleeding profusely.

Next to Vivasvan rode his brilliant son Manu. He was a bit worried for his illustrious father. Along with the servants of Nayantara's mansion and several of his own bodyguard, Manu had seen his father stomping out of Nayantara's private chambers in a visible state of fury. Moments before that

everyone in the reception hall and at the entrance of Nayantara's palace had heard a loud clap, followed by her short
cry, as if she were in excruciating pain. Vivasvan Pujari had
walked out of the reception hall, mounted his horse, and
without a word rode out of the mansion courtyard. His son
and cavalry had followed him. Not one of them had failed to
notice the stains of blood on Vivasvan Pujari's snow-white
robes.

·||ॐ||·

'The devta answers only to the Saptarishi and no one else,'
said Manu sternly to the red-hooded head-soldier. He could
sense his own temper rising, but Manu was not one to react
violently. He maintained his composure despite the unspeakable humiliation he and his family were being subjected to.

'My lord, I am but a humble soldier under the command of
the priestly council. I am here only to do my duty,' replied
the head-soldier with a respectful bow. He knew he stood on
hallowed ground, the residence of the mighty Vivasvan Pujari. But he also appeared to be vilely intoxicated with what
Manu assumed was nouveau empowerment. There was
something amiss in his overly respectful demeanor.

The turn of events was more rapid than the venerated Pujari family could grasp. Within a few minutes of Vivasvan
Pujari and Manu reaching home, almost a whole garrison of
heavily armed Harappan soldiers had arrived at their doorstep, their red turbans fluttering in the breeze. Something
that was unthinkable till only hours ago was unfolding itself
like a carefully drawn game plan. How time alters even the
loftiest fortunes in a matter of moments was once again to

be witnessed. The soldiers carried an arrest warrant for the most powerful and revered man in all of Aryavarta. They had been ordered to take into custody none other than the devta himself!

·||卐||·

Vivasvan Pujari had barely sat down for his daily incantations, when Sanjna disturbed him with a mild clearing of her throat. In an instant Vivasvan opened his eyes, his senses tingling with unfamiliar human anxiety. In over thirty years of wedlock, Sanjna had never once interrupted her husband's daily penance. She was well aware that much of the devta's indescribable powers found their source in the deep recesses of his advanced Vedic meditation and practices. It endowed him with profound wisdom, boundless strength and spiritual supremacy over ordinary mortals. But most of all, it enriched his very soul with deep compassion and humility. He was the only chosen and direct disciple of the great Saptarishi. In fact, for years many in Harappa and even in neighboring Mohenjo-daro believed just what the Saptarishi had promised Vivasvan the previous morning - that Vivasvan Pujari would one day join the celestial ranks of the mighty Seven Sages. And that they would together bless this world as the Eight children of the loving Saraswati, the Eight Sages – the Ashtarishi.

But that was not to be. What cosmic destiny has in store, none can foresee.

Let alone becoming one of them, within one cycle of the moon this devta was going to wipe out the very existence of the Saptarishi, the sacred sages he considered to be the protectors of Harappa and his own divine guardians, from the face of planet Earth.

The succession of horrors and violence that Harappa was about to withstand had never been witnessed before by mankind, but hereon would be endured again and again. Each time man would shed the blood of innocents to quench the unquenchable thirst of one demon. Every era would hear the shrieks of suffering millions, only to satisfy the insatiable hunger of one tyrant who wanted it all for himself. And it was going to begin soon. First when an island's deca-polar demon-king would be vanquished by an avatar of the Lord Himself; then in an epic battle between first cousins for a throne that would be won only after it is drenched in the blood of an entire generation; then in the form of a black plague that would ravage all of known Earth in its wake; then in the central-Earth battle between followers of the fair Shepherd and the worshippers of the divine Prophet who rode into the sky; then in a four-year war that would claim the whole world; to the world battle that would end with the Sun exploding in the very land it rose every morning. And yet, it would not end. The bloodshed would *never* end.

It was all going to begin with the falling of the great devta Vivasvan Pujari. Whether he was chosen to be the cause of planet Earth's darkest curse, or just a medium for Creation to assert itself yet again, even eternity would never know. The universe was going to test him beyond his endurance. And he would fail. He would unleash his deadly wrath on not just his enemies, not just all of Harappa, but also upon anyone and everyone who came in the way - including the Seven Sages from the mountains. But anger is the darkest poison. What he forgot completely during this spell of blind rage was that an act against the Saptarishi - was a declaration of war on the Gods themselves!

But then again, the blackest of depravity and the whitest of goodness, both reside in the same heart, suppressed or bolstered at the behest of the soul. Much as he was destined to preside over the destruction of the great Seven Sages, it was none other than Vivasvan Pujari himself that was going to make the Saptarishi immortal. He was going to make them shine like stars in the night sky till the end of time.

This devta was going to sin like a human. And repent like a God.

Banaras, 2017

MANKIND'S GREATEST UNTRUTH – PART II

Vidyut was relieved to be sitting next to Dwarka Shastri again. More than twenty-four hours had passed since the grandmaster had sensed the presence of an alien object in Vidyut's pocket, and the meeting between great grandfather and grandson had been disrupted. A lot had happened in this time, with Balwanta, with Bala…and with Naina.

'The truth is never sold and *marketed* like lies are, Vidyut. The truth is what gets subdued the most, buried the deepest,' began Dwarka Shastri.

'I know it is hard for you to forget and unlearn what has been systematically fed into you by your modern-day schools and books that find inspiration for their content from European or western influences. So before we proceed, let's consider the following important questions about the discovery and subsequent history of Harappa –

'When did the Harappan civilization exist and when was it discovered?

'Who discovered it?

'What was it originally called?

'What happened there several decades before its officially recorded discovery?

'And most importantly, what happened *after* it?'

Vidyut was listening intently. He was delighted to see words flowing from his ailing great grandfather at a rapid and sharp pace. There was so much to be learnt, and Vidyut knew that time was ticking away.

'Baba, I am not a scholar in this field. But I do know that a British officer discovered the Harappa site in 1921. I think his name was Sir John Hubert Marshall. Other sites like Mohenjo-daro were excavated over the next few years...by 1931, if I'm not wrong.'

Dwarka Shastri was impressed with Vidyut's fundamental knowledge about this nearly forgotten chapter of history. He couldn't help but chuckle nonetheless.

'What happened, Baba? Did I say something that is not correct?' enquired Vidyut.

'No no...you are absolutely right,' responded Dwarka Shastri. 'Now tell me, what else do you know, or should I say, what else have you been *taught* about what you call the Indus Valley Civilization? Tell me everything.'

Vidyut felt embarrassed. Despite being an exceedingly well-read man, he didn't really know too much about Harappa - definitely not enough to have a long discussion with a master like his grand old man. He concentrated hard and gathered everything he could recall from memory.

'Like I said, Baba, I am not very conversant with this topic. But I will try and recollect whatever little I know, and share it with you.'

'Go on,' said Dwarka Shastri with uncharacteristic patience.

'Harappa is believed to be a civilization that thrived in the Indus Valley region, a large part of which is now in Pakistan. The civilization was at its peak during 2600 to 1700 BCE and is considered to be from the Bronze Age. Harappa and Mohenjo-daro are perhaps the most popular among the sites excavated, although over 1,000 such locations were discovered. Some of the other well-known settlements from that era are Dholavira and Rakhigarhi, both these being in modern India.'

Dwarka Shastri was smiling. He always knew Vidyut was no ordinary fellow from a big and heartless city. But he was now admiring his great grandson's knowledge about something as unconventional and obscure as Harappa, especially for an information technology entrepreneur from New Delhi.

'You know more than I expected, Vidyut. Now think hard and tell me the final bits of information you have about

Harappa. What do you know about its culture and its people? And what do you know about its *end*?'

An hour had passed. Vidyut had emptied out every bit of *gyaan* that he had about the Indus Valley civilization. He had recollected pages from his beloved and fantastic NCERT books. He drew upon every chance newspaper or magazine article about the Harappan people, or Dravidians as some texts called their later generations, which he had bumped into over the years.

He described to the great Dwarka Shastri how Harappa had well-constructed buildings, sophisticated drainage systems and extensive use of red baked bricks. He could somewhat describe the seals and the pottery that had been excavated by the reputed Archaeological Survey of India (ASI). He could share how together with ancient Egypt and Mesopotamia, Harappa represented the oldest recorded human settlements. And finally, amazed at his own reservoir of knowledge about this topic, he could tell Dwarka Shastri that while copper and bronze were prevalent in use, there was no evidence of iron.

'That's all I know, Baba. In fact, I didn't know I knew so much!' said Vidyut with a bright laugh. Dwarka Shastri laughed with him. Vidyut couldn't believe he had made the dreaded matthadheesh laugh. Here at this moment, in this massive chamber in the heart of the Dev-Raakshasa matth, Vidyut was simply a little boy, playing with his grandfather.

Before Dwarka Shastri could clear his throat and begin his

end of the narrative, Vidyut interrupted him.

'And yes one more thing, Baba…they found a lot of figurines in the excavations. Among them the most popular ones are those of a dancing girl with arm-length bangles, and a seemingly one-eyed, bearded Priest-King. The latter is on display in a Museum in Karachi today.'

Vidyut was thrilled at himself. He almost rose for a high-five with his great grandfather. But before he could gloat in the vastness of his knowledge, he noticed that the mention of these figurines had disturbed the grandmaster. It seemed as if the brief moment of laughter had turned into vapor in an instant.

'What happened, Baba?' enquired Vidyut. 'What did I say?'

Dwarka Shastri paused for a few moments. He was looking at Vidyut with a strangely tender and inquisitive expression on his wrinkled yet chiseled face.

'These figurines were not unearthed by the chance stumbling of an archaeologist's fossil brush, Vidyut,' said the matthadheesh somberly. 'They were destined for this discovery.'

Vidyut was unable to comprehend what his great grandfather had just said. But he kept quiet. He was not going to interrupt Dwarka Shastri. He could sense something uncanny was about to be revealed.

'The statuettes you speak about belong to two profound characters who changed the course of mankind's fate, Vidyut.'

Vidyut was now on the edge of his seat. He could hear his own heart pumping. He was listening with intense focus on every word spoken by the grand old man.

Dwarka Shastri took a deep breath. And uttered a name that Vidyut had never heard before. But the sound of it sent a shiver down Vidyut's spine. He somehow seemed to know the woman behind this name - from another land, from another time.

'Nayantara.'

There was complete silence in the room. Vidyut had broken into a cold sweat. All this was unreal.

'Who is Nayantara? And...and...' Vidyut could not hold himself from asking, 'and who does the bearded Priest-King represent, Baba?'

Dwarka Shastri turned to Vidyut with a puzzled look. He gestured to him to come closer. Vidyut obeyed immediately and came to sit on the edge of his Baba's bed. He was nearly moved to tears as his great grandfather took his hands into his own.

'Tell me, Baba...who is the scarred, bearded man?' enquired Vidyut insistently.

Dwarka Shastri continued to look at Vidyut inquisitively and asked, 'You really don't know, Vidyut?'

Vidyut looked blank.

The grandmaster then raised his left hand and put it on his great grandson's shoulder. What he said next would change Vidyut's life forever.

'It is you, Vidyut. The bearded Priest-King with the scar across his left eye...is *you*.'

Harappa, 1700 BCE

MURDER

Vivasvan Pujari turned towards Sanjna, only to find his fair and gracious wife nearly shivering with angst. Immediately upon his return from the disturbing visit to Nayantara's mansion, Vivasvan had decided to calm his nerves and composure by retiring to deep meditation. At this very moment of losing his meditative concentration, he heard the heavy clanking of a thousand bronze and copper armors and the rumble of several hundred horses circumambulating his house. Vivasvan was not accustomed to such belligerence. Least of all could he bear the look of fear on his beloved wife's face. He knew something was ominously wrong. But no matter what, he was not going to pardon the audacity of anyone who had disturbed his pious household and his loving family like this.

Stunned and burning with rage at this indignation, Vivasvan Pujari walked out of his meditation chamber towards the entrance of his austere but massive cottage. Anger was not a very familiar state for the great devta. His Vedic penance had long conquered this destructive emotion so well known to the ordinary human. But the events of the last twenty-four hours had been extraordinary and had shaken up even the mighty Vivasvan Pujari.

Even as he paced to meet the unfortunate aggressor, his private guard took vantage positions with bows and arrows at the windows, doors, courtyards and roofs of the devta's villa. The nine of them were handpicked and raised by the Pujari family like their very own children. None other than Vivasvan Pujari himself had trained them along with Manu, on his signature warfare art of sword, shield, twirl and leap – an intense craft that had been propagated as a major martial art by a worshipped warrior-ascetic called Parashuram a few hundred years ago. These nine were enough to defend this household against even a massive army. They held their weapons on stand-by, waiting only for the command of their master.

A few paces away from the door, his strikingly handsome and formidable son politely stopped Vivasvan Pujari. Manu was smiling, with a gentle bow greeting his great father. Two of the house's fiercest warriors were by his side.

Vivasvan noticed that his son, who normally led the life of nothing more than a humble and accomplished Brahmin ascetic, had a gleaming long-sword strapped to his back. His companions had equally ominous weapons at the ready. But what marveled the devta most was the speed at which the young adopt newest produces of technology and craftsmanship. He spotted that Manu's finger-tips were capped with *baagh-nakh* or tiger-claw hooks, that were invented by the principal alchemists of Mohenjo-daro and Rakhigarhi. The tiger-claw was a masterful blend of molten copper on the long extinct saber-tooth's preserved talons. *Baagh-nakh* was the deadliest weapon for close combat.

·‖ॐ‖·

'Maa is such a nervous darling…she never should have disturbed you in your prayers father,' said Manu. 'I would have taken care of it.' The father and son were now footsteps away from the garrison commander waiting at their door. The clanking of armor, swords and spears combined with the cantor of hundreds of horses was now nearly a deafening din. The father son duo could sense that by now soldiers had surrounded their entire residential compound.

Manu's presence gave Vivasvan Pujari a strange and unparalleled sense of confidence. Whether all fathers felt the same in the presence of their growing children, Vivasvan knew not. What he was sure of was that Manu was an extraordinary boy. Something deep within Vivasvan Pujari told him that his beloved and magnificent son was fated for very big things.

'Let me talk to them father,' said Manu as they reached the door.

The mere glimpse of Vivasvan Pujari sent shivers down the

spines of the soldiers that had congregated in front of the entrance to the massive cottage. Not one of them had the courage to look at the *Surya* of Harappa in the eye. Vivasvan Pujari's stature was like the shining Sun and he represented everything good in Harappa. These soldiers, who worshipped the devta like a God, were in a state of complete confusion at what they had been ordered to do. Who can dare capture a God?

Coming straight from his meditation chambers, Vivasvan Pujari stood towering at the raised verandah outside his home's entrance. The majestic built of the bare-bodied Brahmin was awe inspiring, as he held his head high and examined the troops with a sweeping glance. Manu and his two companions were by the devta's side. Despite being in the hundreds, the soldiers were convinced they could never overpower this small but daunting combat unit. Manu and his brotherhood were themselves known for their valiance and skill. But the real danger was the devta himself. In even the most nightmarish of odds, Vivasvan Pujari had never been beaten in battle.

'Who leads this impudent operation? Present yourself!' announced Manu, beckoning the leader of the troops to identify himself.

There was no response, as the soldiers only exchanged glances with each other. Manu asked again, this time raising his voice for all to hear.

'Who leads this audacious procession? Who has the nerve to march soldiers into the devta's house?'

A moment later, a gigantic and monstrous looking commander in the red hooded uniform of the Harappan cavalry, slowly made his way through the soldiers towards Vivasvan Pujari and Manu. He stared straight at them as he arrogantly advanced to the head of the troops. The father and son were alarmed and enraged as they saw one of Harappa's most notorious, corrupt and ruthless army commanders walking towards them.

It was the dubious commander that Vivasvan Pujari had sentenced to rigorous imprisonment a year ago on charges of rape and treason, but had let go upon the direct request of Pundit Chandradhar's wife Priyamvada. It was hard to refuse the princess of Mohenjo-daro. Since then the commander was attached to her as the leader of her personal bodyguard.

The scoundrel was Ranga.

·‖ॐ‖·

How can this be? How can the priestly council issue an arrest warrant against me? Vivasvan Pujari was baffled. Each one of them was handpicked by the devta himself, and they swore allegiance to him at every opportunity. But then Vivasvan Pujari was wise enough to be fully aware of the ways of the world. He knew that fortune and friends visited and left together.

Ranga had served a written notice to Vivasvan Pujari, asking him to present himself in front of the priestly council the next morning. The council was entrusted with both executive as well as judicial powers in running the affairs of

Harappa. This made them the most powerful body across the vast metropolis and its surrounding towns and villages. They were answerable only to the Chief Priest, a position that Vivasvan Pujari had already been chosen for. The morning that was earmarked for the formal seating of the devta as the Chief Priest was now going to see him standing like a felon in front of a bench of judges! Destiny changes its course faster than dunes in a desert.

On the one hand, Vivasvan could not believe something like this could happen and was convinced it had to be a big mistake. On the other he felt deeply alarmed as he observed the garrison surrounding his house in a tight formation, putting him, his family and his household staff under siege. They were following a clear plan.

Manu was seething with anger at the humiliation his father was going through. He charged forward towards Ranga, with an intent to tear-up the council summon and, if needed, the commander along with it. As soon as he lunged forward a raised arm of Vivasvan Pujari stopped him. Vivasvan turned towards his son, and gestured at him to calm down.

'I will come with you, Ranga. But before I do that, please let me know the charges pressed against me,' said Vivasvan Pujari.

'Murder', replied Ranga.

MANKIND'S GREATEST UNTRUTH – PART III

'As expected, you have given me the standard, institutional-ized and well documented information about Harappa,' said Dwarka Shastri, as he muttered a short prayer to *Annapoorna*, the Goddess of nourishment. The old man continued, 'You have simply told me what you and billions of others have been made to believe and accept over the years.'

After several hours of intense discussion, they now sat down for a meal together. It was a rare privilege for anyone to break bread with the mighty Dwarka Shastri. Just like every-thing else in his life, the matthadheesh took his meals like an elaborate spiritual ceremony. He followed every recom-mendation recorded in ancient Ayurvedic scriptures, and ate with his fingers.

Vidyut was in a state of daze. On one end he treasured this opportunity of sharing lunch with his great grandfather, and on the other he was still grappling with all the bizarre tales Dwarka Shastri had just told him. Who was Nayantara? How can a mythical legend survive over thousands of years? What did the grandmaster mean when he said the Priest-King in the Harappan statuette was Vidyut himself? For all his greatness, stature and achievements, *had the old man finally lost it?*

'I am not mad, Vidyut,' said Dwarka Shastri, as if he were reading Vidyut's mind. He probably was.

'I know you must be thinking I am an old fool, conjuring up make-believe stories. But you know what, I thought the same when I was your age and heard of the ancient curse for the first time.'

Now this was new. As if it couldn't get any more mysterious, Vidyut was baffled to hear the term *curse*. *What the hell was going on?!* Since childhood he knew he was a devta. His loving mother had told him so, beaming with pride as her son performed extraordinarily at anything and everything he attempted. His father, the great Kartikeya Shastri, had taught him advanced meditation, Vedic sciences, warfare and the profound *siddhis*. He was also made aware that a dark secret lurked in Kashi. *But a curse?*

·||ॐ||·

Everyone at the matth, especially Purohit ji, was stunned at the visible recovery in the health of the grandmaster. Only three days ago he was in a state of near coma, barely able to speak and totally unable to get up from his bed. And here he was, sitting over a meal, having an animated discussion with his great grandson. It was hard to believe that someone could regain health and vitality at such pace simply due to the presence of a loved one. Even a spiritual force like the great Dwarka Shastri was no match to the power of love.

The meal was both delicious and healthy. The disposable plates made of dried leaves were called *pattals*. As per Ayurveda, the primordial science of life, these were the most suitable utensils to be used for a meal. Rust-brown earthen cups accompanied these green platters. These kiln-baked mud cups were called *purvas*. They smelled of sweet Kashi mud when moist with the water they held.

Every dish on Vidyut's plate was freshly cooked. The basmati rice was fragrant and fluffy. The tomato based vegetable curry was mouth-watering. There was a spinach and cottage cheese mash, accompanied by the ubiquitous north-Indian *daal* or yellow pulses. One corner of the plate had fresh curd with chopped onions and coriander. A separate bowl, again made of dried leaves, held a serving of delicious peppercorn gravy. It was a vegetarian meal fit for the Gods.

Rice was meant to be the main, yet second course. It was the staple diet of the great Aryans. The first course comprised hot *pooris*, or fried flatbread made of wheat flour. It tasted divine. For all their discipline and austerity, the Brahmin priests and monks were known to have a weakness for these puffs of pleasure. Dwarka Shastri and Vidyut were no exception.

The matthadheesh made a morsel of a portion of his *poori*

dipped in a generous dollop of the cottage cheese and spinach mash. He fed Vidyut with his hands. The kitchen servers, Pujari ji, Govardhan, Naina and everyone present at the luncheon were stupefied to see this unprecedented show of affection by the feared clan-leader. Vidyut, on the other hand, was soaking in every moment. He had been deprived of this grandfatherly love ever since his memory had awakened.

Before Vidyut had arrived at the Dev-Raakshasa Matth, no one had even imagined Dwarka Shastri to be a man of sentiment. But here he was. The most dreaded taantric, the most ruthless clan-lord, the most powerful spirit in the solar system – crumbling with emotion while feeding a great grandson.

Clearly, even now…he was half-human.

They were back at the private chambers of Dwarka Shastri. The lunch break was a blessing in every way. The grandmaster had found some visible emotional relief in the youthful company of his long separated but prophesied great grandson. Vidyut, on the other hand, had been able to grab a few moments to deal with the outrageous myths and sagas he had heard over the last few hours. He didn't really know what to believe and what to discard. It was all too over the top, too unscientific, too bizarre.

Dwarka Shastri could sense the confusion and disbelief in Vidyut's mind. He decided to give his young and charming descendent some time. He waited for several minutes, flipping the beads in his fingers.

'Tell me Vidyut, do you really think there were no horses in Harappa?' began Dwarka Shastri. 'Or that some superior race from Europe rode thousands of miles to the East to bring the beast to this land?'

Vidyut sat listening. Every new statement from his great grandfather was opening a whole new box of mysteries for him.

'And that every Harappan was a dark-skinned, uncivilized aborigine, waiting for salvation in the form of a white-skinned army from the West?' continued Dwarka Shastri.

There was silence in the room. The crazy thing was that Vidyut felt the urge to say yes to everything the old man had just asked. But he also knew that his great grandfather would not have posed these questions just for the heck of it. There was something deeper at the core.

'Baba, what they say was that the Harappan people lived in the Indus Valley region till a wave of united, horse-mounted, white-skinned and blue-eyed invaders from the West swept these lands. This supposedly superior race had sharp noses and characters that resemble modern European features.'

Dwarka Shastri was listening intently, although his eyes seemed to be slowly firing up with fury.

'It is believed that it was the invasion of the Aryans from Europe and the contest for agricultural land and water that forced the Dravidians to migrate southwards and settle beyond the Vindhyas.'

'So there must have been a great war?' asked Dwarka Shastri. 'Your so-called Indus Valley civilization is said to have had a population of over 5 million people. Such a vast establishment cannot be defeated without a long and dreadful war, correct?'

'I guess so, Baba...' Vidyut responded unsurely.

'The Harappan people who reached great heights of sophistication in trade, who displayed fine precision in weights and measures, who used hydraulic technologies for water-management, who built cities in scientific architectural patterns and grids, who could build copper smelting plants and gigantic public structures, would no doubt have advanced military prowess also and would not be easy to vanquish, do you agree?'

Vidyut nodded in concurrence.

'Do you know the excavations show that cities of the Harappan civilization were surrounded and protected by mighty walls, which were nearly impregnable for any invading army? Do you think an enormous civilization of 5 million people with such advanced cities and capabilities would simply uproot everything and run away at the mere sight of an invading army? Of course they would not. So if these people were indeed defeated in a military conflict, it would have been a very large-scale and violent clash involving long and powerful sieges of the cities.'

'You are right, Baba.'

'Even those sieges would be nearly impossible for a pre-historic army, given that the major Harappan cities were not only defended by great walls, but also had sophisticated water-supply systems and vast granaries. Any army that laid siege to these cities would take months to starve the inhabitants. So for the moment we have to assume that the invaders actually stormed the cities by sheer military force. And in that case the excavations should have unearthed a massive reservoir of arms used in the war, as well as decapitated and mutilated human skeletons. If baked bricks can survive thousands of years, why not metallic weapons and human bones?'

Vidyut was listening very carefully.

'But none of those things were found Vidyut. Barring a few broken bronze arrows, the archaeologists uncovered absolutely no signs of a war or violent struggle across hundreds of excavation sites,' continued Dwarka Shastri.

It was all very novel and educative for Vidyut. He realized he had never really gone into the depths of understanding how the Aryans actually displaced the Harappan people. He had simply taken it for granted, because he had read so in the books.

'Clearly, if no weapons or signs of a conflict have been found, there never *was* any war. And if there was no war, there could have been no invasion!' exclaimed the great old man like a mathematics professor unraveling a complex theorem.

Vidyut then asked the question that the matthadheesh wanted him to ask. He asked the question the true answer to which had been lost somewhere in the hundreds of years of false propaganda. And the answer to which could change the world forever.

Dwarka Shastri knew that buried in the pages of the Harappan tale, lay mankind's greatest untruth.

'But baba, if there was no invasion, *who were the Aryans??*'

MAD-MEN AND ZOMBIES

'This is absolutely ridiculous!' exclaimed Vivasvan Pujari. He was standing in front of the priestly council, with over one hundred elite soldiers guarding all the exits of the large courtroom.

Despite the garrison siege of his house the previous day, Vivasvan Pujari was confident that the absurd charges against him would be quashed in a matter of minutes, as soon as he explained his meeting with Nayantara to the council. He had presented himself promptly at the court the very next morning. Nevertheless, his heart was deeply saddened as this was originally going to be the appointed hour of his greatest glory. Now his seating as the Chief Priest of Harappa had been substituted by a criminal hearing.

'You must not use this tone with me, O councilman', warned Vivasvan Pujari. He was not going to let his dignity be tarnished by the council or by anyone.

'Yes, I had visited Nayantara. And that was because there was a false summons against my son Manu. I knew it was a terrible mistake and I rode to her mansion only to resolve the matter.'

'And that resolution was the cruel execution of the famous dancer, O devta?' commented one of the council members wryly.

Vivasvan Pujari stared long and hard into the eyes of this council member, who till yesterday did not have the courage to even sneeze loudly in the presence of the devta. Today he had the audacity to question Vivasvan Pujari face to face. In fact everyone was behaving differently. Vivasvan had taken an early repast that morning, which had left him feeling unwell. He attributed the giddiness to his own anxiety about the hearing. On his way he had noticed that several people known to him had looked through him, as if they did not recognize him. As he rode towards the courthouse, he had witnessed street-fights and angry squabbles on the roads, outside shops and even in residential courtyards. All this was not normal in Harappa, the civilized and gentle Vedic city. But today everyone seemed to be restless and aggressive. *What was happening to his beloved city?*

The council members were no different from the city crowd this morning. They were brash, loud and exceedingly disrespectful. The exaggerated swagger in their walk, the uncouth guffawing and the mocking tone of the proceedings were all alien to the normally gracious and brilliant council members, and to Harappa at large. The city, its culture and its people had been groomed under the pious and magnanimous ethos of the Vedas and the Sanatana Dharma. But today the loving and peaceful people of Harappa looked nothing like themselves. Today they all seemed mildly deranged. And it was getting worse with every hour.

'Look council member, I did not even know that Nayantara had been murdered till Ranga informed me yesterday at my residence,' said the devta. 'May God bless her soul and give her noble births till her spiritual journey is over.'

While he said a short prayer for the departed soul of the beautiful dancer, the devta could sense his own temper building. A strange urge from deep within him was tempting him to jump across the hall and brutally decapitate everyone on that bench. He could easily do it, he knew. He even pictured the assault moves in his head. But he was a devta. Within moments he realized it was a manic thought and quickly shrugged it off. This was so very unlike himself, felt Vivasvan Pujari. *What was happening to him?*

Vivasvan could sense that something was not completely okay, although he could subconsciously fight the effect of whatever it was that was making him unnaturally angry. He was a devta and had complete control over his mind, body, nerves and spirit. But the rest of the Harappans were ordinary mortals. The infected water from the wells and tanks of the city was making them mad. They were succumbing to the after-effects of the evil Mesopotamian alchemy of Gun, Ap & Sha.

They were slowly becoming a city of demented beasts.

·||ॐ||·

The hearing was now on for over two hours. It was only during this time that Vivasvan Pujari heard about the circumstances in which the beautiful Nayantara had been discovered by her servants in her private chambers, soon after he had left. She was found bleeding profusely on her great bed, with a thick copper spear pierced right through her chest, literally pinning her to the thick wooden backrest. Only someone bestowed with great physical strength and boundless cruelty could have struck such a powerful blow. Her exceptionally pretty face was contorted with agony and struggle, and her eyes were sunk deep into her head. The daakini had left Nayantara's body. It was useless to her now.

'You do know your white robes were stained with her blood when you stomped out of her chambers, O devta?' asked one of the council members.

'And the servants of her mansion heard her scream with pain, moments before you left her!' yelled another councilman.

Vivasvan Pujari clenched his teeth and closed his eyes to control his rage, now boiling beyond all limits. He responded in a controlled voice.

'I only slapped her once. I agree it was a hard blow for a woman as delicate as her. She fell on the ground, her lower lip bleeding copiously. I instantly regretted my decision of striking a woman, and offered my robe to stop her bleeding.

Hence the stains.'

'And why, may we ask, did you, the great devta himself, choose to physically assault a helpless woman?' asked one of the now half-crazy priests. Vivasvan Pujari did not like the generous dose of sarcasm in his voice.

'She had the nerve to disrobe in front of me,' replied Vivasvan Pujari.

'And…?' asked one of the men from the bench, shifting in his place cockily, winking at his neighbors. The judges now appeared nothing more than a bunch of perverts to Vivasvan Pujari. He was beginning to get worried.

'And she attempted to make intimate physical contact with me,' replied Vivasvan.

'Well that should be rewarded with some love my good Sir, and not a slap. Nayantara was the most delicious dish of Harappa!' screamed out one of the council members, followed by wild and vulgar laughter from everyone in the courtroom. Vivasvan Pujari could not believe his eyes and ears. Not one Harappan would ever speak with such disrespect for a departed spirit. And these priests were some of the most saintly souls on the planet. *Why were they behaving like the mighty warlord Sura's rogue and intoxicated henchmen?*

Vivasvan Pujari concluded that he needed to get out of this courtroom as soon as possible. He would step out and investigate what had gone wrong with everyone. He was convinced that a very dark and sinister enemy was lurking from behind the shadows. The devta had to get to the very root of all this before it was too late for his city and his people. He decided to conclude the court hearing speedily.

Banaras, 2017

'YOU AND ME. HERE AND NOW.'

'We have to find this Romi Pereira', said Sonu. 'But how will this work? Varanasi is a massive city and we have no clue of where to start the hunt.'

Vidyut along with Balwanta, Bala and Sonu had decided to turn tables on this man who called himself Romi. With permission and blessings from the great Dwarka Shastri, they were now planning to unleash a massive manhunt across the ancient city. The construct of the plan was simple. The *Guptachar Sena* (Army of Spies) of the matth would be activated immediately. Nurtured over hundreds of years of painstaking planning and organization building, this *Sena* comprised hundreds of informers of the matth. The ground soldiers of this intelligence unit ranged from small shopkeepers and rickshaw-pullers, to restaurant waiters and even street urchins. This rag-tag, diverse yet supremely effective network covered every lane, every ghaat, every motel and every secret cremation ground of Kashi. This *Sena* had played a key role in the survival of the matth for 1,600 years, and in the numerous bloody battles its inhabitants fought to defend the sacred institution. This spy-army would now be on the lookout for a boyish looking, handsome fellow with round spectacles. They would scan every nook and corner of the city and comb him out.

On the other hand, Vidyut and his newly formed team decided to lay bait by roaming around the ghaats, unarmed and seemingly unprotected. If Romi was here to kill Vidyut, he would not be able to resist the temptation.

Either they would find Romi in the hole he was hiding in, or they would draw him out into the open battleground.

·||ॐ||·

'Absolutely not, Naina!' said Vidyut sternly. 'You will not accompany us on this hunt. This man is clearly a professional. And he may not be alone.'

'And who is asking for your permission *yaa*?' responded Naina nonchalantly. 'You may be the awaited savior and the devta for these people, but for me you are just Vidyut okay?'

The kiss on the terrace had lasted a couple of seconds longer than Vidyut would have wanted. He had unknowingly permitted himself to respond to the passionate lips of Naina, before realizing what was happening and pulling away gently. He was letting Damini down, and he couldn't let that happen. He had just smiled at Naina, given her a soft peck on her cheek and walked away. None of them had spoken about the episode so far, but they both knew they would have to. Soon.

'Look Naina, don't be silly. Out there is no place for a woman.'

'What...? What did you just say...?' Naina nearly shouted back with a deep look of disappointment on her face. 'I never imagined *you* would be such a sexist Vidyut!'

Vidyut wasn't. He admired and respected women deeply. He felt silly and embarrassed at having made that ridiculous statement.

'I'm sorry Naina. I didn't mean it that way. I just don't want you to get hurt.'

'Try me, Vidyut. Let's have a one to one fight. No holds barred,' said Naina calmly. 'I think you forget that the girls of the Dev-Raakshasa Matth train as hard as the boys, and have fought shoulder to shoulder for centuries.'

Vidyut was kicking himself for having said what he did. He vividly remembered the tales of valiance and sacrifice of the womenfolk of the matth. Whether it was battling with other-worldly beings through ethereal conflicts, or taking up arms against invading armies, the ladies of the matth were second to none. And this was true to the very spirit of the Hindu way of life – a great religion that worshipped the Goddess in her most benevolent as well as terrifying forms.

'Let it go *na,* Naina', was all Vidyut could say with an imploring and apologetic expression. By now the others had gathered around, including Sonu, Bala, Purohit ji, Balwanta and few more ladies from the matth.

'No really, Mr. Shastri. I challenge you to a duel. Here and now. You and me.'

Now Vidyut was getting a little amused. Clearly Naina had no real understanding of who he was. Although he did immediately notice that Naina was not in her usual flowing attire of traditional Indian clothing. She was wearing a tight, black sports t-shirt with a low round neck, with army grade camouflage pants and trekking boots. Her hair was tied in a tight bun and she wore a broad belt. She looked devastatingly attractive even in this gear. Vidyut felt she looked like one of those terrific ladies from the Bond films.

'Naina, I know more *kalaripayattu* than anyone here *yaa.* And I am an advanced practitioner of both Jiu Jitsu and Krav Maga. For your kind information I also have the highest degree of black belt in Kung Fu. Bala, tell her man…' Vidyut grinned to his friend who was now enjoying this little quarrel.

Naina stood her ground unfazed. She simply pointed her finger first to Vidyut and then to the ground. 'You and me. Here and now', she repeated.

Balwanta, Sonu, Pujari ji and Govardhan were now having fun. They knew Naina was an ace fighter, but they also knew she was no match for Vidyut. Not that they had seen Vidyut fight. Or even train. They somehow had inane faith in Vidyut's abilities. They just knew. While the entire Shastri bloodline carried traces of divinity, Vivasvan in 1700 BCE and Vidyut in 2017 were the true devtas. With a real God between them.

'Okay look, let's do this. You fight Bala here. If you beat him, we will have the duel you want. If you can't, then you have no chance against me,' offered Vidyut, now almost breaking into a laugh.

Vidyut's non-serious reaction was making Naina angrier.

'What nonsense, Vidyut...' protested Bala. 'Can we please stop this childish exchange and get on with more important things?'

Naina and Vidyut were still staring at each other. Vidyut with admiration. Naina with anger.

'Come on, Bala,' said Naina, still looking at Vidyut.

'This is unbelievable rubbish man,' exclaimed the ex-military veteran, throwing his hands up in the air with exasperation. 'I'm getting outta here.'

He turned to walk away. Within moments he felt like the Shatabdi Express had crashed into his back. Naina had shot a kick and was ready for the fight. Bala turned to see her in a fierce battle stance, one leg in the air, bent so as to fire another kick at a fraction of a second. Her hands were now readied into fists. She was not going to let Bala walk off.

Bala was reeling under the pain.

'Wow…I've never seen a woman strike with such power,' he said. 'Why, I've never seen a *man* hit so hard!' said Bala, now grimacing and rubbing his back furiously to ease the agony.

'Then fight me', said Naina, now concentrating very hard on the fight at hand.

'Look I can't do this, Naina,' said Bala. He couldn't believe what was happening. And the pain was slowly making him very angry.

'I will keep hitting you till you hit back, Bala', said Naina. She was not going to let this go. She was hurt beyond words. *Her* Vidyut had doubted her.

Bala looked at Vidyut, who nodded and gestured with his hand telling Bala to go easy on Naina.

Bala threw off the sweatshirt he was wearing. To the delight of some of the young girls in the audience, a chiseled set of muscles glistened underneath his tight t-shirt and sweat. He wiped the drops on his forehead with the back of his hand, and took a kick-boxer's stance.

Naina attacked again, with twice the ferocity. Her feet landed on Bala's forearms that kept saving his face from the powerful barrage of kicks that she was landing. Suddenly Bala opened up and grabbed her foot. He was a trained fighter and had immense strength in his arms. He was going to twist Naina's leg to drop her to the ground and force her into submission. As he turned her leg, she used the movement to her favor, propelled herself into the air using her other leg and crashed an aerial kick on to Bala's head. He nearly crumbled under the assault.

This was not a friendly fight anymore.

Vidyut tried to intervene when Bala pushed him away. With his nose bleeding, Bala now threw his arms and legs into a quick stretch and got back into the kickboxing pose. Only this time he was all in.

Naina surged forward to punch Bala in the face. Bala swirled and dodged her fist, pushing his elbow into her shoulder as a counter-strike. It was a hard hit. Naina nearly flew two feet away to land on the grassy ground. Bala's raw strength was no joke.

They both swiftly got back into their combat stances and began prancing around in a circle, like gladiators in prehistoric arenas, looking for the best opportunity to strike at the other. So far it looked like a fight between equals. The matth members in the spectators were chanting 'Naina! Naina!' She was one among them, their very own fearless warrior.

As Naina and Bala charged upon each other like lions in a raging battle, Vidyut stepped forward and held Naina's arm. His other hand was on Bala's massive chest.

'Enough!' screamed Vidyut.

A few moments passed, with both sides cooling down slowly.

Bala winked at Naina. She responded with a broad grin.

'You're a tiger *yaar,* Naina', said Bala folding his hands jovially, as an acknowledgement of her intense combat style.

'Well you are no less, Bala. No one has ever come back from my aerial flip-kick,' said Naina, reminding Bala of the crushing blow she landed on his head.

Vidyut was standing quietly with his arms folded, a bit dazed at what he had just witnessed. Purohit ji was smiling at this revelation Vidyut had had about Naina's martial skills. Balwanta was proud of his protégé who had made even a highly trained ex-military combatant taste blood.

'Still worried I'll get hurt out there, sweetie?' asked Naina, turning to Vidyut. Her lips were pouted innocently and her dreamy eyelashes batted quickly to tease him.

'God, no! You can come with us. By all means, lead us, dear *Durga*!' said Vidyut with a cheery laugh and a sincere sense of admiration.

He had addressed Naina as Durga, the slayer of the demon *Mahishasur.*

Harappa, 1700 BCE

THE FALLEN DEVTA

'Because it was not Nayantara in her body! It was a daakini. From Nayantara's breath I could sense the presence of a very potent and exceptionally evil spirit inside her,' explained Vivasvan Pujari.

By now the judges seemed to be far from their judicious best. They were growling in anger, thumping the table needlessly, yelling out orders for intoxicating drinks and hurling abuses at each other. The soldiers of the courtroom, who were normally under a strict code of discipline and conduct, were also chattering and pushing one another like drunk ruffians at a low street tavern.

Suddenly, in all this commotion, Vivasvan Pujari noticed something that made him skip a heartbeat. The judgment book! One of the council members was maniacally jotting something down on the holy book of edicts. This was the ultimate register of judgment in the Harappan legal order. Any edict recorded in this highly venerated book had to be carried out within seven days. It was the law Vivasvan Pujari had himself passed. All that was needed to convert the written text into law was the seal. *The one-horned bull.*

'Stop that councilman!' screamed Vivasvan. He was horrified to see a judgment being noted on the book without the hearing being complete. No one seemed to care.

'Stop writing on that book, you fool!' yelled Vivasvan Pujari again. No response. The demented councilor was now writing at a furious pace, his face twisted in an evil expression of sadism, his eyes not blinking at all.

Enough was enough. Vivasvan Pujari decided to put an end to this madness. He started walking towards the bench and then broke into a run. He was going to pounce on the high dais of the council and snatch the judgment book before something insane got recorded on it. About ten soldiers, one after the other, tried to stop his advance. Vivasvan Pujari could have crushed each one of them in a matter of moments, but despite all the lunacy around him, they were after all his own people. He was not going to harm them. The devta dodged over and glided under every weapon strike at him. His actions were like a dream, his supple body avoiding every blow in an expert move, without counterattacking even once. The council priests, who under normal circumstances could each take on a dozen adversaries at one time, were now staring at Vivasvan Pujari like petrified dolls. The devta was not going to hurt them. He was only going for the judgment book.

Just as he was about to take his final leap, Vivasvan caught a glimpse of something from the corner of his eye. Sanjna! One of the intoxicated commanders had just dragged in his graceful and beloved wife into the courthouse, his hands towing her by the hair.

That was it.

·||ॐ||·

The devta's eyes were now bloodshot with fire that could burn down Mount Sumeru. He turned and bounded towards the grossly erring commander. Sanjna was Vivasvan Pujari's pride, his soul, his promise…his whole world. The devta was not going to forgive this time.

As he approached the exit where his wife struggled with her head being pulled back ruthlessly by the mad commander, Vivasvan Pujari unsheathed the scimitar of a by-standing soldier. In one swift action he pounced on the commander, with his blade tearing through the shoulder of the fool who thought he could get away after insulting a devta's wife. A fountain of blood sprayed from the fallen commander's ripped open flesh. Sanjna was shivering with fright and crumbled into Vivasvan Pujari's embrace. Even before the devta could utter the first word of consolation and comfort to his beloved partner, he felt a crushing blow at the back of his head. The pain was unbearable and the world started spinning before Vivasvan Pujari's eyes. Moments before losing consciousness and crashing to the ground, he caught a glimpse of the coward who had attacked him from behind.

Ranga.

The devta felt his skull had been split into two. The pain from the back of his head was agonizing enough to disable even a God. Vivasvan Pujari could hear sounds of cackling men and screaming soldiers. He wanted to get up. In this slow and painful blur he suddenly remembered Sanjna and the horrible episode that had left him unconscious. For a moment he wished it were all just a bad dream. It was not. The ugly chapter was unfolding in reality.

As he fought the searing pain and struggled to open his eyes to locate his beloved wife, he realized his hands were not free. He felt sharp pain in his wrists. His hands were tied behind him. Not with the regular jute rope used for routine prisoners. His captors had used copper chains that were normally deployed to harness the beasts of battle. They knew that ordinary rope would not be able to contain the *Surya* of Harappa. As the devta slowly opened his eyes, he saw a dozen men looking down at him. The domed ceiling told him he was still in the courtroom.

'Sanjna....' he spoke painfully and broke into a cough. His throat was parched. He could sense he had been unconscious for long hours. All he heard in response was coarse laughter of a hundred men. How much he was missing his valiant son Manu at this time. He would have vanquished them all singlehandedly.

'Sanjna…' he cried out again. Only laughter.

'Sanjnaaaaa…' he yelled with as much strength as his broken body could muster. More laughter.

Tears now broke out from the edges of the fallen devta's eyes. He could not believe how in just forty-eight hours his fortune could turn so much for the worse. From being the most worshipped devta in Harappa, he had been reduced to a plaything in the hands of lesser mortals. He had always been a believer in the power of endeavor over fate. But was fate ultimately the supreme force?

He then felt himself being pulled up from the back of his neck. An extremely strong and gigantic hand was raising him from the floor in the way a hunter picks up a freshly shot rabbit like his trophy. As Vivasvan was regaining consciousness and also fighting the pain, he once again saw his face. He once again saw Ranga's face. In his mind, under his breath, to his Gods – Vivasvan Pujari took an oath. He would not die before seeing the death of Ranga. He would kill him with his own hands. And if for some reason he failed to do that, his son Manu would fulfill this oath.

·||ﷺ||·

'Mrit Kaaraavaas!' announced the drunken priest gleefully.

His pronouncement was greeted with great applause. Every council member, every commander, every soldier and every citizen in the courtroom seemed to be lusting for a violent spectacle. Vivasvan Pujari stood in the center of the courtroom - dazed, hands tied behind his back, bleeding and thirsty. He knew there was no point arguing. This was Satan's gathering.

Confinement in the Mrit Kaaraavaas was the worst incarceration any human could imagine even in the darkest of nightmares. It was a rotting, cold, damp and dark hell of blood, pain, captivity, starvation and torture. The underground prison had been built and administered purposefully. The evolved and peaceful society of Harappa witnessed very few crimes. The classless, spiritual and educated people of this metropolis found little reason or incentive to commit crime. Yet the positive social system that prevented crime was matched equally by the penal framework that punished for it. The Mrit Kaaraavaas was built with a single objective. Deterrence.

The Harappan society believed in equality - wealth for all, opportunities for every citizen, education for everyone and homes for even the poorest. Yet these egalitarian rules did not apply to the prisons. The Dungeons of the Dead were not just punishment in terms of confinement. They were the absolute form of incarceration and banishment. Souls sent to the dungeons were wiped out from the very consciousness of the Harappan society. Even healthcare and medicine did not reach these wretched souls. It was Harappa's own form of capital punishment. Those sent to the Mrit Kaaraavaas never came back.

'The crime of this Vivasvan Pujari fellow has been proven… and he will be sent to the Mrit Kaaraavaas' slurred one of the council members, and stopped to take a big gulp from his glass of flower toddy. Half the liquid found its way from the sides of his mouth to his fine cotton robes.

Others in the room found this hellishly funny and a good enough reason to pick up their own glasses of the inebriating toddy.

By now Vivasvan Pujari was clear that there was no point debating with these delusional hooligans. He was also convinced that his fellowmen had been poisoned with a strong hallucinogenic. He had to get out. He had to find a cure. And if the whole city was going insane, it had to be something that they were all exposed to. The food stocks? Didn't seem likely. The supply came from numerous sources and the distribution was too wide. The meat? No, half the priests were vegetarians. The air? How can that be poisoned? The water? No. All the channels were well guarded.

It all seemed too impossible. Vivasvan Pujari shrugged away the thought.

Had the people of Harappa always been like this? Did they appear kind to him thus far only because the devta saw them from a seat of unquestioned power?

Before he could conclude his thoughts, the continuous bleeding and thirst took their toll on the devta. He once again fell on the ground unconscious.

Banaras, 2017

'WE'RE FIGHTING FOR ONE THOUSAND YEARS.'

'Brahminabad?' exclaimed Vidyut. 'Are you serious?'

He immediately regretted having uttered the last part of his question. He reminded himself that he was speaking to the mighty matthadheesh. He rephrased his question into a more polite one.

'Baba, are you saying that the original name of the Harappan site was Brahminabad?'

'Yes my son. When translated to English it means the Settlement or the *City of the Brahmins.*'

Vidyut was looking bewildered. He did not know what to make of this information. Dwarka Shastri could see the confusion on his great grandson's face. It was time to share the whole truth with Vidyut.

'Why the British officers chose to go with the name Harappa and not Brahminabad, as it was known originally by the locals, is anybody's guess,' explained the grandmaster. 'Also, you said that it was Sir John Hubert Marshall who discovered the Harappan sites in 1921. That is the well-known and well-propagated theory. But do you know that Harappa was actually discovered by another Englishman by the name of Charles Masson *eight decades* before Marshall started the excavations? He even described it in his writings *Narrative of Various Journeys in Balochistan, Afghanistan, and the Punjab.* So clearly, in 1842 the East India Company, and in turn the British crown, had discovered the presence of the Harappan ruins. Why did they commission an excavation only eight decades later in 1922? What were they doing for nearly a century?'

·||卐||·

Vidyut was deeply intrigued at what his great grandfather was telling him. While studying the Indus Valley Civilization back in school and college, he had never thought that the ancient civilization held such significance in Indian history.

'That is still not all, Vidyut. There was another British mission that reached the prehistoric sites after Charles Masson and before Sir John Hubert Marshall. It was a British officer named General Alexander Cunningham, who along with two engineers named John Brunton and William Brunton, visited the Harappan sites in 1856, one year before the great sepoy mutiny of 1857, or as some call the first war of independence. Guess what these Englishman did,' said Dwarka Shastri, looking at Vidyut with an amused expression.

'What, Baba?' asked Vidyut.

'What would you expect educated, civilized and resourceful officers of the East India Company and the British Empire to do if they stumbled upon one of the most ancient relics of the world?'

'I would expect them to preserve the heritage, undertake detailed and careful excavations and eventually gift mankind with a legacy,' replied Vidyut matter-of-factly.

'Precisely. But what if I told you that the British did no such thing? What if I told you that after fourteen years of its discovery by Charles Masson, General Cunningham and the two Brunton brothers blew-up the entire city of Brahminabad to rubble and used its hard-baked bricks to lay the stone-bed for a railway line?' asked the grandmaster, looking straight at Vidyut.

'What are you saying, Baba? This is unbelievable!' exclaimed Vidyut.

'Yes my son. What better way to wipe out an entire chapter of human history? The ancient city of Brahminabad, the first city to be discovered across the Harappan civilization, the most glorious neighbor of Harappa and Mohenjo-daro…today lies crushed and buried under the railway lines between Karachi and Lahore!'

'Why hasn't anybody objected? Why is all this not spoken about more openly?' asked a stunned Vidyut. 'And more importantly, why did the British officers destroy a world treasure in the first place? What did they have to gain from it?'

Vidyut had no idea that a dark conspiracy spreading over centuries and continents lay at the heart of something that appeared to be just an archaeological find about a forgotten people.

'Better than asking what they had to gain from destroying Brahminabad, is asking what they had to *lose* if they let the ancient ruins be discovered,' said the old matthadheesh.

'Consider this Vidyut, several of our ancient scriptures describe rishis and ascetics performing holy rituals and hard penances on the banks of the Saraswati river, supposedly the major river whose tributary was the Sindhu or Indus. Numerous kingdoms of Vedic ethos have been described as flourishing on the mighty river's shores. But none of our history books ever mention this. Agreed the Saraswati vanished from the face of the Earth. But why did it vanish from our books and writing? Billions of dollars are spent the world over to uncover ancient relics, monuments and legends. Then why has the Saraswati been discarded into the dustbins of history?' Dwarka Shastri continued. 'Is it just coincidence?'

After a moment's pause Dwarka Shastri said, 'the forces that wanted to bury the truth behind Harappa are the same as the ones that want the world to forget the Saraswati.'

'Just being a devil's advocate here Baba, but could that be

because there is no real scientific evidence of the Saraswati's existence?' asked Vidyut in a straightforward manner. While he was getting more and more intrigued, he was not going to let go of reason even for a moment.

'That is not entirely true Vidyut. Well-known writer Michel Danino propounded in his 2010 book *The Lost River* that the dried riverbed of the Ghaggar-Hakra was actually the Saraswati river, and that it was the Saraswati that sustained the Harappan civilization and the entire Bronze Age. More recently, the government of Haryana has renamed the *tehsil* (province) of Mustafabad in its Yamunanagar district to Saraswati Nagar, where an underground stream, strongly believed by geologists and archaeologists to be the mythical Saraswati, has been discovered.'

'This is amazing, Baba. One is forced to wonder why such initiatives are being taken only now. What have we been doing for nearly two centuries?!' exclaimed Vidyut.

Dwarka Shastri laughed. Vidyut could make out his laugh carried both sarcasm as well as gloom.

'Not two centuries Vidyut. We're fighting for over one thousand years,' replied the grandmaster.

Another few hours passed and besides further narrating the tale of Vivasvan Pujari, the Saptarishi, Priyamvada and Manu, Dwarka Shastri unveiled several lesser known facts and mysteries about Harappa. Each one of them pointed towards one clear conclusion. Some very influential and powerful force was trying to hide the truth and profound significance of the ancient civilization. Finally, the grandmaster told Vidyut the mysterious story of 1856, Brahminabad.

There was a knock at the door of the matthadheesh. 'Hmmmm…' Dwarka Shastri gave permission to enter. Sonu walked in hesitantly, clearly nervous in the great matthadheesh's presence. But he also had a mischievous smile on his face, which he was trying in vain to hide.

Sonu folded his hands and bowed in reverence to the grandmaster. He then turned impishly to Vidyut and announced, 'Vidyut dada, you have a visitor.' Vidyut noticed that Sonu was going red in the face, and was trying very hard to control a giggle.

'A visitor…? How can I get a visitor? Except for Bala no one even knows I am here,' replied Vidyut. He was in deep conversation with his great grandfather and did not want to be disturbed. There was much left to be learnt and discovered. The painful and gripping tale of Vivasvan Pujari and the last days of Harappa was only mid-way. Neither did Vidyut entirely know how he was connected to it. The mystery behind the Aryan invasion was still not fully uncovered. Why the Saraswati Civilization was named the Indus Valley Civilization and why the British officers conspired to undermine the discovery was yet to be discussed. But most of all, Vidyut was still grappling with what his great grandfather had said about the statuette of the priest-king being that of his own. This was not the time Vidyut wanted to get up and receive a visitor.

'Who is it Sonu?' enquired Vidyut a bit irritably.

Even before Sonu could respond, Dwarka Shastri kept his hand on Vidyut's shoulder and spoke with an affectionate smile, 'Go Vidyut. It is an important visitor.' The great matthadheesh could sense every presence, every new vibe in the Dev-Raakshasa matth.

'As you say Baba. But I will seek more time with you very soon,' said Vidyut and touched his great grandfather's feet. The old man mumbled a blessing, a blessing more powerful than any other on the planet.

'Who is it, Sonu?' Vidyut asked again. He was very amused to see that Sonu was shy of even telling him who it was. With his snickering young friend by his side, Vidyut strode out of the grandmaster's cottage and began walking towards the reception area of the matth situated in the outer precincts. But he didn't have to walk all that way. His visitor was standing at a distance in a walkway between the monastery's gardens. Even after a reasonably long journey, Damini looked beautiful.

THE PRINCESS OF MOHENJO-DARO

'But I don't want to be a king, you wicked wicked woman! How on Earth could you steal the holy seal?' shouted Pundit Chandradhar, even as Priyamvada strolled out of the room. He was trembling with anger and emotional defeat. He was used to it.

Chandradhar was a fine soul. Perhaps among the finest the Earth had ever hosted. He was a priest, a warrior, an ascetic, a statesman, a scholar, a military general, an architect and a master astrologer. He had been in battle numerous times, and had defeated the mightiest of enemies. He had planned towns and built metropolitans. He had co-authored the constitution of Harappa and contributed to even the Vedas. After the devta Vivasvan Pujari, he was the most revered man across Aryavarta. Everyone loved Pundit Chandradhar. Everyone held him in great esteem.

Except for his wife. Priyamvada treated him no better than a slave. The bold and brilliant Chandradhar, who impressed and dominated the whole world, was nothing but a scared puppet at home. There is a hidden streak God grants women, which has the power to change the world. Whether that is for the better or for the worse, depends on the woman who yields that influence. It is a woman that is the progenitor of entire creation. Yet it is often a woman that has led to the bloodiest of wars. Man is but a conduit for the will of the woman.

·||༄||·

Chandradhar did not know what to do. His wife had just confided everything in him, to his horror. The shav-saadhana of Gun, Ap and Sha, the evil possession of Nayantara, the fake summon, her brutal execution, the Mesopotamian alchemy and the poisoning of Harappa's water sources. Chandradhar could not believe his ears. He could not believe someone could be so demonic in her intent and actions. He felt like a sinner and his heart was ready to explode. And when the thought of his sister Sanjna hit him, he crumbled down to his knees, sobbing and screaming with mental agony.

The husband and wife had had a turbulent wedded life. Chandradhar was a large-hearted, brilliant and able man. But he was so deeply in love with Priyamvada that all his wisdom and sense of propriety took a backseat when it came to her. She was an unbelievably beautiful woman, with a regal upbringing as the princess of Mohenjo-daro. While there were no kings in Harappa and its great ally city, the daughter of the Chief Priest of Mohenjo-daro was known across Aryavarta as a princess. She behaved like one. She expected everyone to behave like she was one. The painful part, as Chandradhar would discover a few months into his marriage, was that despite being the revered Chief Priest's daughter, she had the soul of a serpent. And what she considered to be a personal shortcoming would soon make her dark persona worse. She was a personification of hate, envy and greed. Moreover, deep down she was extremely violent and cruel. Never once pricked by even a pin herself, she did not think twice before inflicting inhuman pain on others. And yet Chandradhar was in her complete emotional captivity.

The rise of Vivasvan Pujari had always been a bone of contention between the husband and wife. Chandradhar knew Vivasvan Pujari was an extraordinary soul, a devta, whereas he was himself just a commonplace mortal. Priyamvada had not witnessed all the things he had. He had seen Vivasvan Pujari in battle and knew that no one untouched by divinity could combat like that. The devta had fought and defeated hundreds of armed tribesman of the west singlehandedly. He had fought dangerous beasts and once struck a massive horse along with its rider to the ground with one single blow. He could shoot an arrow and find his mark from miles away. He could slice through the trunk of an oak with one shot from his machete. But more than his physical superiority over every man on Earth, it was the devta's spiritual power that bedazzled Chandradhar and made him Vivasvan Pujari's devoted friend and follower.

While all of Harappa and especially its priests were sophisticated practitioners of Vedic meditation and ethos, no one came close to Vivasvan Pujari's spiritual prowess. It was believed that the devta was the bloodline of the primordial *Rishis* who existed at the time of Creation. And Vivasvan lived up to this reputation. He had mastered all of the eight *siddhis* that existed. This achievement provided him with extraordinary resistance against fire, hunger, thirst, injury, alchemy, illness, gravity and exorcism. The devta was a master taantric who could use the craft for the betterment of the individual and the society. He could study the space-time continuum and had intuitive vision into the past and future. It was the intensity of his penance combined with the goodness of his heart that made the devta dear to even the profound Saptarishi.

After all of this, Chandradhar found it ridiculous that Priyamvada wanted him to compete with Vivasvan Pujari. She was blinded by her ambition to become the first woman of the metropolis. *Why didn't she understand? How can a human compete with a God?* And he knew that even as a human, Vivasvan Pujari was the better man. By far.

Priyamvada was in her private chambers, bathing in milk and rosewater. The plight of Vivasvan Pujari's family, the gruesome killing of Nayantara, the madness of thousands of Harappan men, women and children had no effect on the princess of Mohenjo-daro. She hummed her favorite *gand-*

harva (celestial musicians) tune as she enjoyed her luxurious bath with half a dozen maids at her service.

Chandradhar walked in unannounced. His eyes were blood-shot and his breath was heavy with rage. The maids immediately bowed out of the bath, leaving their mistress and master to their privacy.

'What, Pundit Chandradhar? You don't have to run into my bathing suite just because you want to see your poor little wife naked!' teased Priyamvada, pretending to cover her breasts with her palms, ignoring the obvious fury on her husband's face. She was a temptress par-excellence, and used her beauty and sensuality as potent weapons.

'I am not going to let this happen. I am leaving now to rally physicians, *ayurvedacharyas* (Ayurvedic doctors) and alchemists from all the surrounding provinces. We will disinfect the waters first and then cure our people of this frenzy.'

Priyamvada was listening quietly to her husband. She had handled such rants many times before. Yes this one was exceptionally challenging, but she knew in the end she would have her way.

'In parallel, I am going to summon an emergency meeting of the council, and get all the orders against my friend Vivasvan Pujari annulled. Let them punish me any way they like. I deserve every bit of it. You have shamed me like never before you wicked woman! Are you not scared that the heavens are watching?'

Priyamvada slowly got up and stepped out of the rose-milk with the grace of a mermaid. Stark naked with her skin glowing under the wetness of the fragrant immersion, she came closer to Chandradhar and started planting soft kisses on his neck and shoulders. She whispered into his ears, 'Isn't heaven here and now, my lord?' Her hands slowly reached down to undo her husbands lower robe. Chandradhar grabbed her wrist, twisted it in an instant and pushed her away to the floor.

Okay, so that didn't work, thought Priyamvada.

Banaras, 2017

DAMINI

Vidyut could not believe he was seeing Damini at the Dev-Raakshasa matth of all places in the world! She looked gorgeous in a white sleeveless vest tucked into her tight blue jeans. Her checked cotton shirt was tied around her waist. She wore black sunglasses, big round earrings and her beautiful brown hair was tied behind her head in a bun. Even in this casual clothing Damini looked smashing.

Vidyut could instantly figure out why Sonu was gushing with bashfulness. Damini's outfit was a wee bit bold for the traditional matth clothing. He couldn't care less. He was delighted to see her.

Damini shrieked with bubbling happiness as she saw Vidyut coming towards her. She dropped her backpack and ran towards her dashing boyfriend. The residents of the matth were pleasantly embarrassed when they saw Damini jump straight into Vidyut's arms, her hands and legs wrapped around him. They were both laughing and in pure bliss. Young Sonu stood there mesmerized, observing the couple. Somewhere in his heart he wanted a girlfriend like Damini. *What a life that would be!* He immediately admonished himself for entertaining the thought even for a moment. Damini was the devta's better half, and hence worthy of worship.

'Hi babyyyyyy…' shouted Damini in a shrill voice almost tearing through Vidyut's eardrums. Vidyut laughed in sheer delight and kissed Damini twice on her cheeks. Even though they were meeting after only a couple of days' gap, they were both somehow relieved to be in each other's arms.

·||卐|·

'How on Earth…how did you find this place Damini? How did you know I was here?' asked Vidyut as he gently eased Damini down from her high perch. He could sense that coy laughs and wide glares were being exchanged between the matth dwellers.

'Well you know how resourceful I am, baby…I'm a journal-ist after all!' replied Damini, melodramatically whistling at her fingernails. The brilliant and astute Damini found only one person with whom she could shed her intellectual skin and be the crazy girl she was deep down. It was Vidyut.

'No seriously, how Damini? Bala wouldn't tell you without asking me for sure,' enquired Vidyut again, still wondering.

'Oh come on, *yaar*...don't be such a silly boy. I called Rhea... she told me you were in Varanasi.'

'*Arey*, but even Rhea doesn't know this place,' said Vidyut.

'Yes but she knows the cab company that sent you the taxi. And the cab company knows which driver was on duty for you that day. Simple!' replied Damini, quite pleased with herself.

'Paras Pandey!' exclaimed Vidyut, fondly remembering the interesting fellow who drove him from the airport.

By this time Sonu had taken Damini's bag. As he swung the bag around his shoulder, Damini noticed how desperately shy the young man was. She could also see the honesty on his face. She decided to tease him a bit.

'Oh my God, you have really good-looking guys in this monastery, Vidyut,' she said loudly, staring at Sonu with an expression of excessive admiration. Sonu couldn't look at Damini in the eye, but his heart was pounding. 'The girls in Delhi would go nuts meeting him,' Damini pressed on. The gruff and valiant Sonu, who had challenged even Vidyut at the great gate of the matth, was no better than an ecstatic puppy by now. He almost crumbled to the ground, so weak were his knees.

'Okay that's enough, Damini,' intervened Vidyut with a laugh. 'Sonu will make girls go nuts wherever he goes,' he said putting his arm around his blushing friend. Damini pulled Sonu's cheek affectionately. She had won not just Sonu over with her gregarious and loving self, but also everyone around who were watching.

Or *almost* everyone. Naina stood at the window of her room, her eyes ablaze, staring at what was happening.

Damini was a golden soul. Unfortunately, her purity and power of goodness was no match to the grotesque and dark forces at play in Kashi this hour.

·‖卐‖·

As Vidyut and Sonu led Damini towards the guest quarters of the matth, Purohit ji greeted them on the way. Vidyut muttered 'Purohit ji' to Damini so that she knew who this revered person was. Vidyut immediately bent down to touch Purohit ji's feet and receive his blessings. Damini felt that was her cue and followed suit.

'No…no…please *beta* (child), girls don't touch anyone's feet,' said Purohit ji, stopping Damini mid-way, affectionately but surely.

'But why is that Purohit ji? If Vidyut can touch your feet and win your blessings, why shouldn't I get the opportunity as well?' asked Damini with a smile, softly and respectfully. Sonu and Purohit ji were both deeply impressed to see this sharp metropolitan girl, so willing to embrace their little nuances of tradition.

'My blessings are always with you *beta*. But in Sanatana and Hindu dharma, women represent the Goddess Herself. And the Goddess bows to no one. We bow to Her,' said the old priest.

'That unmarried girls don't touch anyone's feet, not even

their parents', was something I knew Purohit ji,' said Vidyut. 'But then why are married women seen touching the feet of the elders?'

'First of all Vidyut, there is no edict of any kind. Hindu dharma champions free will of the individual. Touching of feet is only symbolic. It simply represents affectionate deference to an elder. Quite like the westerners kiss hands. If a woman wants to touch the feet of elders, it is her choice. If she does not want to follow this tradition, it is absolutely her choice again. Isn't this liberty and freedom of choice what makes our ancient dharma distinctive, Vidyut?' asked Purohit ji with a proud smile.

'For sure Purohit ji,' Damini spoke politely. 'But then why this differentiation between married and unmarried women? Why are married women advised to bow to elders, and not the unmarried ones?'

Purohit ji smiled and kept his hand on Damini's head as a gesture of blessing. 'Because with marriage comes responsibility and partnership, my dear. After marriage women are free to embrace this tradition as the inseparable halves of their husbands, just like they share all other duties. But then again, there is no compulsion. Like I said, our dharma places the woman on a much higher pedestal than man.'

'How do you say that, Purohit ji? Aren't women still exploited in the name of tradition?' asked Damini. She was thrilled to have found someone she could fearlessly clarify her doubts with. Vidyut was enjoying the conversation. In fact he had started it purposefully. Damini was a devout Hindu at heart, but with firm views and objections about the many regressive so-called traditions. She couldn't have met anyone better than the wise Purohit ji to allay her doubts.

·||ༀ||·

Purohit ji had invited Damini to sit down on a bench next to the gardens. Sonu took Damini's bag to the guest quarters to get everything ready for her stay. Vidyut stood and listened as Purohit ji and Damini sat on the bench and spoke with great affection and candidness.

'Religion is a great cleanser *beta*, but it is also vulnerable to the dirt it aims to clean,' spoke Purohit ji. 'Tell me this – if you take a snow white muslin and use it to clean dirty vessels, what will happen to the cloth after some time?'

'The cloth would become dirty, Purohit ji,' replied Damini.

'Exactly. Same is the case with dharma or religion. It is pious and spotless in its original form, but as years, decades and centuries pass, the dharma itself gets tarnished due to the vested interests of rogues who twist and misinterpret it in order to gain political or economic mileage. Exploitation of women in Hinduism is a preposterous distortion. Consider this, everything we hold dear in material or spiritual life, is worshipped as a Goddess, NOT as a God. Wealth is worshipped through *Maa* (Mother) *Lakshmi*. Valor through *Maa Kaali*. Nourishment through *Maa Annapoorna* and knowledge through *Maa Saraswati*. Why, even day to day blessings like wellness and courage are sought from *Maa Seetla* and *Maa Durga* respectively!'

Damini was listening very carefully. She knew a lot of what

Purohit ji was explaining, but his conviction and integrity were impeccable. She could have this conversation for hours. Purohit ji too was now on song. He wanted Damini to grasp every nuance carefully.

'This is not all Damini. Have you seen any other religion where God is considered to be incomplete without his better half? Probably not. It is only in Sanatana dharma that we worship *Lord Ram* essentially with his wife, *Maa Sita* by his side. We don't worship *Krishna* without his beloved *Radha* or *Lord Shiva* without his consort *Parvati*. So how can anyone in his right senses say that Hinduism has anything but boundless respect and love for women?'

Damini was amazed at the clarity with which Purohit ji reminded her of the inherent fabric of equality in Hinduism. She knew about the Gods and Goddesses he had mentioned, but she had never fully appreciated what Purohit ji had just elucidated. She mentally ran through all of the other religions she could think of, and realised that a male God dominated almost all of them! Hinduism was the only refreshing change.

'And don't forget Damini, not only does Hindu dharma offer equality to its ladies, it also makes the men duty-bound to stand by their women and protect them. Lord Shiva entered his universally destructive *taandava* dance-form only to avenge the self-sacrifice of his devoted wife *Sati*. Lord Ram waged war against the demon-king *Raavan* only to rescue his beloved wife Sita. Damini *beta*, our dharma has the woman, the Goddess, the female form of Shakti (power) at its very core.'

Damini was touched. She realised she had been focusing

more on what she was consuming as media stories and on the propaganda around her. She was unknowingly blaming it on the religion without really diving deep into its essence. She knew almost everything that Purohit ji had described, but she had never tried to assimilate and grasp it the way he put it. She was conveniently bashing this profound religion all this while, when it was perhaps a bastion of sanity in a world full of faiths based on conquest, forced-conversion and bloodshed.

'Hinduism was born thousands of years ago, when there *was* no other known religion, *beta*. In fact no one can say when a profound way-of-life took the form of an all encompassing and all-embracing refuge called Hinduism. We never competed with anyone. We never tried to travel far and wide to convert people. We never took to the sword to compel people to follow our God. Because for us there is no *our* and *your* God. For us all Gods are our God – the mighty *One*. And here we are, perhaps ten thousand years later, still around,' concluded Purohit ji with a gentle smile. He was clearly passionate about the subject.

Here in the most prehistoric city of the world and in the heart of the Dev-Raakshasa matth, Damini saw a side she had never witnessed before. Sanatana dharma or Hinduism passed no judgments, gave no diktats, told no one what to wear and when to worship. It was not a martial code based on dark regulations imposed by a handful of so-called holy men. It was a glowing way-of-life. To each his own.

THE FIRST KING OF HARAPPA

Chandradhar was getting ready to leave his residence. He stood in front of a polished copper mirror, strapping his sword to his belt. These were dark times. He did not know what the day held in store for him or for anyone. He could not rely on any of his bodyguard. They were all behaving like zombies. The only people in Harappa unharmed by the water were Priyamvada, her trusted maids, the crooked Ranga and his select henchmen. And of course Pundit Chandradhar, who was kept away from the poisoned water by his wife, as part of her meticulous conspiracy. She wanted him to be in his senses for what lay ahead of them.

Just as Chandradhar was about to leave, Priyamvada entered his room. She was in a different color now, somber and graceful.

'What is so wrong in what I have done, Chandra?' she enquired innocently.

Chandradhar could not believe what he was hearing. He looked at his wife with that disbelief clearly showing on his face. 'You *really* don't think there is anything wrong with what you have done, Priyamvada?'

'Okay I know a woman lost her life. But isn't that a sacrifice we must endure to build a great future for this glorious kingdom under your able leadership?' she replied.

'Harappa is NOT a kingdom, Priyamvada!' shouted Chandradhar.

'But it will soon be Chandra. Don't you see? You will be the first king of Harappa!' Priyamvada walked up to her husband and looked into his face with imploring, ambitious eyes. 'And I will be your queen! We will rule this prosperous province as our own. And after us our children, and their children…'

'We have no child, Priyamvada!' interrupted Chandradhar in a loud voice. There was silence in the room.

Priyamvada's face had turned pale, as if bitten by a cobra.

'Wake up and accept the reality my dear. We are childless and we have to accept our fate!' said Chandradhar more affectionately, fully aware that he had cut open his wife's most gangrenous wound.

Priyamvada was now quivering with hate, her eyes welling

up with tears of poison.

Chandradhar tried to hold her, only to be pushed away. He could see his wife turning into a witch again. Every time she was reminded of her fruitless womb, she transformed into a monster much more heinous than her normal self.

·||ॐ||·

'I will kill her son!' screamed Priyamvada like a woman possessed. 'That bitch Sanjna thinks she can be the first-lady only because she has that boy?! I will kill them both!'

Chandradhar knew he had made a big mistake. He had awakened the evil sorceress inside his wife at the worst possible time. It was not going to be easy to contain her hate and fury now.

'It is my sister and nephew you speak about Priyamvada. Be careful.'

Priyamvada charged towards Chandradhar and clawed at his face and chest with her long fingernails. 'You also don't find me worthy of becoming queen because I couldn't give you a successor, don't you, Pundit Chandradhar??'

'That is not true, Priyamvada. You know I love you more than anything or anyone in this world,' said Chandradhar.

'Then do as I say. Put the seal on the judgment book and let that devta die the death of a rabid dog!' insisted Priyamvada hysterically.

'You know I cannot do that. Vivasvan Pujari is an innocent

man. He is a great man. He is my friend and he is the husband of my sister. And how can you forget, *he saved my life!* I am standing here in front of you because of the life gifted to me by Vivasvan Pujari'.

Priyamvada threw her head back and laughed maniacally, her head swinging from side to side. She stopped suddenly and growled at her husband, 'You are so naïve, you old fool! That devta saved you to serve him like a slave for the rest of your life.'

'Kill him,' she continued, now whispering as if someone was listening. 'Kill that devta. Kill his fair son. Kill his wife. Make me the queen of this kingdom.' Her lunatic expression was as if she had just arrived at this novel plan and was sharing it for the first time.

·‖卐‖·

Chandradhar had left the room. He knew there was no use speaking to his wife when she was in this state. Much as he was enraged at her cruel plan, deep inside he shared her horrible pain. He had seen her suffer and long for a baby. Seeing her without a child was Chandradhar's greatest source of agony. In trying to compensate for this great sorrow, he permitted Priyamvada leeway on many other fronts. Sometimes, he didn't know where to draw the line.

As he was about to mount his horse, a maid came running at him from inside his mansion.

'My lord, please rush. Please rush!' was all she could exclaim in a fit of panic.

'Calm down and tell me what the matter is!' said Chandradhar.

'Lady Priyamvada...she...she...'

Even before the maid could complete her sentence, Chandradhar was dashing towards his private quarters. He knew what had happened. It was not the first time.

As soon as he entered the bedroom, he saw Priyamvada sitting on the ledge of a window. Her hair was thrown open, her upper robe lay on the floor, the kohl of her eyes was smeared across her eyelids and tears rolled down her cheeks. Her wrists were slit and she was sitting in a pool of her own blood.

'What have you done, my love?' cried out Chandradhar, as he tore his angavastram to make bandages with which to cover the bleeding wrists of his beloved wife.

'Don't bandage them, Pundit Chandradhar,' said Priyamvada softly. 'I will cut them again. If I cannot have a child, and I cannot see my husband as king...what do I have left in this world to live for?'

Chandradhar looked into her weeping eyes and her fading complexion as she lost more and more blood. He knew even if he succeeded in stopping her bleeding now, Priyamvada would do it again. She was stubborn, and this was her ultimate weapon against him. He was left with no choice.

'It is time to choose, Chandra,' said Priyamvada with a weak smile. 'Them or me?'

Chandradhar slowly nestled his head into his beloved wife's lap. With her blood oozing all over his face, he repeatedly kissed her bleeding hands. His eyes were also wet with tears of pain and helplessness.

'You, Priyamvada...I choose you.'

Banaras, 2017

ARDHAANGINI

Vidyut and Damini sat inside a cheap but clean Tibetan food joint very close to the matth. Varanasi, one of the hottest tourist hubs of India and a haven for the international spiritual seeker, was also a carnival of food and drink. There was no cuisine on Earth that was not on offer in this mystical city.

The devta had been advised against leaving the monastery, given the highly sophisticated assassination attempt that had been made against him, by a man who had introduced himself as Romi Pereira.

But Vidyut needed to get out, even if it was for a couple of hours. Before they launched a full-scale counterstrike against Romi and whoever else was with him, Vidyut had to confide in Damini. He had to tell her the bizarre but true realities of his past, present and maybe his future. *Their* future.

They sipped on pints of cold beer. Much to Damini's displeasure, Vidyut was smoking again. Sonu, who sat two tables away with Bala, also had his second glass of beer in front of him. He had secretly confessed to Bala that he had never had alcohol, and wanted to try some. Much as he was an austere warrior-monk, Sonu was also just a young boy who wanted to try a few crazy things in life. Bala, the supremely fit yet heavy-drinking ex-army man, was happy to oblige. Every once in a while Vidyut would turn from his table towards Sonu, and smile or wink at him. He was delighted to see the monastery youngster breaking at least one rule! He also knew that with Bala he was in safe company. His veteran friend would not let Sonu go overboard. Also, while Sonu was enjoying the new sensation to the fullest, the youngster was well aware of his responsibility. Every couple of minutes his fingers checked his belt for the deadly Colt .380 Mustang that he was carrying.

Besides Sonu, there were four more fighters from the monastery who shadowed Vidyut and Damini as their bodyguard. Little did they know that if there was indeed an enemy that could vanquish Vidyut, they anyway stood no chance. There was no way they could stop an adversary strong enough to harm the devta himself.

'The dim sums are getting cold, sweetie,' said Vidyut. 'These are your favorite kind, babe, and this place is pretty authentic Tibetan.'

Damini sat staring at Vidyut. She could hardly believe that Vidyut was speaking about steamed chicken dim sums after all that he had narrated to her! She was not even listening to him now. Either her boyfriend had gone mad or something really sinister was unfolding itself. Who was this Vivasvan Pujari? Why did he sound so nervously familiar? Why did she feel like crying even at the mention of this mystical name? Chandradhar was again a name that was disturbing her. Who was General Alexander Cunningham? Who were the British Brunton brothers who destroyed Brahminabad? Why was the place called Brahminabad in the first place? Did the East India Company and the British crown really not know about a whole prehistoric relic town being blown up to provide for railway ballast? And worst of all, what did the great Dwarka Shastri mean when he told Vidyut about the priest-king statuette? Damini always knew there was something mystical, something extraordinary about her boyfriend. But she had no idea that it was going to turn out so complicated and unreal.

'I can't believe all this yaa...' said Damini after a long pause. 'Before I ask anything else tell me this – is your great grandfather really a man who can conjure spells, summon spirits and unleash exorcisms?'

Vidyut smiled tiredly. 'We all can do all of that, babe,' he replied.

Damini was stunned. *What did her boyfriend just say?* And least of all could she accept the nonchalance with which Vidyut had uttered these words.

'Sorry...did I hear you say *we all?* I mean...are you part of that *we all,* baby?' enquired Damini, amazed at the ease with which her man was speaking about spells, ghosts, spirits and the netherworld. She picked up her pint of beer for a split second to check which brand it was that they were having, hoping it was the alcohol working on Vidyut. Her strapping and socially sought after boyfriend, who was best known for the cutting edge digital security company he had built from scratch, was now speaking like a mystical occult practitioner.

·||卐||·

Vidyut picked up his fourth pint of beer and emptied half of it in one long swig. Damini sat across him, a bit concerned about how much Vidyut was drinking and smoking. She let him. She knew that despite his brave demeanor, his nerves were jangled too - uncovering all that he had in the last two days. Also, deep inside her wicked side, she loved it. Vidyut became quite an erotic enchanter once he was drunk. She did not know if he was truly a devta or not. But after a few drinks, she knew his fingers worked pretty divine. She realised she was smiling to herself. She shrugged off the thought for the moment, confident that those expert fingers were hers to have anyway, *all her life.*

Back from her fantasyland, Damini realised that there was much at stake.

'So why exactly did the Brunton brothers decimate Brahminabad Vidyut?' asked Damini.

'It is quite simple Damini. They were trying to wipe out the evidence of an ancient Vedic civilization,' replied Vidyut. 'By using the bricks of the primeval city as ballast, they ensured that it would never be found again. Don't you see Damini? They were looking for something! And when they did not find it, they ensured neither would anyone else.'

'Wow...!' gasped Damini. 'This is all so...so...crazy.'

'That was just the first in a series of systematic steps taken to wipe out the truth. Do you know that General Alexander Cunningham, who was present when John and William Brunton were laying the city's bricks as ballast under the Lahore – Karachi railway line, was later rewarded by the British with the post of the Director General of the Archaeological Survey of North India?'

'What? An officer who quietly witnessed the ruthless destruction of a precious legacy, was actually made in-charge of such heritage?!'

'How do you know he was just a witness, Damini? How do we know he was not being rewarded for what he not just witnessed, but *oversaw* at Brahminabad in 1856?' replied Vidyut.

Damini was listening with her mouth open in daze.

'For over half a century after all of this, the Harappan cities lay buried. Brahminabad was forgotten as two generations changed. And a new campaign, with a new name was commissioned in 1921.'

'But baby, what was the truth they were trying to bury?' asked Damini.

Vidyut grinned. 'You still haven't understood, Damini?' he asked.

His exceptionally intelligent girlfriend shook her head.

'To legitimize their imperial onslaught on the subcontinent, the British had to prove that Indians were an inferior race – nothing more than a brown, semi-tribal people who had been vanquished and civilized by a superior race of white-skinned, blue-eyed invaders riding from the west. It was the perfect psychological warfare to cripple the Indian consciousness. And make them believe that white western supremacy was destined and divine.'

'I don't fully understand, Vidyut,' said Damini, now concentrating very hard on every word Vidyut was saying.

'How do you think that just a few thousand British officers and soldiers conquered and controlled an entire subcontinent of tens of millions? Do you think it was only by military might?' asked Vidyut.

'Military might, superior economic strength, modern weaponry, disciplined bureaucracy...' added Damini with a quick shrug.

'Yes Damini, these were some of the advantages they enjoyed. But none of these was the definitive game-changer. Their most potent weapon was something else. It was *psychological imperialism*. They actually succeeded in subduing not just the land, wealth and politics of India. They crushed the

Indian mind into submission.'

'*Dogs & Indians Not Allowed*' kind of signboards were a frequent phenomenon outside British clubs and officers' messes even as late as the early twentieth century. What do you think such communication was aimed at Damini? Were they really trying to keep dogs out with signboards? Or was it a slow and continuous assault on the Indian psyche?' asked Vidyut.

Damini was listening intently, her fingers playing unknowingly with a strand of her beautiful hair.

'The British knew they could never keep three hundred million people enslaved by the power of the gun alone. There was only one way of doing it, and that was by ensuring mass psychological submission of the entire populace. And this systematic effort started far back in time from the muddy ruins of Brahminabad. But that was not all, Damini. The conspiracy is much murkier than just British dominance over India.'

Vidyut was now looking at the burning cigarette between his fingers, deep in thought. He had not taken a puff since he had lit it. Damini was cold with nervousness. She had to know how Vidyut was connected to all this.

'What do you mean conspiracy, Vidyut? Please explain with clarity,' implored Damini.

'It all began over one thousand five hundred years ago, in

the medieval city of Constantinople. It was here that followers of one faith decided among themselves that they were meant to rule over all the others…forever.'

Vidyut paused for a few seconds before he spoke again. He was now almost in a trance, as if teleported to another land, very far back into time.

'It was all happening just like the dying Saptarishi had prophesied, ' he said.

·‖卐‖·

Vidyut took a gulp from his beer. As he placed the glass back on the table, he noticed that Damini was in a state of deep duress. He knew instantly that she had had enough for one day.

'Come on let's go, we're quite late already,' he said to Damini, signaling to one of the old Tibetan waiters for the bill. He also gestured to Sonu and Bala that they had to leave.

'Nooooo…' protested Damini. 'How can you stop now, Vidyut? I need to know everything!'

'Yes yes…you will get to know everything, Damini,' replied Vidyut, 'but it is best that you listen to the rest from Baba directly.'

'Baba? You mean the great Dwarka Shastri ji…?' asked Damini, clearly in immense awe of the matthadheesh.

'Yes, Damini,' replied Vidyut with a broad grin.

'No…no…I'm scared of meeting him, yaar. And what…you will actually introduce me to him?' asked Damini with her eyes wide, secretly delighted that Vidyut was going to introduce her to the only family he had.

'He has asked for you himself. He asked me to bring my *ardhaangini* (inseparable half) along,' replied Vidyut, smiling charmingly, looking deep into Damini's eyes.

Damini's eyes welled up and a moment later she grabbed Vidyut's hand in her own. 'I love you, Vidyut.'

'I love you too, Damini.'

They sat there, clutching each other's hands, lost in each other.

A minute or two passed in pure bliss. Finally one of the restaurant waiters disturbed their moment of togetherness. He had just slipped the invoice folder on their table. Vidyut and Damini broke into a loving laugh.

'Let's leave now, it's late,' said Vidyut, as he slipped a two thousand rupees bill into the invoice folder. Something caught his eye. The folder did not have the restaurant's food and drinks invoice. It had a note, written in a stylish, slashing handwriting.

Tomorrow 7 pm, Ganga aarti.

Yours truly,

Romi

Harappa, 1700 BCE

MRIT KAARAAVAAS

Vivasvan Pujari woke up to a hideous stench. As he opened his eyes, all he could see in the dim flickering light were walls of rough, black stone. His head wound was still fresh and he felt a cold and wet surface under his bareback. He tried to get up. The stink in the air was unbearable.

As he sat up and looked around, he could not get a clear sense of where he was. His vision was still blurred. His throat felt like it was infested with cactus thorns. He had not had a sip of water for what seemed like days. He turned to see a thick wooden door tightly shut on the suffocating space he was holed up in. His ears were filled with his own dried blood, but could catch distant screams of people enduring great suffering. The hellish smell of the place was making him nauseous.

Slowly the devta was gaining consciousness and memory. He realized his hands were resting on wet and squishy ground by his sides. He raised one of them only to see his palm smeared with brown filth. The cries of people continued to pierce through what appeared to be thick and impregnable walls. Vivasvan Pujari sensed that his palm was also reeking of the same stench that filled the air, only stronger.

The devta shook his head to get more clarity of his surroundings. The smelly air was going to make him sick. As his senses returned to him, he recognized that the stench was a gruesome mix of human sweat, faeces, blood and rotting flesh. The realization made him vomit instantly. Only blood came out from his gut. He had not eaten or drank for over two days now. He noticed that the ground he sat on was flowing with blood and human excrement. In a sudden jolt he figured where he was. But he refused to believe it. He tried frantically to get up and open the thick door. It was locked. The only light in this dark cell was from a lone flame flickering on a wall-mounted lamp. Vivasvan Pujari got up to see that he was in a stifling cell smaller than the size of a cot. The air was thick with the smell of decay and death, and the cries and moans of inmates were never-ending.

Vivasvan Pujari could hardly breathe. He was now shivering in the cold dampness of the cell where he could not even stand up without his head hitting the low ceiling. The ghastly stench, the black walls, the chilly dankness, the macabre screams…all were telling the devta where he was.

Vivasvan Pujari was not ready for this. Despite all his strength, courage and spiritual profundity, the devta was not willing to accept that he was in the most ghoulish prison on Earth. That he was in the mrit kaaraavaas – the dungeons of the dead!

·||ॐ||·

Somdutt could not believe his eyes as he saw the conditions and suffering of the mrit kaaraavaas. Unbeknownst to Priyamvada and her associate Ranga, the chief engineer had escaped the infected water. When Ranga and his men, who had placed themselves on guard duty that night, spiked the central cisterns and tanks of Harappa, Somdutt was out on a site inspection on the banks of the Saraswati. He and his handful of trusted men had come back to a city and people they did not recognize. They had come back to a city of madmen.

He had heard about the trial of the mighty Vivasvan Pujari with disbelief and gloom. Somdutt was convinced, as any Harappan would be in his right senses, that the devta was being framed. He had decided to take corrective measures. But first, he had to meet the devta and find out what was going on.

The mrit kaaraavaas had no policy or procedure for visitors. Even a graveyard allows people to connect with their departed near and dear ones. But not the dungeons. The dungeons were a dark hole from which nothing came back. A hell where every entrant had to abandon all hope.

Somdutt was an enterprising man. As Chief Engineer he also had access to vast vaults of wealth. In the current state of collective insanity, it was not going to be hard to bribe one of the officers in charge of the prison. No matter what needed to be done, Somdutt knew he had to meet the mighty devta. If there was any hope for this manic metropolis, it was Vivasvan Pujari.

·||᭧||·

Sixteen hours since he came back to the city of Harappa, Somdutt was climbing down the dark stairs of the mrit kaaraavaas. He had succeeded in arranging a short meeting with the most influential inmate those prison walls had ever seen.

Somdutt vomited thrice before he could reach the cell of the devta. The air of the dungeons was worse than a human could imagine. As he vomited, he also wept. He could not visualize the glowing, white-robed, divine and benevolent Vivasvan Pujari being held captive in such torment. He also realized how sometimes people in power and prosperity lose touch with the horrible realities of those less fortunate. Or in the case of the dungeons, those who were condemned to suffer till their mortal bodies decomposed into the sewage slurry of the prison. He wondered if any human had the right to subject another to such a merciless fate.

When the door of Vivasvan Pujari's cell was flung open by the intoxicated guard, Somdutt saw what he expected to. Even in the pathetic and inhuman conditions of the dungeons, the devta sat cross-legged, in a deep meditative trance. Somdutt could not help but fall at the feet of the mighty Vivasvan Pujari, the savior of Harappa.

'Somdutt…my friend…Somdutt…' the devta said, clasping Somdutt's hand in his own, resting his forehead on his friend's fingers and weeping profusely. He could not express the relief he found as he saw the face of his noble friend. In the last two days Vivasvan Pujari had forgotten what a friend looked like. All men he considered friends had abandoned him and his precious family when he needed them most. The engineer was overwhelmed himself. The devta, who was impeccably dressed, groomed and smelled of fresh sandalwood at every occasion, was sitting here in a rotting cell, bleeding, dirty, wounded and betrayed.

'What is going on, my lord, my Surya?' asked Somdutt, wiping his own tears as well as his mentor's. 'We need to take quick action.'

'Yes we do, Somdutt…yes we do,' replied the devta. 'But before we discuss anything, tell me where my Sanjna is. Tell me where my Manu is!'

'They are safe, O devta…at least for now,' replied Somdutt. 'Sanjna was rescued by Manu and his Magnificent Nine in a daring raid on the courtroom. She is safe now, and they are all in hiding. They wanted to extract you too, but by then the courthouse was reinforced with hundreds of cavalry. They could not reach you.'

Vivasvan Pujari heaved a sigh of relief. He was ready to die a thousand deaths, as long as his wife and child were safe.

After a few moments of respite, Vivasvan Pujari spoke again. His voice now had a glimmer of hope. The devta was ready to fight back!

'So what is the course of action now, Somdutt?' Vivasvan asked.

'My lord, I hear Manu is planning an all-out attack on the mrit kaaraavaas. But O mighty devta, he does not stand a chance. The ten of them will not be able to overpower the three hundred trained fighters protecting this hell hole.'

Vivasvan Pujari gave a tired smile. He was not so sure about the odds Somdutt had described. Manu himself, and each of the nine gems of his family, could shoot forty arrows from their bows before a commoner could complete a single cycle of breath. Each one of them could engage and rout twenty opponents in a sword-fight. If the ten of them attacked the dungeons, it would be a fifty-fifty chance.

However, with his beloved Manu and the magnificent nine, Vivasvan did not want to gamble. In any case he was certain that he and his family had a lot of battles to fight in the coming days. If there was an easier way of escaping the dungeons that no one had ever escaped, Vivasvan Pujari wanted to take it.

Banaras, 2017

TRAITOR!

The drunk owner of the Tibetan restaurant had no clue how the note had reached Vidyut, or who dropped it there. With dirty caps and similar uniforms, the waiters looked more or less the same. None of them appeared to know anything, even when threatened by a revolver muzzle peeping out from under Bala's jacket. None of them anyway had the courage to mess with visitors from the feared Dev-Raaksha-sa matth. Romi was either one of the unnoticed guests at the restaurant, or he was a master at disguise.

Vidyut asked Sonu and two of his fighters to escort Damini back to the safety of the matth. Damini tried to protest, but in vain. Vidyut was not going to let her stay at a place that was clearly being watched and controlled by an expert killer with exceptional abilities. Sonu and his team drew their handguns and swiftly made their way to the monastery, keeping Damini between the three of them at every step.

The clock had struck half past nine and it was dark. The busy street, however, was still buzzing with thousands of tourists filling the seats of scores of tiny restaurants lining both sides of this flea market. Offering everything from Japanese sushi to Indian *masala dosa*, these eateries were packed with tourists of all nationalities, age groups and ethnicities. Possibility of finding their deadly stalker in these myriad thousands offered worse odds than a needle in a haystack. And clearly, he was watching them, even now. This assassin had outsmarted even the highly effective *guptachar sena* (army of spies) of the matth. He was more dangerous than Vidyut had imagined… and he was a step ahead.

·||卐||·

Back at the matth, Vidyut kissed Damini goodnight. Given the matth's regulations and code, it was not prudent to spend the night in the same room. The one thing Vidyut was certain of was that Damini was in the safest place she could be. No one, not even this extraordinary assassin, could dent the perimeter of the mighty Dev-Raakshasa matth.

'What now, Vidyut?' asked Damini, as Vidyut was about to leave the neat guest suite she was lodged in.

'Well, the guy has asked me to meet him at the *Ganga aarti* tomorrow. How can I decline the invitation, especially after his gift from our first meeting?' replied Vidyut, clearly burning with rage. Tonight Romi had made the mistake of coming near Vidyut when he was with Damini. And this Vidyut was not going to forgive.

'But why has he called you to the Ganga aarti, Vidyut? What is so special about it?'

'The Ganga aarti takes place at 6.45 pm at the overcrowded Dashashwamedh ghaat…same place I met Romi the first time. The only difference is that during this divine aarti or collective worship with incandesced sacred lamps on the banks of the loved river, the crowd becomes a sea of human heads. The Ganga aarti is a surreal experience, where Lord Shiva, Maa Ganga, Surya (Sun) and *Agnee*, the God of fire, are worshipped. Devotees throng the ghaats to partake in this holy ritual.'

Vidyut paused for a few seconds and said, 'In other words, there will be over twenty thousand people at the ghaat tomorrow.'

·||ॐ||·

It was a huddle of the warriors. Balwanta was furious, breathing heavily, his massive shoulders heaving like giant mechanical pistons. He was angry with himself at letting Vidyut leave the matth. There was Bala, now fully aware of the dark talent of this master-assassin. Sonu had washed his face and was chewing several bundles of the famous *Banarasi paan* – betel leaves flavored with betel nuts, lime paste, spices and sometimes tobacco. Sonu couldn't let any of the matth elders know he had had beer that evening. There was Govardhan and of course Purohit ji. Vidyut had just joined in.

'How could the *guptachar sena* not find him?' fumed Balwanta. He was the leader of the ancient intelligence network and took its failure very personally. 'We cover every motel, every guesthouse, every restaurant and every shop. More than three hundred rickshaw pullers and two hundred auto drivers are part of the network. Why, we even keep an eye on the graveyards and the taantric monasteries! There is no way this rascal could have escaped our clutches. What is one man against an entire covert army?'

Balwanta was right. From whatever Vidyut had described, Romi was clearly not from Banaras. His language, his clothing, and his demeanor…everything suggested that he was an outsider. How could one man, and that too in a new city, beat a vast network as old as the Dev-Raakshasa matth itself?

'Unless…' muttered Bala.

'Unless what, Bala?' enquired Vidyut.

'Unless he is not alone in Banaras, Vidyut. Why are we being so naïve as to imagine he is a lone wolf? Maybe he is not. Maybe he is backed by a whole organization with deep-rooted presence in Varanasi. If we are going to take him on, we better consider all possibilities.'

Bala instantly made sense to everyone present, most of all to Vidyut. In a flash Vidyut knew Bala was right. *How could he have been so silly?*

'He is not alone,' said Vidyut. His statement had no element of doubt.

'Now let's not jump to conclusions either, Video…' started Bala, only to be interrupted by Vidyut.

'He is not alone!' repeated Vidyut, this time a bit sternly. His hands rested on his waist and he was looking straight at the ground, shaking his head. 'We have been so stupid...' he muttered, before breaking into a big laugh.

'Oh God...we have been so stupid!' shouted Vidyut as he began guffawing uncontrollably. The others exchanged glances, clueless about what Vidyut suddenly found so funny.

'For God's sakes man, Video...would you care to share your thoughts with us?' enquired Bala after half a minute of Vidyut's laughter.

'I'm sorry...I'm sorry everyone...just that I can't believe we didn't see it before,' said Vidyut. He was slowly turning serious.

'See what, dada?' asked Sonu.

'It is very simple, Sonu. Romi met me, or should I say Romi was in my vicinity today when the outing was totally unplanned. How did he know I was going to be there?' explained Vidyut.

Balwanta, Bala, Govardhan and Purohit ji froze as they heard the last devta's words. *How did they miss something so obvious?*

Sonu was still a little baffled. 'What do you mean, Vidyut dada?' he asked. 'Romi must have been waiting for you at a vantage point close to the matth entrance, and would have followed you.'

'You are right, Sonu. But there are two issues with your theory. First of all, as we all know, a large force of armed warrior-monks defends this monastery. It would not be possible for anybody to hold on to a vantage point for three days at a stretch and not be caught. Secondly, both times he met me he was very well prepared. The first time he had a sophisticated explosive and detonation device ready. The second time around he was in perfect disguise or had infiltrated the restaurant staff. So it can still be what you are saying, but that would be hard to believe.'

Sonu understood what Vidyut was saying. He said his thought out loud, 'So Romi knew exactly when and where you were going!'

'Yes,' growled Balwanta, his eyes on fire. 'There is a traitor among us.'

·‖卐‖·

Vidyut was now walking back to his room. It was a chilly night and the inner sanctum of the matth looked beautiful with its vast lawns, fountains and dim lighting. After the long and eventful day, Vidyut was looking forward to a few hours in his warm bed. He knew getting sleep would be difficult though, given that he had a dangerous rendezvous the next day. *Dangerous for Romi.*

'Hey!'

Vidyut turned around to see Naina leaning against a corridor pillar at a distance.

'Oh hi, Naina. What are you doing here at this hour? It's past midnight,' said Vidyut.

Naina didn't speak. She just kept staring at Vidyut. The devta noticed she was clad in a well-fitting white *salwaar kameez*, with a bright orange *dupatta*. Her opulent hair was tightly parted in the center and tied in a long and fashionable *Punjabi* plat. A small *bindi* sparkled on her beautiful forehead and, as usual, her large eyes were made over neatly with mascara. Ornate earrings accentuated her gorgeous features.

'Whaaaat…?' Vidyut asked her jovially as he walked across the little green patch towards her. 'Are you just going to stare?'

'No. I don't think I can do that anymore, can I Vidyut?' she asked with a bewitching grin. Her smiling face was clearly hiding her pain behind it. Vidyut knew what she meant. He decided to ignore it nevertheless. *What else could he do?*

'Oh come on, Naina. Walk with me *na*,' he said as he took her hand in his own and gently pulled her next to him. They started strolling leisurely towards Vidyut's room. The bubbly and gushing Naina was unusually quiet this evening.

'Something bothering you, Naina?' asked Vidyut. He knew he couldn't avoid the topic forever. And as a childhood friend Naina was very dear to him.

'Why? Should something be bothering me, O great devta?' replied Naina, pretending to not understand Vidyut's question.

'No, of course not. Just that you're not talking as much as you usually do,' he said, turning and looking at her. Naina did not respond. She kept looking straight at the path ahead of them, hands covered under her *dupatta* on this cold evening. Had it not been for the tension between them due to

Damini's arrival, this was a romantic setting to perfection.

·‖ॐ‖·

Vidyut's room was the guest suite closest to the great Dwarka Shastri's cottage. Naina and he were now right outside its door. Vidyut couldn't help but notice how devastatingly beautiful Naina looked on this moonlit night.

'Good night, Naina,' he said, 'and thank you for walking me to this room.'

'No problem, Vidyut. Night.'

Naina turned around and began walking towards her own quarters. Vidyut felt an uncontrollable urge to hold her and kiss her. Clearly, he was still half-human.

As he turned to unlock his door, he heard Naina's voice call out his name.

'Vidyut…?'

The devta turned around to see Naina standing a few steps away.

'Yes, Naina?'

'You know what…you should've sent a reply to at least *one* of my letters. You should've told me about Damini. She's beautiful by the way!' she said, her voice now trembling, her eyes moist…though her face still braved a smile.

Vidyut didn't know what to say. Naina looked more desirable than the *apsaras* of the heavens. Deep inside for a moment, he wished he could lift her in his arms and make love to her. Even the most righteous of men can be vulnerable to a heady concoction of unquestioned love and unparalleled beauty. But then again, Vidyut was not just a man. He was the last devta on planet Earth. He fought the temptation and kindled Damini's picture in his soul. After a few rare moments of weakness, he was back. Nevertheless, he did want to comfort Naina. He really did love her as a dear friend.

'Naina...my dear dear Naina...' he said in an exasperated, unsure tone, his head tilted to one side.

'Because if you did...I wouldn't have waited 26 years, 9 months and 18 days for you, Vidyut,' continued Naina, before giving Vidyut a longing glance and turning to leave.

·‖卐‖·

Vidyut had too much on his mind tonight. He smiled at Naina's departing silhouette and entered his room. He was in no frame of mind to go after her and indulge in a draining emotional conversation at this time, even though he felt terrible about it. But something totally disconnected with the whole situation was disturbing Vidyut. He was not fully sure, but he felt he saw Naina holding a bulky electronic device under her dupatta. It was not a cellphone. It in fact looked like a device not very many people had access to. Vidyut ran a technology company with digital and telecom security at its core. He knew this stuff.

From whatever Vidyut could make out in the dark, the gadget Naina held nearly wrapped under her stole, was an advanced Iridium 9555 satellite phone.

Harappa, 1700 BCE

THE DAGGER OF
BETRAYAL

'Where is Chandradhar in all this? Why has he not come to
my rescue?' asked Vivasvan Pujari. 'He was missing in the
courtroom as well.'

Somdutt was quiet. Vivasvan Pujari stared at him expectantly. If there was anyone he knew could get him out of this
quagmire, it was his partner, his brother-in-law, his friend...
Chandradhar. The devta was certain that Pundit Chandradhar would leave no stone unturned and would wage war with
any force of this world or another to save him.

The chief engineer remained silent. Vivasvan Pujari was getting anxious, as he wanted to quickly get on with the plan to
counterattack.

After a moment of hesitation he put his filthy hand on Somdutt's shoulder and spoke again, 'Believe me Somdutt, it will not take Chandradhar more than a few hours to find out who is behind all this. While of course that scoundrel Ranga is involved, he does not have the intellect or the capability to conjure up such a byzantine conspiracy. There is definitely a dark and potent force behind the shadows.'

Vivasvan Pujari was stunned to see his friend Somdutt sobbing softly. His heart froze. *Had something happened to his beloved friend Chandradhar?*

'Speak up, Somdutt! What is matter? Have they got Chandradhar too??'

The chief engineer looked up, regaining his composure. 'No my lord, Pundit Chandradhar is perfectly fine.'

'So why didn't you contact him? I know you are very capable and resourceful Somdutt, but Chandra would have been a big help. He would have taken control of both the priestly council as well as the army.'

'He already has full control of the council and the army my lord,' replied Somdutt coldly.

Vivasvan Pujari didn't know what to say. He was a bit exasperated at Somdutt's short responses and refusal to react positively to his advice about seeking help from Chandradhar, his most trusted ally and partner.

'Look Somdutt, I don't think you understand. Pundit Chandradhar is like a brother to me, and he will fight till his last breath to save me and my…'

Somdutt couldn't take it anymore. 'Stop it, O great devta!' he shouted, interrupting Vivasvan Pujari mid-sentence.

Vivasvan could see Somdutt was breathing heavily, and appeared both dejected and angry.

After a moment's pause Somdutt leaned forward and placed both his hands affectionately on the devta's bloodstained shoulders. He spoke softly, looking straight into Vivasvan Pujari's eyes.

'You really don't know, my devta?' he enquired softly, clearly unable to hide his emotions. Tears were once again rolling down his eyes.

Vivasvan Pujari could now sense something sinister. If Chandradhar was alive and he was in control of the council and the army, why was he not here instead of Somdutt?

'Tell me what you know, my friend,' asked the devta nervously.

Somdutt nodded softly and spoke, 'Who do you think is commanding the army against you, my lord?'

Vivasvan Pujari was looking at him blankly, never for a moment imagining what he was about to hear.

'And who do you think is rallying the entire priestly council to make sure you and your family are declared felons of the worst order?'

'Who, Somdutt?! Quit knitting puzzles and tell me!' Vivasvan Pujari implored

Somdutt tried to speak but was startled by a bloodcurdling shriek that tore across even the thick stonewalls of the dungeons. Someone was being tortured beyond human endurance.

Both Vivasvan Pujari and Somdutt muttered a healing mantra in their mouths, aimed to alleviate the pain of the poor soul.

'Brace yourself my lord, for now I will reveal the name of the person who put the holy seal of approval on your incarceration in this living hell,' said Somdutt.

He did not need to take the name. There were only two people in all of Harappa who had the authority to put the seal of approval on all judgments passed in the court, for those to be carried out within seven days. One of them was locked deep in the dark belly of the mrit kaaraavaas. He was Vivasvan Pujari himself. The other was the man this devta trusted with all his heart. The man whose life he had saved. The gem of Harappa whose sister he had married.

'Chandradhar!' screamed out the devta in disbelief. 'It cannot be. You lie to me you wretched scoundrel!' he barked at Somdutt. 'You are also a part of the web of treachery being spun around me. Get out of here!'

Somdutt was not offended. He expected this reaction from the noble devta. And yet he knew he had to convey the whole truth, no matter how venomous it was.

'It was Chandradhar who sent you to the dungeons. It was Chandradhar who released arrest warrants for your son Manu and the gracious Sanjna. It was Chandradhar who influenced the city council to confiscate all your property, land and assets. Your household workers have been declared complicit in your crimes, and have all been sentenced to death.'

Vivasvan Pujari sat frozen in the dark cell. A blunt arrow of deceit had pierced right through his very soul. The dagger of betrayal had been sunk deep into his very existence. He looked nothing more than a lifeless corpse. His face had no color, his eyes any life. The devta who looked like a strapping young man even at his ripe age, was suddenly looking like a very old man.

·||卐||·

Vivasvan Pujari was now sitting with his face buried between his raised knees, weeping profusely. He had wept so much in the last few hours that his eyes seemed to have run dry. Yet he could not help but convulse into heavy sobs. The devta was an exceptionally strong man. He could cry with as much honesty as he did love.

The onslaught was not over yet for Vivasvan Pujari. Somdutt braced himself and began delivering the final blow.

'There is more, O devta. Pardon me for being the bearer of such devastating news,' said Somdutt, nearly breaking down himself as he submitted the disclaimer. Vivasvan Pujari did not move or react, although his heavy sobbing was now quieting down.

The engineer continued.

'A massive manhunt has been unleashed to capture and kill Manu, lady Sanjna and your nine warriors. Moreover, Chandradhar has passed a decree through the council, declaring himself as the first monarch of Harappa and his wife Priyamvada as the royal queen. He is going to end the rule of the people in our beloved metropolis, the city you have built so meticulously, O devta.'

Somdutt was expecting a violent response from Vivasvan Pujari, but there was none. The devta sat in the same posture without any reaction, his face buried deep into his knees.

'There is one more thing, my devta,' continued Somdutt. 'Chandradhar has passed special instructions to make a public spectacle out of you tomorrow morning. It is to set a precedent, he says.'

He knew the devta was listening to every word. He broke the last bit of bad news he was the harbinger of.

'A great public feast and procession have been organized for the people of Harappa at the Great Bath tomorrow morning. As you know, our bath is twenty times larger than that of Mohenjo-daro. They are working overnight to convert it into a gigantic arena with seating for over fifteen thousand spectators.'

There was still no response from Vivasvan Pujari.

Somdutt dropped his head backwards and let out a short cry of grief. His world was spinning, as he could not believe how his happy and glorious Harappa could turn into this hideous nightmare within hours and days. After a few seconds he pulled himself back and prepared to speak the unspeakable. He slowly bent forward, close to the devta's face, and spoke as if every word he uttered was a profound sin.

'They are going to torture you brutally tomorrow morning, O mighty devta. And all of Harappa will watch.'

Banaras, 2017

THE GREAT VEDIC CIVILIZATION

Damini was hellishly nervous at the prospect of meeting the great matthadheesh, the mighty Dwarka Shastri himself. It was a double whammy for her. On one end, meeting the most powerful and mystical saint and taantric in the whole world was making her terribly anxious. On the other hand, the grand old man was the only real *in-law* she was ever going to have. So Damini was flustered at what to wear, what to say and when to shut up.

However, both Vidyut and Damini knew that today was not going to be a regular day. The devta's evening appointment with Romi Pereira loomed over their minds every second. Damini was deeply concerned about Vidyut's safety. Vidyut on the other hand wanted to know why Romi wanted to kill him. He was yearning to know which organization or institution was behind this lethal assassin. He was hoping to discover at least some part of the plot during his impending meeting with his great grandfather this morning.

Damini loved the fact that she was being treated like a queen at the monastery. On her flight to Varanasi she had imagined the matth to be a dark and suffocating prison of stifling rituals and boring, stuck-up people. She was overjoyed to see the exact opposite happen. While indeed the matth looked intimidating and fortress-like as one entered it, the life and people inside were positively glowing. As she woke up in the morning, Damini was welcomed by the chanting of divine mantras with an intensity and passion she had never seen before. She was treated to a hot cup of rich herbal tea, the finest brew she had ever had. It gave her energy and elation she had never experienced before. This was followed by a session of rigorous yoga on a sun-kissed terrace, led by beaming and vivacious instructors.

Damini was pleasantly surprised when she was served a hot breakfast fit for an empress. Her crunchy fresh fruit salad and farm fresh yoghurt were accompanied by not only Indian delicacies like *aloo paratha* and *poha matar*, but also by baked beans and cornflakes. The Dev-Raakshasa matth, its teachers, its profound disciplines and its infrastructure in no way appeared inferior to western educational establishments. The only difference being the advanced spiritual, warfare and occult training imparted at this ancient institution as part of the essential curriculum.

As they walked towards the great Dwarka Shastri's massive abode, Vidyut couldn't stop laughing. Damini had attempted wearing a *Banarasi saaree* (traditional Indian outfit) that had been gifted to her by Purohit ji's gracious wife that very morning, as a gesture of her affection. Much as Damini marched with great poise and dignity towards the cottage of the matthadheesh, every thirty seconds she felt that her cumbersome attire would dismantle itself and grossly malfunction. She was relieved when she finally reached the grand old man's doorstep, her dress in one piece.

The moment of truth was here. She had to now enter the medieval looking cottage and meet the phenomenon her boyfriend considered to be the most powerful man on Earth.

'Okay, Vidyut baby…you ready *na*?' asked Damini nervously as she took some deep breaths. Vidyut nodded innocently, barely able to hold back his laughter. He knew Damini was panicking needlessly. He knew his Baba was a *trikaaldarshi* or the viewer of all the realms of time and space – past, present and future. He knew the grand old man would see through the beautiful heart of Damini in a matter of moments. What Vidyut did not know was that the mighty Dwarka Shastri already knew Damini.

He knew a lot more about her than even Vidyut did.

The devta knocked on his great grandfather's door and was greeted with the now familiar 'Hmmm…' Vidyut gestured Damini to follow him.

As soon as Damini entered the massive living chamber of the world's most powerful spirit, she could sense the presence of more than just the grandmaster in that room. She could almost hear the hissing of an ethereal being. She somehow felt that Dwarka Shastri, Vidyut and she were not the only people in the room. She tried to ignore this intense instinct. She was meeting her in-laws for God's sake!

Dwarka Shastri once again lay perched on his tall bed, raised to his regal posture by a dozen pillows and bolsters. Damini was nearly hypnotized as she caught the first glimpse of this extraordinary man. His flowing white hair, his battle-torn face and his royal appearance overwhelmed her to numbness. His fingers were flipping rosary beads like an automated counting machine.

'*Pranaam,* baba,' said Vidyut. *Pranaam* was among the humblest and most respectful of salutations in Indian culture.

'*Yashasvi bhava…*' replied the grandmaster. *May you be the glorious one*, was what the matthadheesh had replied with as a blessing.

'Baba, I have Damini with me,' said Vidyut, feeling stupidly shy. 'I think you knew about her the moment she entered the matth.'

Damini found this to be her cue again. This time she was right.

'*Pranaam,* baba,' she said in a gentle voice, her hands folded in veneration.

Dwarka Shastri opened his eyes and looked at Damini.

Within moments his signature glare melted into a look of profound love and familiarity. He then said something that neither Vidyut nor Damini could comprehend.

The great matthadheesh smiled and uttered just two words in a loving tone.

'*Swagatam,* Sanjna.'

Welcome Sanjna.

·||卐||·

The bejeweled necklace sparkled brilliantly. Damini was dumbstruck when the great Dwarka Shastri asked Vidyut to open his old mahogany cupboard and pull out an intricately carved sandalwood box. It was a present for Damini. The diamond studded gold necklace inside was the most expensive piece of jewelry she had ever set her eyes on. It looked like an antique treasure, like it belonged to some ancient queen.

'Baba…Vidyut…how can I accept something so…expensive…' Damini said hesitantly, as she looked at Vidyut for guidance. Vidyut smiled and nodded at her to keep it. It was the grand old man's show of affection.

'I am glad you both are here together,' said the matthadheesh after a few moments of silence. 'Before we speak about anything else, tell me Vidyut, are you sure you want to meet this assassin at a time and place of his choice? He will be fully prepared.'

Purohit ji had briefed the grandmaster about the events

of the previous evening. Dwarka Shastri was cautious but not overly worried. He knew his grandson was no ordinary mortal. He knew from the moment Vidyut had set foot in Varanasi that a final face-off was unavoidable – a clash between demon and devta; evil and good; Romi and Vidyut. It was prophesied three and a half millennia ago. The time had come. And the grandmaster knew that the battle with Romi was only the beginning.

'Yes, Baba. I will meet him and set things right once and for all. The Ganga aarti is a holy hour. We will vanquish the forces of evil,' replied Vidyut.

Dwarka Shastri smiled with pride and raised his hand to bless Vidyut.

·||ᴕ||·

'But Baba, Vidyut…there are too many questions that are still unanswered,' spoke Damini softly. 'While I comprehend that the East India Company's conspiracy to bury the truth of Brahminabad was part of a larger game-plan of psychological imperialism, but I don't understand how destroying Brahminabad or undermining the Harappan or Saraswati civilization would help that cause.'

Dwarka Shastri turned to Vidyut, 'Why don't you answer the question, Vidyut?'

'Like I was explaining to you last evening, Damini, the absolute dominance of one race over another first needs the total submission of the ruled to the ruler. This becomes possible only when over generations the entire populace is made to believe that the rulers have the moral, historical and cultural right to be the sovereigns.'

Vidyut paused for a moment to see if Damini was following. She was.

'So sowing seeds of a past that showed a legacy of western superiority was an important element in their strategy. It worked wonders for them to propagate to the Indians that they were always inferior, and even since the time of the Harappan civilization it was actually riders from the west that brought in development and prosperity. However, the entire scheme of the imperialists would fall flat if the people they are trying to suppress into submission suddenly discover that it was *they* who actually established mighty civilizations, cities and trades, when their current rulers were living in caves and wearing animal hide!'

'And Harappa would do exactly that! It would remind Indians of a glorious past. It would inform them that it was in fact their very own ancestors who brought civilization to this world!' exclaimed Damini, as she slowly grasped the whole maze.

Dwarka Shastri nodded. 'There is more to it, *beta*. Do you know that there were numerous *havan-kundas* or ritual-pits discovered in the excavations? That the Gods worshipped by the Harappans were actually *Pashupati* and Shakti, which are other names of Lord Shiva and the Goddess Durga? How many times have you read that seals and pottery depicting yogic postures were unearthed in the hundreds at the Harappan sites?'

'Quite honestly, Baba, I have not really read about these details,' replied Damini. 'In fact, very few people would have.'

'Damini, *havan-kundas* are essentially used for Vedic rituals. Even today Hindus across India and Nepal worship deities like Pashupati and Shakti. If *Yoga* existed even in Harappa, what does it all mean?' asked Dwarka Shastri animatedly.

'It means that the Harappan civilization was nothing but a vast Vedic settlement on the banks of the mighty Saraswati...' mumbled Damini as she deciphered the truth.

Both Dwarka Shastri and Vidyut were pleased to see that Damini had finally understood the truth behind Harappa. *Or at least some of it.*

'So you see Damini, reducing Brahminabad to rubble, ignoring further excavations for half a century, propagating half-truths and hiding facts about the glory and achievements of the Harappan civilization were all part of a concerted effort to darken an entire eon from the pages of history. White-skinned men riding horses through the Khyber Pass was a picture slowly imprinted on the entire sub-continent. Harappa was the perfect ploy to disconnect India with its ancient glory. *Indians would never know that it was they who civilized the world!*

Damini nodded in agreement. She had never in her wildest dreams imagined such a profound conspiracy around something as obscure as Harappa. Tea had been served and the three of them sat in silence for a while. Damini needed time to internalize the truth.

Suddenly Damini turned to Dwarka Shastri and enquired in

a tone of urgency, 'But then Baba, who were the Aryan invaders?'

Dwarka Shastri looked at Vidyut and they exchanged grins.

'My dear Damini,' said Vidyut leaning towards her.

'There *were* no Aryan invaders.'

Harappa, 1700 BCE

PRATISHODH

For several minutes the devta had not moved or spoken a word. Somdutt gave him that time to assimilate the horror the Gods had sent his way and to nurse his deep angst. The engineer was worried that the time he had bought at the mrit kaaraavaas was running out. Just as he was about to reach out and comfort the devta with a friendly arm around him, Vivasvan Pujari spoke with his face still sunk into his knees.

'The mountains...what about the mountains of brick and bronze that were to be made to change the course of the raging Saraswati?'

'Chandradhar is going ahead with that project on war footing. Within hours he has gathered the other engineers to build the mountains of brick and bronze as per your plan and drawings. It is a massive undertaking, and thousands of men, women and beasts of burden are being deployed.'

Vivasvan Pujari suddenly looked up. The chief engineer skipped a beat at what he saw.

The devta was looking more manic than the recently intoxicated and deranged inhabitants of Harappa. In the blackness of the cell all Somdutt could see was Vivasvan Pujari's eyes gleaming red like those of a panther caught in the darkness by a fluttering torch. In the same body, with the same limbs and the familiar face – Vivasvan Pujari was a different creature. Whether his own soul had twisted into its darkest manifestation or that he had summoned a black spirit from the netherworld into him, Somdutt couldn't say. But Vivasvan Pujari was certainly not himself.

·||卐||·

'Uuurrrrraaaaaaaaarrrrrrgggghhhhhh!' the demonic devta screamed so loud and hideously that all the moaning and crying in the mrit kaaraavaas stopped for a few brief moments. Every inmate of the death-prison could sense the presence of someone whose profound grief was greater than their collective suffering. The deep agony in Vivasvan Pujari's cry cut through the hearts and souls of the condemned wretches, and for now they wept for this unknown sufferer amidst them.

'Aaaaarrrgggghhh…aaaaaarrrrgggghhh…nnnaaaaaarrrrgggh-hhh' Vivasvan Pujari kept yelling, his eyes rolled-up, his arms outstretched on his sides and his hands twisted into claws, as if possessed by the devil himself. To Somdutt's horror, the devta turned and started smashing his forehead against the sharp edged rocks of the cell's walls. The engineer leapt forward to grab hold of him and pull him away. But he was late. The walls were already smeared with the devta's blood, and his eyes and face were once again dripping with his pious bloodstream.

Somdutt held the devta and with great difficulty made him sit down on the dirty floor. As he held his friend and till recently the most powerful man in all of Harappa, he panicked. Vivasvan Pujari's skin was as cold as ice and he was mumbling some ethereal chants like a bumblebee high on *Somras* (flower-toddy). The engineer was considering calling for help. Much as he respected the devta and his divinity, *had Vivasvan Pujari finally lost it?*

'I am fully in my senses, Somdutt,' said the devta in a hissing voice, as if he was reading Somdutt's mind. He probably was. 'May I borrow your dagger for a moment please?'

'We...we will rescue you from the Great Bath arena tomorrow, my lord,' said Somdutt. 'Even if it means we fight to the last drop of blood in our veins.'

'May I borrow your dagger please, Somdutt?' insisted Vivasvan Pujari as if he had not heard what his engineer friend had just said.

'O great devta, please don't worry about your wife and son. They are as revered for us as you are. We will not let them be harmed,' said Somdutt, now sitting next to the devta, cleaning his face with his own fine angavastram.

'May I borrow your dagger, Somdutt?' repeated Vivasvan.

He was not relenting.

Somdutt pulled out his gleaming blade from the scabbard, went down on one knee and held his dagger up with both hands towards the devta, like he was submitting an offering to a God. As far as was concerned, he was.

·‖卐‖·

'What are you doing, my lord?' exclaimed the engineer.

Vivasvan Pujari had slit open his right wrist and the blood was oozing out profusely. Somdutt was as shocked as he was deeply concerned. The loss of blood that the devta had suffered over the last one day could prove fatal.

'Don't worry, Somdutt,' said the devta. 'Don't you remember, I cannot be harmed by fire, hunger, thirst, injury, alchemy, illness, gravity or exorcism.'

'But, my lord…'

'You must leave now,' interrupted the devta. 'Keep archers and horsemen ready tomorrow morning. Intercept them when they are bringing me back here from the Great Bath. I will take care of the rest.'

Somdutt had to obey the devta. But he was horrified to see that the devta had turned his back towards him, and was using the blood from his right wrist as ink to inscribe something on the stone wall of his cell. Although Vivasvan Pujari appeared to be stable and calm as he continued to write on the wall, Somdutt noticed that the devta's hands were shivering.

'Guard!'

Without turning even for a moment, Vivasvan Pujari had called out for the prison security. Within seconds they could hear the stomping of a drunken guard walking towards the cell. Just before the cell door was flung open, Vivasvan Pujari turned his head partially towards Somdutt and whispered, 'Remember my friend, on the way back tomorrow. Keep archers and horsemen ready. We will pull off the greatest rescue of all time.' He tried to smile.

In the flickering light of the tiny lamp, Somdutt saw one side of Vivasvan Pujari's face. It was a horror of a sight. A face that was once illuminated with love, brilliance and Godliness, was now a concoction of sweat, blood, pain and hate. Something told the sharp engineer that a fierce and gory battle was going to rage across Aryavarta soon. The devta was not going to be vanquished easily.

·‖ॐ‖·

As Somdutt took leave and the inebriated guard swung the massive wooden door so as to shut the cell, the engineer noticed what was being smeared on the wall in the color of blood. It was a word. A split second before the door finally slammed shut and Somdutt lost the view of the back-wall of Vivasvan Pujari's cell, he got a glimpse of it.

The prison wall of the mighty devta was now painted with his own blood, spelling out one lone word – *Pratishodh*.

Retribution!

THE LAST SAPTARISHI

'The word *Arya* is from Sanskrit, which roughly means *the noble one*. In ancient times all of northern India was called Aryavarta, or *the abode of the noble ones*. It did not mean abode of the Aryans as a specific creed,' clarified Dwarka Shastri.

'So you can say that the people who were original inhabitants of Aryavarta or ancient north India, were called the Aryans. They were builders of great cities, ports, metals and trades. But the theory of sharp-nosed, blue-eyed horsemen from the west is nothing but a figment of imagination...a lie propagated so widely that it almost became the truth,' added Vidyut.

Damini nodded thoughtfully. She was still in a daze, but glad to have seen the hidden end of the Harappan mystery unravel itself.

'This is all so unreal. You know Vidyut, we owe it to our great nation, to our fellow Indians. We must share this knowledge with everyone!' said a delighted and charged-up Damini, looking at both Vidyut and the grandmaster expectantly.

Vidyut and Dwarka Shastri exchanged glances. 'It is not that simple, Damini,' said Vidyut. 'What you have discovered to-day and I heard from Baba yesterday is just the tip of the ice-berg. This conspiracy is not restricted to just the East India Company and the Indian subjugation. It is far deeper and more ominous than that. It involves the whole world, the entire human race.'

⁞∥卐∥⁞

'Our bloodline is cursed,' said the mighty Dwarka Shastri.

That didn't sound very heartening to Vidyut and Damini. It was like they were in a thriller movie. Only this was all real, they both knew.

'Vidyut, you must tell Damini whatever you know till now about the painful and chilling saga of our greatest ancestor, the devta Vivasvan Pujari,' continued Dwarka Shastri, 'but at this point it is important that you both know about the curse of the Saptarishi.'

His two-member audience was staring at the grandmaster, spellbound.

'It will take me many more days to narrate the full tale of Vivasvan Pujari, Pundit Chandradhar, Priyamvada, Sanjna, Sara Maa, Manu and the eventual fall of Harappa. I will also tell you about the events that unfolded immediately after the devastating deluge of the river Saraswati, and how these events changed the course of mankind's destiny. But we don't have that kind of time today. The enemy stalks us from very close,' said Dwarka Shastri. Vidyut and Damini assumed he was referring to the showdown with Romi, which was now only a few hours away.

In all of what Dwarka Shastri had just said, Damini caught the name Sanjna. This is what the grandmaster had welcomed her as when she had stepped into his room. She had ignored it as perhaps a slip in the grand old man's aging memory. But now he had taken the name again, and that too in the context of a cruel tale.

While Damini was still groping with that one name, Vidyut's mind was running at lightning speed. He was putting the two and two together. It struck him like a thunderbolt that his great grandfather would have referred to Damini as Sanjna for one and one reason only. As the scion of the Dev-Raakshasa matth and the last devta, Vidyut could see the picture clearly. He also now knew why Dwarka Shastri had said that the statuette of the bearded Priest-King of Harappa was of none other than Vidyut's himself.

The matthadheesh was quiet, as he closely observed his great grandson's pensive face. He knew Vidyut had figured it out. The grandmaster intoned a couplet from the Bhagvad Gita.

:|| *vasamsi jirnani yatha vihaya*
navani grhnati naro 'parani
tatha sarirani vihaya jirnany
anyani samyati navani dehi ||:

Vidyut translated it for Damini without looking at her –

'As a person puts on new garments, giving up old ones, similarly, the "soul" accepts new material bodies, giving up the old ones.'

Damini was not able to understand what was going on. But Vidyut was fully enlightened.

Punarjanma, he thought.

Reincarnation.

·‖ॐ‖·

Vidyut shook his head slightly at his great grandfather, who immediately understood what Vidyut was trying to say. Damini was not ready for everything just yet. That the three of them had met before, millennia ago, in a distant and violent land was something she would not be able to comprehend.

'Baba, please tell us about the curse of the Saptarishi and about the web of this conspiracy,' began Vidyut. 'Tell us what happened in Constantinople.' Besides his keenness to know more about what was plaguing his divine bloodline and humankind at large, he also wanted to steer the topic away from Sanjna and her connection with Damini. He would tell her one day. But not today.

Before the matthadheesh could respond, there was a knock at the door. It was Balwanta. He folded his hands in reverence as he bowed to the grandmaster.

'What is it, Balwanta?' asked Dwarka Shastri.

'Gurudev, pardon my intrusion but it is well past noon. Vidyut must come with me so we can prepare for the evening encounter. Only a few hours remain. This adversary must not be taken lightly,' replied Balwanta, his hands still folded. He worshipped Dwarka Shastri like a God. And while the assassin was here in Varanasi for Romi, Balwanta believed it was his own fight. For centuries his forefathers had protected the Shastri clan. He was not going to let them all down.

'Thank you, Balwanta dada. Please give me some more time. Baba is about to make a vital revelation, which might tell us more about this Romi,' replied Vidyut instead of Dwarka Shastri. He was now more and more connected to his great grandfather, and could take some liberty.

'But, Vidyut…'

'Just one more hour please, dada, then we will begin the preparations,' insisted Vidyut.

'As you say, Vidyut. But one hour it is.'

Balwanta bowed to the matthadheesh and left.

·‖卐‖·

'It was in 312 AD that the powerful Roman king Constantine embraced Christianity. Whether it was the popularity of the faith that encouraged him to enter its fold, or whether it was his own powerful influence that made the religion even more widespread, cannot be said with surety. But one thing is certain; Constantine did for Christianity what the great

Ashoka did for Buddhism. He rallied the power of the king behind the word of the priest,' narrated the grandmaster. 'It was all happening just like the curse said it would.'

Both Damini and Vidyut were stunned to hear the great Dwarka Shastri speaking about a Roman king, about the spread of Christianity and events that had no connect with Harappa whatsoever!

Or so they believed.

'Anyhow, it was not under Constantine that things went out of hand. It was in 445 AD under Emperor Valentinian that one faith was officially declared as the faith of the empire. This political gamesmanship, deceit and eventual bloodshed in the name of God was exactly what the curse had banished mankind to.'

Vidyut and Damini were blank. They had no clue why Dwarka Shastri was talking about Constantine and Valentinian, when their concerns and questions were around Harappa and the killer that was stalking them.

'I know your concerns and questions are around Harappa, and around the killer that is stalking us,' said Dwarka Shastri, as if he were reading their minds. He probably was. 'But what I am telling you is equally material to the bigger web of treachery, power and hate that is being spun for centuries.'

'Please go on, Baba,' said Vidyut. He did not want to rush the matthadheesh.

'The burying of Harappa's glory and truth by some officials of the East India Company was in comparison just a tiny manifestation of a much larger disease – one that would time and again unleash unbridled and unstoppable blood-shed, only to maintain the political superiority of one people over another. And this disease has nothing to do with Christianity, which is a great religion with peace and love as its bedrocks. It is the religion of *Yeshu* or Jesus, the fair and benevolent Son of God who never spoke of anything but love. Therefore I am talking about the dark corruption of men, not any particular religion. Scoundrels are not restrict-ed to any one faith. They are born under every creed, every race. If it was Christianity unleashing holy wars during the Crusades, it is some other religion now. Tomorrow there will be another. This murderous lust would spread from one faith to another – and each will justify killing their fellowmen in the name of God. These men would use religion and their own interpretation of the word of God to inflict unthinkable atrocities on their own kind. And this is *precisely* the destiny the Saptarishi had cursed the human race to endure.'

Vidyut and Damini's mouths went dry as they tried to grap-ple with the new revelations Dwarka Shastri was making. In fact Damini felt her head would explode, and wanted to run away from the massive cottage of the matthadheesh.

Dwarka Shastri could make out that his beloved children were fatigued with information overload. But he had little choice. Vidyut was the prophesied savior and he had to bear the burden.

'We will speak about the rest later, my dear Vidyut and Damini. For now there is only one more aspect I want to share with you both.'

'Please go ahead, Baba,' said Vidyut. He could have sat in this room for days together. But he knew Damini was reeling under the conspiratorial information onslaught. He had to get her out.

'There were in fact two dark curses, Vidyut,' continued the grandmaster, 'one each from two dying sages. They were the fifth and sixth of the Saptarishi. One curse was for Vivasvan Pujari's descendants and one for mankind at large, as I have been describing,' said the grandmaster.

This was going too fast, even for Vidyut. *Who were the Saptarishi? Why were they dying? What made them cast such ghastly spells? And how was everything connected?*

There was another knock at the door. This time it was a long and urgent one. Upon Dwarka Shastri's permission Balwanta entered the room again. He was clearly annoyed.

'Vidyut we need to leave…*now*,' said Balwanta. He was in no mood to dilly-dally. There was a battle awaiting them. And the warrior chief was not going to go into it underprepared.

·||ॐ||·

Damini bowed to Dwarka Shastri, who smiled at her with fatherly love. Both of them had moist eyes. Vidyut was fidgety, as he wanted to know more. He decided to squeeze in his one last question.

'Baba, I will listen to the rest of the tale upon my return. For now I have only one question – who is Romi Pereira and why does he want to kill me?'

Dwarka Shastri nodded and replied, 'Remember Vidyut, there is a very powerful force lurking in the dark that does not want the curse on mankind to end. The bloodied fault-lines and manic killing suit its black and malicious design. We have been fighting this monster and protecting the se-cret for centuries across the land and beyond, from Harappa to Kashi to Goa, Calcutta, Delhi, Rome, Vatican, Syria and beyond. This dark force's lust for power has transcended all frontiers of greed, and they want to use the name of God to establish what they call a New Order.'

Vidyut was listening intently.

'They have sent him,' said the old matthadheesh. 'Romi Pereira is just the first soldier from a whole legion of de-mons you will need to annihilate, Vidyut.'

·‖ 卐 ‖·

They had touched the grand old man's feet and left his room. Damini was a bundle of mixed emotions. On one end she was delighted at having met and won the affection of Vidyut's great grandfather, but on the other she was pet-rified at everything she had heard. The name Romi Pereira was driving her mad. Vidyut was her lifeline and she could not afford to lose him.

Vidyut could sense Damini's anxiety and put a reassuring arm around her. 'I'll take you to *Sarnath* tomorrow, my love,' he said with a beaming grin. 'I'll show you where the Buddha gave his first sermons.'

Damini stopped and turned towards her man. 'You know I cannot live without you, Vidyut. Promise me that you will not let anything happen to you,' she implored, ready to break into tears.

Vidyut put his hands on her cheeks, looked into her eyes lovingly and said, 'I promise, Damini. No harm will come to me. Don't you remember, *I am half-human, half-God.*'

·‖卐‖·

Damini was back at her room and Balwanta was summoning fighters to the matth's armory. Vidyut stole a moment and ran to Dwarka Shastri's cottage, again.

The grand old man was waiting, and had not moved an inch from where he sat before.

'*Pranaam,* Baba. My apologies for running back in unannounced, but I felt there was something you wanted to tell me.'

'Yes there is, Vidyut,' replied the grandmaster gravely. 'And it is this. Someone is going to betray you tonight, my son.'

·‖卐‖·

'I sense the presence of a black soul around you,' continued Dwarka Shastri. 'Romi is not alone.'

Vidyut clenched his teeth. He could not help but think about the satellite phone in Naina's hands. *Who was she speaking to?* He did not want to say anything to the grandmaster though.

Naina had been raised at the Dev-Raakshasa matth since childhood, and was like family to Dwarka Shastri.

'I will be careful, Baba. With your blessings on my side, no one can hurt me,' said Vidyut.

He touched his great grandfather's feet again and took permission to leave. As he reached the door, he turned to ask his Baba one last question for the day.

'Baba, I now understand why you said the statue of the Priest-King was me. It was originally Vivasvan Pujari's I am sure. After over three thousand seven hundred years the great devta's soul has taken rebirth as me, as your Vidyut. The same is with Damini. She is the reincarnation of the pious Sanjna. I see how karmic debts and bonds are interconnected over thousands of years. And I am blessed to be the chosen one.'

Dwarka Shastri held back his tears, as he smiled at his great grandson. He had fought his entire life to guard the secret of the *Black Temple,* and had waited nearly three decades for Vidyut to come and take his rightful place. That day had finally arrived.

'But Baba, if I am Vivasvan Pujari and Damini is Sanjna, *who are you*?' asked Vidyut with a twinkle in his eyes.

Dwarka Shastri grinned. After a moment he replied.

'I am the last Saptarishi.'

Harappa, 1700 BCE

THE MIDNIGHT RAID

'We must sack the prison tonight!' said Manu, as he paced up and down the rocks around the bonfire that lit their camp for the night. They were now twenty miles away from Harappa's city gates. The Sun banner, that represented Vivasvan Pujari, was fluttering in the dim glow of the fire.

Upon his return from the mrit kaaraavaas, Somdutt and his men had managed to locate Manu, Sanjna and their handful of companions. The engineer's own trusted soldiers, Manu, his nine companions and himself made all of thirty-six fighters. While he had promised Vivasvan Pujari a daylight rescue raid the next morning, Somdutt was not sure how it could be pulled off. Harappan soldiers, priests and people had become even more aggressive than the previous day. Vegetarians were chopping horses and eating raw meat. Mothers were intoxicating their own children with Somras. Temples were being used for gambling and prostitution. Granaries were being looted and *havan-kundas* were being desecrated. But worst of all, the givers of nourishment in the form of divine milk, the worshipped cows of Harappa were being slaughtered. Both Manu and Somdutt were convinced, that the end of the metropolis was near.

·‖ॐ‖·

'Don't be silly, Manu,' retorted Somdutt with the authority of a godfather. Much as he admired the boy, Somdutt could not put him at risk. He had met Manu's divine father earlier that evening and had witnessed suffering and degeneration beyond description. He had sworn to protect Sanjna and Manu, even if it meant sacrificing his own life. *How many people get to serve a living God anyway?*

'We can take them, uncle,' replied Manu. 'There are three hundred guards around the prison. They are all hallucinating. An assault under the cover of darkness will allow us to eliminate all of them. We have only a few hours left uncle. Permit us to attack!' insisted Manu.

Somdutt was intently sharpening his copper long-sword on a stone. He stopped, inspected the blade for a moment and kept it aside for later. It needed more work.

'The security of the prison is far more impregnable than it looks. I agree the soldiers are drunk on whatever is making this city go mad, but I observed them closely this evening. The beastly aggression of the intoxicant more than makes up for the sluggishness it causes. They may be slow tonight, but they are free of fear and pain. You cannot defeat such troops, Manu. They are not human anymore. They are *raakshasas.*'

'But, uncle…' Manu tried to protest.

'Enough, Manu,' said a loud but graceful feminine voice. Sanjna had spoken from a corner of the bonfire camp. She was listening to the entire conversation and had decided to go with the opinion of her husband's trusted friend. Somdutt was the last word she had received about the well being of her doting husband. She valued that above all else.

'If brother Somdutt says we should attack only tomorrow, we must go by his wisdom,' said Sanjna.

Sanjna's word was treated like the word of the devta, sometimes even more than that of his. She was a golden soul. Unfortunately, her purity and power of goodness was no match to the grotesque and dark forces at play in Harappa this hour.

·||卐||·

Manu sat down with a plate of rice in his hands. He was terribly tired and had been on horseback for over twenty hours. He needed this meal and a short rest to prepare him for the impending battle the next morning. He had to snatch away his beloved father from the clutches of the beastly Harappan soldiers.

As he ate a mouthful of the freshly cooked rice, Manu winked boyishly at one of Somdutt's soldiers sitting across the bon-fire. The soldier grinned back, delighted at being greeted by the scion of the devta himself. Even before Manu could take his eyes off, a lethal arrow pierced right through the head of the smiling soldier. Within split seconds there was a rain of metal. Ranga was here with four hundred of his manic fight-ers growling and screaming like goblins. The camp of Manu and Somdutt was completely surrounded with the attackers shooting arrows from all sides.

As more of Somdutt's men fell, Manu and his nine com-panions moved into a battle-formation at the center of the camp, their backs towards each other in a huddle, shields up and bows ready. The ten of them were each facing the ten different directions that Vedic scriptures divide the space around into.

The five girls among them shot a volley of arrows back at the raiders, while the five boys glided and spun shields so as to block every arrow and spear coming towards their for-mation. Each one of the five archers was unleashing four arrows at one time, nearly each arrow finding its mark. The ten fighters appeared to be one single organism, their battle moves choreographed to perfection. Ranga's men fell by the dozens at this vigorous counterattack. This also gave time to Somdutt and his men to take striking positions.

Manu and Somdutt knew that this battle of bows and arrows was soon going to give way to a close, face-to-face conflict with the enemy. Ranga's men were closing in from all sides and despite the loss of scores of their men, they still out-numbered this small squad by one is to ten.

·||卐||·

Manu broke the formation and dashed towards the cluster of rocks where he noticed his mother hiding. Dodging the arrows and spears flying around, he leapt straight into the corner where Sanjna sat crouching.

'I'm fine…I'm fine…go out there and fight,' urged Sanjna as soon as Manu reached her.

'I can't leave you here, Maa,' replied Manu. 'I can't let you get hurt!'

'We will all get hurt if you don't show them your valor to-night, Manu. Remember who you are, my son! Remember your illustrious father!' insisted Sanjna, smiling proudly and looking straight into her son's eyes.

'But they are too many, Maa. We may not be able to defeat them!' argued Manu.

'Do we have a choice, Manu?' asked Sanjna calmly. She bent forward and kissed her son on his forehead. 'Now go. Do what you have to. That's my commandment.'

'I shall do as you say, Maa. Don't worry about me and stay here. I will come back for you Maa, I promise…I will come back for you,' said Manu as he drew his sword and darted back into the thick of the combat.

He made a promise to his mother. A promise he resolved to not let anything in the world stand in the way of.

Banaras, 2017

SANKAT MOCHAN

The motorcycles roared. Vidyut was the pillion rider with Sonu. Naina sat behind Bala. The warrior Balwanta rode his own bike. The five of them rode out of the Dev-Raakshasa matth at around 6 pm, with the powerful Enfield Bullet engines revving. Eight of the matth's elite fighters had already been dispatched an hour before.

The *guptachar sena* had been active for forty-eight hours now, but there was no lead on Romi. However they did find something unusual. Around fifteen foreigners, all of who had a muscular, military built and unusually heavy bags, had checked in to seven different hotels of the city. No ordinary observer could connect these bulky 'tourists' with each other, since they arrived into Varanasi at different times and moved into a variety of hotels – from the cheapest lodge to the sparkling five star hotels of the city. But the *guptachar sena* was by no means ordinary. They had not only spotted the unusual visitors but had also informed the matth that they were all seen taking different transport options earlier that evening. While they were travelling separately, they all had the same destination – the Dashashwamedh ghaat.

As the group left the matth gates, Purohit ji noticed that his great mentor Dwarka Shastri was unhesitant in sending Vidyut out to the riverbank to hunt for the hunter. Much as he worried for the well being of his great grandson, he also had boundless faith in his bloodline. He had seen Vidyut rise and speak two evenings before. Dwarka Shastri was an astute judge of men's abilities. The demons would have to conjure up something extraordinary to be able to harm even a hair on Vidyut's body.

Upon Purohit Ji's express instructions, the group took a very small detour to pay obeisance at the mighty *Sankat Mochan* temple. Literally translating to the 'Destroyer of Distress' or 'Reliever of Troubles', this temple was a stone's throw from the famed Assi ghaat. Believed to have been established by the great poet-saint Tulsidas just where he had a vision of the Lord, this temple belongs primarily to the powerful Hindu deity *Hanuman*. An omnipotent form of God, with His idol being a permanent companion of none other than Barack Obama, the ex-President of the United States, this sanctuary was hallowed territory of Hanuman, the supremely powerful ape-God.

Vidyut stood in front of the bright orange and strangely disfigured statue of Lord Hanuman. The courtyard of the divine temple was thronging with devotees. The famous *Besan Ka Laddoo* (sweet balls of gram flour in condensed sugar) was the most popular offering to the Lord. There were all creeds, classes and sorts of people in this melting pot of human beings. There were the middle-class housewives walking amongst those who were stricken with abject poverty. There were flashy young girls stepping out from luxury cars rubbing shoulders with handicaps and the destitute. There were the nonagenarians walking in step with the millennials. There was no one rich and no one poor in this temple compound. There was none too beautiful and none too ugly here. Sankat Mochan was a great leveler. Everyone here was a beggar, a seeker.

On one end was the twisted yet endearing sculpture of Hanuman Himself, and on the other was a deeply magnetic shrine of Lord Rama, the greatest God of the billion plus Hindus of this planet. Vidyut stood bewitched in front of the statue of Hanuman. Something drew him to the great deity. The blanket of hundreds, thousands of people around him started to feed an inexplicable streak of energy into Vidyut. He stood in front of Hanuman motionless, but every devotee seemed to be adding to his inner light. It was surreal. Vidyut stood embracing the energy for several minutes, before he fell down on his knees, in complete submission to Hanuman. The Lord was speaking to Vidyut, or so the last devta felt.

Vidyut was now present in front of the *durbar* (Court) of Lord Rama, or so the Hindus called the set of statues of Rama Himself, His beloved wife Sita, His devoted brothers Laxman, Bharat and Shatrughna, and Hanuman at His feet. For people uninitiated into the unconditional love of Lord Rama, this sight may not mean much. But for a billion worshippers of Rama, He was the very essence of creation, the symbol of goodness, love and hope.

Vidyut touched his forehead on the steps of Lord Rama's durbar. He didn't ask for anything. He never did. He knew the Lord was watching over him every moment of his existence. All he muttered under his breath was, 'Help me Rama. Bless me with the valiance and propriety that you taught the world when you vanquished the demon Raavan.'

Vidyut opened his eyes as he stood up, only to notice a very old temple priest dressed in saffron robes staring at him in amazement. Vidyut turned to the priest and folded his hands as a sign of respect. The priest raised his right hand to bless Vidyut and said just one word.

'*Utthishtha!*'

Rise.

·‖卐‖·

The plan was simple. Vidyut would break away from the group a few hundred meters before the ghaats. He would walk around on the riverside, smoke, speak on the mobile phone and wait for Romi. All this time his combat team would keep a close watch, each one of them maintaining a distance of barely a few seconds from him. If Romi was watching, he would come for Vidyut.

Vidyut did not really want Sonu, Naina, Bala, Balwanta and his fighters to accompany him at all. He did not want any one of them to come in harm's way, and was prepared to take on Romi alone. But this suggestion from him had been shot down immediately by his fellowship, and they were now here in the battlefield with their devta.

As he stood on the massive stairs of the Dashashwamedha ghaat watching the crowd building up, Vidyut dialed Bala's mobile number. Bala was only twenty feet away but understood that Vidyut wanted to speak from a distance.

'Ya, Video?,' answered Bala.

'Just a quick one, Bala,' said Vidyut. 'I know this will sound absurd, but keep an eye on Naina, will you?'

Bala was stumped for a moment. 'What? Naina? You gotta be kidding me, man!'

'Just do as I say, Bala,' requested Vidyut before disconnecting the call.

The number of people on the ghaat was increasing steadily and lights were coming on all around. There were tiny shops lining the top of the ghaat, selling flowers, garlands of marigold, lamps, sweetmeats and incense. A whole battery of young and old priests was busy preparing for the Ganga aarti. The beloved river Ganga was now reflecting the lights from the ghaats like a gleaming black mirror, mesmerizing the visitors on both land as well as those who were enjoying a boat ride before the aarti, and would participate in it from the boats itself. The place looked like a noisy and colorful carnival.

And there, amidst hundreds of people moving up and down the stairs of the ghaat, Vidyut saw that handsome, childish face.

Romi stood smiling at Vidyut from a distance.

Harappa, 1700 BCE

MANU

Somdutt was right. The intoxicated soldiers of Harappa were indeed free of fear and pain. Even those among them who had been shot with arrows multiple times, were fighting on like delirious ghosts. One thing was clear to both Manu and Somdutt – these demons were not going to retreat. Manu will have to kill them to the last man. *But how?* They were too many.

The battle raged on, with the smaller unit inflicting far greater casualties on the enemy. It was now a no-holds-barred spectacle of brutality. Swords tearing into throats, daggers ripping up faces, eyes were being gouged out and hearts being torn open.

Soon the perpetually black and purple clouds burst violently, and the midnight encounter was now swept by heavy wind and rain. Fighting in the heart of the mayhem Manu suddenly saw Somdutt at a distance, surrounded by fifteen or twenty enemy soldiers. He could not let anything happen to his father's last real friend. Manu pounded across the camp towards Somdutt, slashing and decapitating anyone who came in the way. He yelled out a fierce battle cry as he pounced upon the soldiers surrounding Somdutt. In a matter of moments he had drawn all the soldiers towards him and was moving his sword at the speed of light. Blood sprayed like fountains as Manu massacred the deranged villains like a lion slaughtering a herd of sheep.

'Enough!' came a deafening snarl. Ranga stood glaring at Manu.

'Fight someone your own size, O son of the devta!' challenged Ranga loudly for everyone to hear. He held a massive spear with ominous spikes at both the ends. He was twirling this heavy weapon around his shoulders in swift, expert moves. At over seven arms in height and broad as the one-horned rhino from the far East, Ranga looked like a bloodthirsty monster.

'I was waiting for you, you malevolent commander!' replied Manu defiantly. 'I heard you struck the mighty Vivasvan Pujari from behind at the courtroom, like a coward. Today is your judgment day, Ranga!'

By now Ranga and Manu had come closer, walking cautiously towards each other and preparing for what both knew was going to be a herculean battle. To the death.

All fighting had stopped and combatants from both sides paused to watch the titanic clash between the cruel monster Ranga and the young ascetic Manu. The evil commander and chief henchman of Priyamvada had picked the double-spiked spear as his weapon of choice. Manu on the other hand held two heavy short-swords, which he swung like they were made of straw. The two warriors were now moving in a circle, waiting to pounce upon the other at the first opportunity. The lightning and the lashing rain continued relentlessly.

Ranga made the first move. He moved to one side to mislead Manu, and suddenly leapt back to the other, attacking Manu viciously with his powerful spear. The young lad twisted his full torso at a dazzling speed and avoided the spear completely. In the same flow of movement, he slashed Ranga's waist just below his armor. The commander yelped in pain. Within moments of the duel, Manu had stamped his superiority over the oversized beast. He was now going to make him pay for his sins. Manu could not get the picture of his dear and noble father being assaulted brutally by this man out of his mind, and he was going to make him suffer.

Ranga charged again, this time swirling his lethal spear in gigantic circles. Manu ran towards the rushing monster and a moment before contact he slid down into the slushy mud, gliding past Ranga and hacking a deep cut on the commander's thigh. The scoundrel shrieked in pain. As he crashed to his knees, Ranga was convinced in his black heart that he had underestimated the young warrior-priest.

It was now Manu's turn. Under the clapping thunder and punishing rain, he lunged forward with the swagger of unmatched supremacy and swung both his swords across at Ranga's chest, tearing it open. The giant commander was now completely overpowered. Blood oozed out of his chest like it were a leaky bucket.

Manu was now prancing around Ranga like a harpy eagle flies above its prey before launching into the final dive. He wished his mother and father could see this sight. He wished they could see how easily he had vanquished this unworthy foe. After a few moments of waiting, Manu decided to deliver the killing blow. He leapt forward and struck the red headgear off Ranga's head. He grabbed the hair of the colossal fiend and pulled his head backwards. Manu stared around at everyone watching this gory exhibition. He wanted to make sure everyone was seeing. He hailed from a family that detested violence and embraced love. But this was not the time. Ranga had sinned against the last devta on planet Earth. And Manu was not going to forgive him.

Just as Manu was about to slit the throat of the beast, Ranga raised both his hands and begged for forgiveness.

·‖卐‖·

Raindrops were spluttering on the wounded commanders face. Although Ranga could barely keep his eyes open, Manu could make out they were begging him for mercy.

'Mercy!' whimpered the once brazen Ranga. He was shivering with fear.

'Mercy, O mighty Manu Pujari!' he repeated.

Manu was in no mood to relent. He was thirsting to punish the man who dared to strike his father Vivasvan Pujari and who conspired to send him to the dungeons of the dead. He decided to ignore the pleas of mercy and was about to dig his blade into Ranga's jugular.

'Have mercy, O son of the devta Vivasvan Pujari! Do not malign your good father's name by executing an unarmed man,' begged the treacherous rogue.

The sound of his father's name held Manu back. *Would his father have killed an unarmed and defeated man, no matter what his sin was?*

No.

Manu looked up at Somdutt. The chief engineer was himself a man of high values and righteousness. He nodded at Manu. This impeccable morality was the Harappan way of life before everything was poisoned by the vicious lust of one ambitious woman. Love, compassion and forgiveness were the bedrocks of the Harappan people.

Manu let go of the commander's hair. He stretched himself straight, threw his head back and let the pouring rain wash his face. Even though he could see that the hallucinating Harappan soldiers were still growling with hate and madness, he dropped his swords on the wet ground. Expecting the maniacal troopers to appreciate this magnanimity, Manu started to walk towards Somdutt. He wanted to take his mother and get out of this graveyard of fresh carcasses. He was very close to Somdutt and could see his father's friend smiling with admiration for his act of kindness and generosity. However, as he came just a few short steps away from Somdutt, he saw the engineer's expression change to one of petrified shock. In this briefest of moments Somdutt could only raise his finger and stare at Manu. But the devta's son was no ordinary warrior. In a split moment he could see that Somdutt was not staring at him. He was staring at someone behind him.

Manu did a full split and dropped starkly to less than half his height. But it was too late. Ranga had slashed his back deeply with a thick machete. Manu convulsed with pain. He struggled back to his feet before the giant attacker could strike again. Ranga was now charging in with renewed madness.

Manu stepped on one side in an expert move to dodge the mad man's assault. In one seamless flow of trained *kalaripayattu* routine, he landed his fist in a claw-formation into the gut of Priyamvada's bulldog. Manu's fingers were equipped with lethal tiger-claw hooks, which would one day be inherited by one of his ablest descendants. Within moments he disemboweled Ranga, tearing out his heart along with his intestines.

This duel was not between equals.

The delirious soldiers of Harappa were now in disarray without their cruel leader. While there seemed to be no letting-up in their blood-thirst and aggression, they certainly were retreating slowly. The handful of fighters with Manu and Somdutt broke into a cheer. Manu had displayed every quality expected from a warrior and a hermit — valiance, skill, fearlessness, composure, but most of all…compassion.

The rejoicing was transient. Just when Manu, Somdutt and their fellowship thought the worst was over, they heard the long and haunting blare of Harappan army's battle-horns from a distance. They could hear a massive battalion approaching the campsite. The reinforcements for Ranga and his crew had arrived. They exchanged exasperated glances. *How could the remaining twenty-five of them take on a thousand riders of the Harappan cavalry?*

Even before Manu could think what their response should be, he heard Tara scream out his name. Tara was one among his magnificent nine and unlike her brave and balanced self, she was shrieking with dread. Manu looked at her and his blood froze. Tara was near the cluster of rocks where Sanjna had taken refuge.

In the heat of the violent battle, Manu had forgotten about his promise!

Banaras, 2017

RISE OF THE DEVTA

Just as he was about to go after Romi, Vidyut heard a blood-curdling scream. It was a battle cry. On the now completely packed ghaat Vidyut saw Balwanta and Sonu swinging massive swords and charging into the crowd. They had clearly spotted something. In two minds whether to chase Romi or to rush to their help, Vidyut turned to see that Romi was gone.

As Vidyut dashed towards the direction in which he had seen his companions running, he saw what had spurred his team into action. A menacing group of men dressed in black combat outfits was heading directly towards Vidyut. In an instant the devta knew it was the same unit that the *guptachar sena* had cautioned them about. These men were clearly not ordinary street fighters. They were muscular, trained and disciplined, and were moving in a commando formation. In the flicker of a glimpse that Vidyut caught of them, he could see they were ex-military veterans from perhaps Iran, Russia - he couldn't say for sure. But he was certain of one thing - they had grossly underestimated the foe. It was only now Vidyut could see what they really were. *Mercenaries!*

·||ॐ||·

Vidyut suddenly felt worried for Sonu. While Balwanta was an accomplished warrior, these mercenaries were beyond Sonu's league. Vidyut tore his way through the crowd towards the men in black. He had to reach them before Sonu or anyone from the matth got hurt. He was relieved to see Bala also pounding towards the battle scene. If there was anyone beside himself who could match the skill of these trained fighters, it was Bala and Balwanta. And from what he had seen back at the matth, perhaps Naina.

In the background the Ganga aarti had been commenced, drowning the noise of the clash of blades and knuckles that had begun. Both sides knew that gunshots would attract immediate and needless attention, and were relying on swords, machetes and military-grade knives, at least for now. The loud chanting of mantras by scores of priests combined with the devotional striking of cymbals and blowing of conches, was now rendering a deafening and haunting din. Tens of thousands of devotees thronged the Dashashwamedh Ghaat, their eyes shut and their hands folded in devotion. Hundreds of massive lamps swung in the hands of the priests and threw mystical reflections on the holy river's water. It appeared as if the entire ghaat, the sacred river, the thousands of pilgrims and the mantras of the priests were all working in harmony to quell the power of evil this night.

They were fifteen. Even as he covered ground towards the fight, Vidyut counted the number of adversaries. Sonu had succeeded in slashing one of the mercenaries around his rib-cage and Balwanta had inflicted a deep cut on another. By now Naina was engaging two of the attackers at once, fighting like a warrior-princess. *Whose side was she on?* Vidyut was now running at lightning speed even through the crowd and launched himself into the heart of the fight, leaping at the throats of two of the mercenaries. He noticed that two of the matth's fighters were badly wounded by the commando knives of their attackers, and Sonu had been struck hard on his face with a pistol butt, tearing his lower lip. Bala had also reached the fight zone.

'Bala…take our fighters and Sonu away from here,' instruct-ed Vidyut, as he was slowly surrounded by twelve of the fifteen mercenaries.

'We will fight by your side, Vidyut,' protested Balwanta fiercely. He was like a raging bull, ready to take on an entire army. Balwanta was not going to leave Vidyut alone. These men in black were among the most skilled fighters he had ever confronted, and they were too many of them. Vidyut did not stand a chance.

'Do as I say!' commanded Vidyut. He suddenly carried the authority of the matthadheesh in his voice. He was not re-questing them. As the scion of the Shastri bloodline, he was passing a diktat.

Bala took Sonu and the two wounded fighters aside. Balwan-ta and Naina stood next to their injured companions, ready to witness the encounter between Vidyut and twelve deadly adversaries. The odds were by far not in Vidyut's favor.

Surrounded on all sides by the mercenaries, Vidyut's con-centration was so intense that it looked as if he were medi-tating with his eyes open. The twelve ex-commandoes had pulled out lethal military knives and short machetes. Vidyut was unarmed. The twelve men in black showed no excite-ment or rashness. They were moving with the cold precision of trained soldiers.

One of them closed in on Vidyut with his machete. Vidyut swung at stunning speed and landed a crashing kick on the attacker's jaw. The hit was so powerful that the merce-nary collapsed in an instant, letting out a short, agonizing grunt. For a moment the remaining adversaries stood shell-shocked. They had never seen a teammate from their elite squad be overpowered so swiftly and comprehensively. Two more of them attacked Vidyut, this time in a coordinated move, attempting to catch their prey from two sides at one time. In an expert counterattack maneuver Vidyut blocked the attacking arm of one of the strikers, twisted it in a flash and with a swift blow from his elbow, broke his arm into two. The other attacker had been met with a ramming kick into his diaphragm, sucking out the last whiff of breath from his lungs. Three of the black unit's members now lay on the ground, writhing in pain. Less than half a minute had passed since the fight began. Despite being veterans of several brutal wars and face-to-face conflicts, the black mercenaries had never come across a fighter like Vidyut.

His team watched the proceedings with their jaws dropped. In a matter of seconds Vidyut had summarily crushed three of the twelve dangerous enemies. Balwanta was delighted to see this one-sided assault. Naina's heart was beating faster than an express train. She was both worried as well as deeply attracted. Sonu was nearly jumping with excitement. The matth's fighters were overawed. Pilgrims and worshippers had now started gathering around, a commotion building up. Vidyut knew he did not want any police or paramilitary around. He had to finish this quickly.

As he glided into a typical low stance of advanced *kalaripayattu*, Vidyut tied his long brown hair into a short ponytail behind his neck. He went very low on his left knee, his right leg straightened out to his side. And then he pounced on the black squad like a panther, landing fatal kicks and crushing blows at devastating speed. Balwanta and Naina immediately noticed that while Vidyut's initial stance was a traditional *kalaripayattu* posture, he was attacking with a unique combat form combining Japanese Jiu Jitsu with Israeli Krav Maga. The martial art Vidyut was deploying was unheard of, unthinkable. He was fighting with a masterful technique that could not be beaten.

Apart from a shallow dagger slash across his chest, Vidyut had suffered no injuries and no blows. It had been mayhem for the black squad. As Vidyut inspected the squirming and moaning mercenaries littered around him like dolls thrown about in a little girl's play area, one of the attackers got up and pulled out a Beretta 92fs pistol. Before he could pull the trigger, Balwanta rammed into his ribcage like a bulldozer. The fight was over in less than three minutes. The supremacy of the devta was palpable. He nodded at the warrior-chief to acknowledge the timely help. Vidyut caught his breath and slowly undid his hair. He ran his fingers through them as he looked up at the sky and mumbled a short prayer. He then gestured to Bala to call an ambulance for the fallen mercenaries. Only Vidyut could have a heart large enough to care for even his darkest enemy. The night wind was blowing hard from the river and the chanting of mantras and striking of cymbals had reached their zenith.

As members of the Dev-Raakshasa matth witnessed this extraordinary man, this astonishing warrior and this fabulous leader standing tall amidst fallen foes, they were mesmerized by his sheer presence. As they saw Vidyut's chiseled face glowing even in the eclectic lighting of the Dashashwamedh Ghaat, his hair blowing in the sacred wind against the moonlit sky, they all had only one thought etched on their minds.

Vidyut was, beyond doubt, the savior they had been waiting for over centuries.

He *was* the last devta.

·||ॐ||·

Balwanta ran towards Vidyut and nearly lifted him up in his arms with glee. Vidyut laughed and winced at the same time, blood now oozing out from his chest wound on to his checked shirt. Sonu was clapping away from where he lay injured, his lip wound still bleeding profusely. Naina ran up to Vidyut and hugged him tightly. She did not get any response. Vidyut looked away towards Balwanta. It did not matter. Naina was relieved that Vidyut was okay.

'We must stay alert Balwanta dada, and get out of this place as fast as we can. Let's move towards the lower ghaat, away from these wounded mercenaries,' said Vidyut to Balwanta. 'Romi is still out there. And that coward will not attack from the front.'

'Yes,' agreed Balwanta, 'yes we should. Let's also send Sonu and the other wounded fighters back to the matth.'

'That's a good...'

Even before Vidyut could complete his sentence, they heard a shrill scream. They turned to see Naina leaning over Sonu, who was gurgling in his own blood. In the chaos of the crowd, an expert killer had slit his throat in just a centimeter long gash. But a gash that was sure to kill the man, slowly and painfully.

Balwanta and Vidyut ran towards the struggling Sonu. They were horrified to see the strapping young boy in extreme suffering, gasping for breath. *How were they going to face Purohit ji?* Naina was sobbing heavily, her eyes filled with horror. Enough was enough. Vidyut could not hold himself back any more. He grabbed Naina's hair and pulled them violently. The devta had never hurt a woman in his life. *But then he had never encountered a murderous witch like Naina.* His great grandfather had warned him about a dark betrayal. He was sure Naina had betrayed him. She had betrayed the whole matth.

'Why did you do this, Naina?' hissed Vidyut, completely unlike his dignified self.

'What are you doing, Vidyut?' protested Naina. 'Have you gone mad? Sonu is like my brother!'

Balwanta was alarmed at what Vidyut was doing. 'No Vidyut, Naina will never betray us. She is one of us, O mighty devta!' he said, as he held Vidyut's wrist, gently tugging it in order to set Naina free.

'You don't know anything, Balwanta dada! She hates Damini. She wants to harm us. If she was not working for our enemies, why would she carry a satellite phone in the middle of the night? She is the one who has been informing the enemy about our movements!' replied Vidyut, his face sweating with anger and hate.

By now Naina had stopped struggling. She was just holding Vidyut's hand to try and loosen his grip and ease the pain of her hair being pulled. She stared at Vidyut with helpless eyes and an irreparably broken heart.

'Don't be silly, Vidyut. It was *I* who gave her the Iridium 9555 phone. That is the only way we stay connected with the guardians of the Black Temple!' yelled Balwanta.

Balwanta's words hit home. Vidyut suddenly felt a biting pang of guilt as he let go of Naina's beautiful brown hair. She did not move. Something was lost forever.

Vidyut realized he had made a big mistake. 'I'm so sorry,

Naina…' he began, but he was interrupted by a deafening bang.

Almost instantly Vidyut felt a tearing sensation in his left shoulder. He turned around to find the smoking barrel of a Webley Scott revolver a few feet away.

His most trusted friend Bala had shot Vidyut from point blank range.

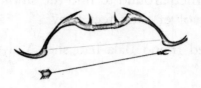

Harappa, 1700 BCE

THE SCION OF THE DEVTA

Manu stiffened as he saw what Tara was trying to draw his attention to. His mouth opened, struggling with asphyxiation and cold sweat broke all over him. He forgot all about the pain he was enduring because of the sword wound across his back. This was the day he had dreaded most ever since he was born.

Sanjna lay in front of him, her chest pierced deeply with a copper arrow. Despite her robes and her skin drenched fully in blood, she looked calm and peaceful. Devta Vivasvan Pujari's wife was half the force behind his divinity. Her shivering fingers were gesturing to Manu. Her eyes were crying but full of love. Even now, she had a soft smile on her face.

'Maaaaa…..!' shouted Manu as he crashed into the sludgy

ground and grabbed hold of his dying mother.

'Maa I'm sorry…I'm sorry…Maa I'm sorry…' sobbed Manu, clutching his mother like his embrace would hold back her soul from departing.

Sanjna caressed her son's cheek with her nearly limp hand. 'My time has come my son. But I leave this life with the satisfaction of being the wife of this planet's greatest man and the mother of this world's noblest son. History will never forget me.' She coughed blood even as she completed this sentence.

'No Maa…we will leave this place soon and get you to an *ayurvedacharya*. You will be fine Maa. You cannot leave me, Maa!' By now the wounded and bleeding Manu was crying profusely. 'How will I face father, Maa? What will I tell him?? I cannot live without you Maaaa….' Manu was devastated. Most sons love their mothers deeply. But Manu believed his love for Sanjna was boundless. His mother was his very existence. His mother was his God.

'Remember this, my son…you are the bloodline of the last devta on Earth. You have been sent for a larger purpose. Fulfill it. No matter what…find your destiny.' Sanjna's world was going dark as she uttered her last words.

'Tell your father, tell my Vivasvan…that I will meet him on the other side'.

She slumped into her son's arms.

The light of Manu's world went dark forever.

·||卐||·

'You must leave now, Manu!' shouted Tara. She and two of the magnificent nine were sheltering Manu and Sanjna from the barrage of arrows that were again showering on the campsite, using three massive shields. But it was clear now. They were going to be overrun by the inebriated garrisons of Harappa in no time.

Manu was refusing to move. He was sitting like a statue of stone, with his departed mother's head in his lap.

Tara could not wait any longer. She knew that the only hope of keeping the devta's bloodline alive lay in Manu's escape from this nightmare. She ducked under the shields and grabbed hold of Manu.

'Wake up, O son of the devta! Today is not when you die!'

Manu turned to her slowly. He was in deep shock. *He had promised her he would come back for her. His mother must have waited. He had promised her!* Manu was never going to forgive himself. In fact he was okay if they just beheaded him tonight. This world was not worth living without his mother.

Tara tried to shake Manu into his senses. Just as she bent forward, an arrow made its way through the shields and tore into Tara's shoulder. She cried with pain and fell on the ground next to Manu. The sight of Tara falling and writhing in pain was just what was needed to pull the grieving son back from his trance.

'Run, Manu…escape while you can…' insisted Tara as she

tried to get up and draw her sword. 'You are the devta's only son Manu. Your survival is critical for all of mankind.'

Before Manu could respond, Somdutt came running to this makeshift shelter. He was panting with exhaustion and panic.

'You must leave NOW, Manu!' he ordered the devta's son like his own. 'We will not be able to hold them much longer.'

Manu was not going to leave his friends behind on this battleground that was almost certain to be their graveyard. He lovingly shifted his mother and placed her gently on the soil. With tears rolling down his eyes incessantly, he bent down to kiss her cheek. He then slowly stood up and picked up his sword.

'I will not leave you all here, uncle,' he said, 'we will fight and die together.'

·||ᴊ卐||·

'But what about your father, Manu? Will you just let him rot in that ghastly prison?' enquired Somdutt angrily. 'And don't you see, if you perish here tonight, these monsters will not even give your mother her last rites. You owe it to her, Manu...you owe it to your parents!'

Manu was unsure of what to do, but his duty towards his living father and his departed mother was above all else.

The Harappan soldiers were now fighting through the remaining of Somdutt's men, being slowed down only by the hail of arrows being unleashed by Manu's fighters. But it was not going to be enough. Within minutes Somdutt, Manu, Tara and the rest of their comrades would be confronted by an ocean of brutal Harappan troops.

'Leave now, Manu! Take your mother with you. Head east and look for the Black Temple. You will find help there,' said Somdutt as he repelled a dagger attack by a manic Harappan soldier.

Tara readied a horse for Manu, even as two of his comrades lifted Sanjna's body with gentleness and reverence.

Manu looked around at his devoted fellowship and said his last words before mounting the horse, 'I will come back for you, my beloved ones. And this time I will not break a promise. But before I leave, may I give you one last commandment as your friend and as the mighty devta's son?'

The fellowship nodded in unison. 'What would that command be, O valiant Manu?' asked Somdutt.

Manu braced himself to hold back his tears. He then shouted like a military commander addressing his platoon, in a hoarse voice, heavy with emotion, 'I order each one of you to get out of this fight alive. Tonight, I order each one of you to SURVIVE!'

His fighters broke into tears, gritted their teeth and nodded again. They then darted off to their respective positions. Manu's words had given them renewed resolve to live through this trial by the sword.

Vineet Bajpai

As Manu mounted the horse and lovingly laid Sanjna's body on his lap, Somdutt gave parting instructions, 'If there is any place across the known world that can protect you, it is one of the Black Temples Manu. If we survive this night and tomorrow's rescue raid, we will meet you at the Mountain of the Saptarishi a fortnight from now…hopefully with the devta by our side!'

'Yes uncle, and thank you for everything,' said Manu, before spurring his horse towards the opposite direction as the enemy.

But nothing that night was favoring the noble family of the devta. Manu's horse had not even broken into a gallop when one of the hysterical Harappan commanders spotted him.

'There goes the son of Vivasvan Pujari!' he yelled. Pointing towards Manu he barked orders to his troops, 'Archers… take him down!'

Somdutt, Tara and the rest of their fighters charged towards the battery of Harappan archers. They had to stop them from releasing their arrows. But the archers were far away. Even as Tara charged upon them like an angry serpent, she was late. The massive volley of arrows had been shot.

And three of them had found their mark.

·||ॐ||·

The last view that the wounded Tara and Somdutt got was of Manu riding into the rainy mist, the dead body of his beloved mother in his lap. Three arrows were pierced through his back and neck, and the machete wound bled profusely. Tara's eyes welled up. No man could survive such fatal wounds. Somdutt shut his eyes in grief as he bid farewell to the scion of the last devta.

'This is the end of Vivasvan Pujari's bloodline. Never again will a devta walk on planet Earth,' whispered Somdutt to himself.

He was wrong.

Banaras, 2017

THE TAANTRIC FUNERAL

Before he could squeeze the trigger for the second time, Naina pounced on Bala and threw him off balance. The gleaming Webley Scott revolver fell from Bala's hand. It was now a duel between the man who had betrayed the devta, and the woman who had loved him all her life. And this time, the duel would not be stopped. It was going to be to the end.

Balwanta held Vidyut in his arms, shocked at the turn of events. The devta was bleeding copiously, the bullet lodged deep into his shoulder. The warrior-chief of the Dev-Raakshasa matth now had to save both Sonu as well as the great grandson of Dwarka Shastri. *He had to rescue the last devta at any cost.* He had to get them to a hospital as fast as he could. He was not worried about Naina. He had trained her. He knew it was the end of Bala, the man who thought he could get away with betraying the devta himself.

·‖卐‖·

Vidyut was in intense pain, almost dizzy with the loss of blood. More than his physical suffering, it was the shock of being shot at by the one person he had always trusted that was killing him. He now understood clearly. This very afternoon his great grandfather had warned Vidyut about the presence of a black spirit. *How could it be Naina?* Naina lived within the matth since the day she was born. If she were the traitor, the great Dwarka Shastri would have known it years ago. Why did he sense the black spirit only now? That black spirit was Bala's!

The evil that the great matthadheesh had felt had arrived at the matth residing deep in the malicious heart of Balakrishnan. Romi was not the only soldier sent by the Order.

'I must take you and Sonu to Govardhan immediately, Vidyut,' said Balwanta, as he and the fighters of the matth lifted Sonu. Vidyut gestured at him to tie up his wound. 'No Vidyut,' protested Balwanta, 'you have to see a doctor. You have a bullet in you, for God's sake!'

·‖卐‖·

Bala pulled out a knuckle-blade that was hidden in the left sock under his corduroy pants. He placed it between the index and middle fingers of his right fist. Every blow from this hand would now be a severe stab. Naina did not flinch and was the first to attack. She started circling Bala in a swift jog and pounced on him landing a powerful punch on his lower jaw. Bala slashed back wildly with the lethal blade in his fist, but missed Naina completely. By this time Naina had crashed an elbow into Bala's spine, sending him crashing to the ground. It was a bad beginning for him, but the veteran fighter was not going down so easily.

Bala spun around on his hands and in a lightning fast move ripped into Naina's right leg just above her knee. It was a deep cut from the knuckle-knife, and it had wounded the gorgeous and deadly Naina's favorite attack limb. Bala then rammed into Naina's gut with his powerful head and sent her flying back before she fell hard on the concrete surface of the ghaat. Just when Bala felt he was going to go for the kill, Naina raised both her legs in the air and sprung back up like a gymnast. In the same flow she smashed a punch right below his throat. It was a deadly strike. Bala could not breath and grabbed his throat in pain. In the same instant Naina swung a lethal uppercut on Bala's chin, which made his head drop backwards and he crashed on his knees. It was all over.

But the warrior-princess of the Dev-Raakshasa matth was not done. She was furious like a wounded tigress. Naina moved to one side and flung her bleeding leg around Bala's throat in a death-lock. She was going to break his neck.

'Enough, Naina!' shouted Vidyut.

Naina did not listen. Her grip was tightening around Bala's neck and his eyes appeared ready to pop-out of his squeezed skull.

Vidyut rushed towards Naina and pulled her by the arm. 'No Naina, we're not murderers. Besides, once I am done with Romi I want to ask my trusted friend some questions,' said Vidyut, looking at the traitor who was once his greatest ally.

Naina loosened her grip slightly.

'Take him to the matth, Balwanta dada,' instructed Vidyut. Naina unlocked her leg and kicked Bala on the shoulder, making him slump to the ground. Vidyut went down on one knee and looked at Bala's battered face. He shook his head with disbelief and asked the question that was eating him from within, 'Why Bala?' asked Vidyut. 'We were like brothers. *Why?*

'Because all is fair in love and war, Vidyut,' replied Bala, his mouth sputtering blood but his eyes gleaming with hate. 'You have no idea…the war has only just begun. The New World Order is here, O devta, and even you cannot stop it!'

·||卐||·

Vidyut was now alone on the ghaat, where the crowd was gradually thinning. Reporters and investigators had reached the spot where the black squad lay struggling, although Vidyut and his fellowship had slipped away from the scene by this time. The police and city ambulances had carried away the wounded and Vidyut was relieved to hear that Sonu was stable. The devta had insisted that everyone from the matth leaves for the safety of the monastery. Bala was taken for questioning. It was important to keep him in the matth's custody. For now he was the only link they had to whoever was unleashing such ominous attacks against them, both open and covert.

The full-blooded, frontal assault of the mercenaries was menacing as it was, and yet it was no match for the under-cover treachery of Bala. It showed how deep the enemy had infiltrated Vidyut's work, home and life. He was deeply scarred with the ghastly betrayal and didn't know whom to trust here on. *Since when was Bala working against him? Was he a carefully crafted implant by those he was calling the Order? Were they watching and tracking him for years? And if they were, why didn't they try to kill him sooner?* It was clear to Vidyut that just like Dwarka Shastri had warned him, there was a very powerful force at play against them.

Even in the state of mental blur and deep agony, Vidyut's eyes were darting around, scanning every corner of the Da-shashwamedh Ghaat as far as he could see. He knew Romi would be watching, and Vidyut was not going to leave the ghaat tonight without crushing the assassin once and for all.

Their eyes met. It was as if the hunter and the hunted were both looking for each other, only now the roles were unclear. *Who was the predator and who was the prey?* Romi was watching the proceedings from the far corner of an old temple, stand-ing coolly with his hands in his jeans pocket. Only this time he was not smiling.

His childish eyes were ablaze with fear and rage.

Vidyut ran towards the lonelier section of the ghaat, where Romi had stood behind the cover of an old temple pillar. Once again, the assassin had vanished. Vidyut ran around all four corners of the temple but could not see Romi anywhere. This section of the ghaat was comparatively darker than where the Ganga aarti took place. The Ganga was now just about twenty feet away. At a distance the funeral pyres of the Manikarnika ghaat flickered continuously, constant reminders of the transience of human life. Several groups of taantrics and *aghoris* (a darker cult of taantrics known for their questionable practices like corpse worship, cannibalism and even necrophilia) sat by the riverside beginning their occult rituals. Their low but haunting chants and intonations filled the air with a fearsome mystique.

Vidyut decided to search the entire area. He knew Romi had eyes on him and he did not expect much honor and bravery from the assassin who believed in striking from behind. The devta's wounds were weakening him with every passing second as he ran from one old temple to another on the ghaat, parallel to the holy river. He had now left the Dashashwamedh ghaat behind and was nearing an old fortress wall very close to the flowing Ganga, glowing orange under the dim sodium vapor lights illuminating it.

'Hello, Vidyut,' said a smart voice from behind a dark end of the fort wall.

Vidyut took a second or two to figure where the voice had come from. It was Romi all right.

Just as Vidyut spotted the silhouette of the killer and advanced towards him, two dull thuds and bright flashes greeted him.

With the poise of an expert marksman, Romi had fired at Vidyut with a Walther PPK handgun, the noise of the shots suppressed by a SilencerCo Spectre 22 attached to the muzzle.

·||卐||·

To Romi's horror, the devta lunged forward nevertheless. Thanks to Vidyut's swift movement, one of the bullets had missed him. But the other found its mark and hit Vidyut straight in the gut. This was his second bullet shot for the night, apart from the dagger gash on his chest. So many grievous wounds and such uncontrolled blood loss could turn fatal even for a devta, who was now struggling to keep going.

Before Romi could fire another shot, Vidyut had smashed head-on into the skillful yet weak assassin. Without explosives, detonators, mercenaries, infiltrators and silenced pistols, Romi was nothing more than a scrawny and pathetic scoundrel. Vidyut struck his face with a punch so hard that it inflicted a deep cut across Romi's cheekbone, sending his innocent spectacles flying into the dark night. The devta then crashed his powerful fist into the assassin's upper belly, making him spit blood within moments. This was a one-sided punishment and Vidyut was not showing any mercy.

'Wait!' yelled Romi. 'Wait, please Vidyut…please…' he pleaded.

Vidyut was worried he could pass out any moment. The last

bullet fired by Romi had torn into his abdomen, and blood was oozing out generously. The devta stopped for a moment to hear what the crooked assassin had to say.

'How will killing me help, O great devta?' blurted out Romi, his hands folded in a plea for mercy. 'I can tell you everything you want to know.'

Vidyut was listening, his right hand grabbing Romi by the collar in an iron grip.

'I am very weak, Vidyut. I have haemophilia…my…my blood…doesn't clot. Please don't hit me,' begged Romi. Vidyut could not believe his ears. This hardened and ruthless murderer was shivering and begging like a wet puppy. Romi's face was smeared with his own blood, and he was even coughing blood every now and then. Vidyut's onslaught had been too much for the fragile expert.

Vidyut loosened his grip. He was feeling giddy himself and wanted to reach Govardhan as soon as possible. Without immediate medical aid, the devta knew he wouldn't last long.

'Thank you, thank you, Vidyut…' muttered Romi, who was now sobbing like a child who had just been thrashed by his father after failing an exam. He was a pathetic sight. Vidyut almost felt pity for the scoundrel.

Just as Vidyut was taking a breather, giving time to Romi to recoup, the master assassin moved with the speed of a wild cat. Before the exhausted and wounded Vidyut could react, Romi had pulled out a gleaming surgical scalpel from nowhere and glided it at the speed of a bullet towards Vidyut's throat. But this time his adversary was not the burly man in the train or the young Sonu. This time it was the devta.

Vidyut responded with lightning speed and blocked the attack, the scalpel's edge now only a hairline away from his throat. The expression on Romi's face had changed. He was scowling and his features contorted in a manner as if he were evil personified. *This* was his real face. Vidyut twisted Romi's wrist sharply that made him drop the scalpel and twist his torso in pain.

'This one's for Sonu,' whispered Vidyut as he clenched his teeth and tightened his grip. In one swift blow from his open hand, Vidyut rammed into Romi's badly twisted arm and dislocated his shoulder. Romi's hand dropped limp as he fell on the stairs of the ghaat, yelping in pain.

·‖ॐ‖·

Holding him by his collar, Vidyut was now dragging the crumbled Romi back towards the Dashashwamedh ghaat. Much as he wanted to end the life of this ruthless and unscrupulous killer, he decided otherwise. There always had to be a difference between the good side and the bad. Always. That is what held the world together.

'What…what are you going to do with me, O great devta?' asked Romi in a broken, struggling voice. Vidyut did not answer.

'Do you know why the Maschera Bianca wants to kill you, Vidyut?' offered the assassin. 'Because you have no right to disrupt what has been lying dormant for fifteen hundred years!'

Vidyut kept walking, pulling Romi along. He did not answer,

but was listening keenly.

'Do you even know why you are here in Banaras after three decades? Why they didn't kill you years ago? It is because eleven days from now an ancient prophecy will come true, O devta - a constellation and juxtaposition of planets in the night sky awaited since 1,700 BCE. You have been kept alive for a reason, Vidyut, and you don't even know it!' said Romi as he tried to laugh. He spat more blood and moaned in agony.

'I saw you fight today. You truly are the demigod they believe you to be. But even you cannot fight them, O mighty devta. Their power and reach is beyond your imagination. The Order will change the world. You cannot stop them!' continued Romi, nearly delirious with pain.

Vidyut had to stop. The excruciating agony from his wounds was now unbearable. He took out his mobile phone and dialed Balwanta's number. The warrior-chief was relieved to hear Vidyut's voice. Vidyut requested Balwanta to pick them up from the pier where the *aghori* taantrics sat for their night rituals. It was just a few steps away and Vidyut was going to wait there along with his prisoner.

'They are coming for you, Vidyut. They are coming for the Black Temple,' whispered Romi.

Vidyut started dragging the killer towards the ghaat of the taantrics. He suddenly felt Romi breaking into wild convulsions. His body was twisting violently and he dropped to the ground writhing in agony. Vidyut turned him over to notice thick yellow foam coming out from Romi's mouth. His eyes were rolled up completely.

That was the end of Romi. A capsule of potassium cyanide that he had bitten into at the taantric ghaat sucked out his evil soul. This was the assassin's funeral.

·||卐||·

Vidyut sat on the ghaat's steps, with Romi's twisted body lying a few yards away. Two *aghoris* had taken great interest in it. Balwanta had called again, reassuring Vidyut that they were reaching him in a couple of minutes and were equipped with immediate medical aid for him.

The night was now darker than before, with lights of the ghaats, *bajdas* (houseboats), shops and boats much fewer. A fragrant breeze laden with the scents of marigold and ritual incense whiffed across Vidyut's face and hair. The Ganga was flowing in its loving and sacred path, kissing and touching the ancient ghaats gently on its way. Tonight, the Ganga aarti had indeed blessed the devta in his quest against evil.

Vidyut stared into the night and the Ganga, with the breeze soothing his nerves. He had no idea what the New World Order was and what their ominous designs were. Neither did he know who was this Maschera Bianca that Romi was referring to. What was the mystery of the Black Temple? His instinct told him that a long and hard battle awaited him in the coming days. But there was one thing the devta was sure of. No matter how potent and treacherous the forces of evil may be, they can never defeat the power of love, the supremacy of goodness.

Kashi was, after all, Lord Shiva's own city.

Harappa, 1700 BCE

THE GREAT *BLOOD* BATH

The ten gigantic prison guards hauled Vivasvan Pujari on the rough ground of the Great Bath of Harappa, ready to drag him all the way to Harappa's dreaded mrit kaaraavaas or dungeons of the dead. The bath of Harappa was in tradition with the townplanning of the time. Despite the fact that Mohenjo-daro was also a powerful province and was Priyamvada's home before she wedded Pundit Chandradhar, the Great Bath of Harappa was by far the biggest community bathing and assembly facility across all of Aryavarta. It was over twenty times the size of the great bath at Mohenjo-daro.

Just that today the beautiful and wicked Priyamvada had turned this public bathing and assembly pool into a torture arena. And all of Harappa was invited.

The last devta was by now drenched in thick layers of sweat, blood and tears. He had never imagined such brutality. Vivasvan begged incessantly, pleaded, even folded his hands at the commoners he passed. He could do anything to save his beloved Sanjna and Manu. A thick wooden beam crushed him under its weight, even as he was whipped to pull its backbreaking bulk along. As he was pulled brutally by nearly a dozen thick chains and ropes, these shackles strangulated him from head to toe like the embrace of a hundred pythons. Yet no one responded. Vivasvan Pujari was not just alone in his suffering. He was a spectacle of sadistic entertainment for the Harappan people.

After hours of torture, public stoning, spitting and cheering, Vivasvan Pujari could now sense the hopelessness of his situation. Gradually, one kick after another and one stone too many, his mental state changed rapidly from disbelief to desperation to that of pleading, and finally to one of demonic hatred. Vivasvan stopped begging. His hands slowly unclenched themselves and clasped the thorny ropes instead. He started digging his wounded heels into the ground and began exerting counter pressure against the ten enormous guards that were guffawing as they dragged him like a dead animal.

Vivasvan Pujari was now pulling them all back into him. And they were losing ground, their strappy sandals scrubbing against the dry soil. Suddenly, the entire circus came to a silent standstill.

The devta was finally resisting.

The ten guards were dazed at the sheer strength of this man

they had so easily written off a couple of hours ago. Vivasvan Pujari was pulling at the ropes and chains with the power of twenty horses. The guards doubled their effort and called in reinforcements. Some of the new entrants added hands to the ropes, while the others attacked Vivasvan's knees with clubs and staffs. To no real affect. By now the lacerated and breathless Vivasvan Pujari had upped the ante. He was now harnessing the power of a *hundred* horses. He could not be stopped.

Finally a guard's baton came crashing down on his head from behind, splitting his already bleeding scalp like a knife. Vivasvan Pujari fell with a painful gasp. They then pounced on him like hyenas and began showering him with hits from multiple batons and clubs.

Chandradhar could not hold himself back anymore. He knew he had participated in perhaps the worst sin ever committed under the Sun. He knew the Gods would never forgive him for this horrendous crime. Any which way, he was not going to let it go on. Without looking at Priyamvada, Chandradhar ran out of the counsel pavilion and sprinted towards his oldest friend and dearest brother-in-law. He dived to cover the devta with his own body, unmindful of the scores of blows that came crashing down. The manic soldiers took notice and immediately held back as they saw the first King of Harappa lying under their mindless assault.

Vivasvan Pujari appeared lifeless. Chandradhar could not hold back his tears. He held his friend's bleeding head in his lap and could utter only three sobbing words into the apparently dying devta's ears.

'Forgive me, Vivasvan…'

From under his robes Chandradhar took out a small leather pouch filled with spiced vinegar. He unknotted it and pressed it on the devta's lips. 'Drink this, Vivasvan', whispered Chandradhar. 'This is the only help I can provide on this cursed day my friend. Drink this vinegar and it will all be over. My men are carrying cartloads of ayurvedic aloe and myrrh to resuscitate you. A cave in the estate adjacent to this arena is ready to see you rise again.'

Vivasvan Pujari suddenly opened his eyes like a man possessed. He could not speak clearly as his cracked teeth had filled his mouth with bone, blood and mud. But his eyes, filled with tears and pain, shone like those of a vindictive serpent.

'Go now, Pundit Chandradhar. I give you the opportunity to bid farewell to your loved ones…and to this entire ghost town.'

If there was anyone in all of Aryavarta who knew the real power of Vivasvan Pujari, it was Chandradhar. He had never seen that manic look in Vivasvan's eyes, and he now knew that apocalypse was near for the people of Harappa. All he could muster the courage to say was, 'Don't do it, Vivasvan. Punish me. Punish Priyamvada. But spare the rest.'

Vivasvan Pujari did not pay attention to Chandradhar's plea. He tried to get up, and was greeted with more blows on his face and neck. He could hear his own collarbone cracking.

And then one of the prison guards tore into his rib cage with a spear. Vivasvan Pujari screamed in agony, but forbade the blood from his body to spill any further. All that emerged was the weeping water of the Saraswati...thick and colorless. The pain was excruciating. Vivasvan got up nevertheless. The time had come. Chandradhar shouted an order to the guards to stop their brutality. Then there was a pin-drop silence.

·||卐||·

The devta lifted himself in a labored struggle, the soil around him reddened with his dripping blood. Even before he could stand up fully, his body started shaking. To the disbelief of the maddened audience, Vivasvan Pujari began laughing maniacally. He stood up and looked around the entire Great Bath complex, pausing a moment as his eyes met Priyamvada's. With the heavy wooden beam still strapped to his shoulders, and his arms outstretched in a prophesizing gesture, he screamed out an agonizing pronouncement —

'Hear me one and all! Hear me you city of sinners! I, Vivasvan Pujari, the Surya, will come back with devastating vengeance you ungrateful, bestial people of Harappa. I devoted my entire life in the service of this metropolis. And today you stone me like a rotten animal!'

Vivasvan now broke into loud and uncontrolled sobs. He could not believe this was happening to him. Even as he said these last words, a sharp rock came flying and smashed into his left eye, which started oozing thick, deep-red blood profusely.

'Aaaaaarrrrggghhhhh…' Vivasvan yelled again, weeping continuously in extreme pain, and almost passed out. Only the thought of Sanjna and Manu was keeping him alive even after such ghastly punishment. And it was only the devta who could hold on to life even after his body was broken in every way possible.

The ten thousand people in the crowd cheered in gleeful unison. Something thus far unfamiliar and alien to the righteous Harappans was showing itself this blood-red morning. The individually calm and pious citizens were now displaying uncharacteristic mass hysteria. The animal, the jealousy, the *raakshasa* in each one of them was rearing its ugly head, as they collectively witnessed and enjoyed Harappa's tallest man writhing and struggling in inhuman suffering.

As the chains dragged the devta's body like a wretched animal against the dirt of the Great Bath compound, Vivasvan Pujari gathered the last ounce of his strength and let out a final, frightening warning for all to hear.

Remember my words, you cruel Harappans! My revenge will be as ruthless and as brutal as your collective conscience is today. No loving mother among you comes forth to save me. No son raises his arms in my defense. No kind brother comes to my rescue. Not even a child sheds a tear. So be it. So be it! Every son, every mother, every child of Harappa will suffer in the same manner as my pious wife and my beloved son do today. You all will be mercilessly destroyed you undeserving children of the Saraswati, you scoundrel flock of the Saptarishi!'

Vivasvan Pujari now rose against the weight of the wooden block, against all the whips and chains that bound him from head to toe. His eye was still oozing a repulsive mix of blood and flesh, his torso was all but skinned, he wept with power-ful jerks of his bleeding chest and he was soiled in a slurry of dark mud and of his own sweat and blood. He raised both his arms against the pull of the ten prison guards and his biceps appeared ready to burst. His chest muscles stretched like iron cables as he beckoned every drop of physical and spiritual strength from within him. A man once known for his glowing and God-like appearance, looked ghastlier than the devil himself. He looked up to the sky and sent out his last, bloodcurdling words to the masses of Harappa –

'Listen you who are already dead. Listen you congregation of corpses. Listen you fools.

I am half-human, half-God!'

TO BE CONTINUED...

Vineet Bajpai

TO BE CONTINUED...

Available now in all leading online & retail stores.

ABOUT THE AUTHOR

Vineet is a first-generation entrepreneur. At age 22 he started his company Magnon from a small shed. Today Magnon is among the largest digital agencies in the subcontinent, and part of the Fortune 500 Omnicom Group.

He has led the global top-ten advertising agency TBWA as its India CEO. This made him perhaps the youngest ever CEO of a multinational advertising network in the country.

He has won several entrepreneurship and corporate excellence awards, including the *Entrepreneur of the Year 2016*. He was recently listed among the *100 Most Influential People in India's Digital Ecosystem*.

Vineet's second company talenttrack is disrupting the media, entertainment & creative industry in India. It is the fastest-growing online hiring and networking platform for the sector.

He has written three bestselling management & inspirational books — *Build From Scratch, The Street to the Highway* and *The 30 Something CEO*.

He is an avid swimmer, a gaming enthusiast, a bonfire guitarist and a road-trip junkie. He is 39.

www.VineetBajpai.com
facebook.com/vineet.bajpai
twitter/Vineet_Bajpai
instagram/vineet.bajpai
Write to Vineet at vb@vineetbajpai.com